SAVING EVEREST

D0123144

SKY CHASE

wattpad books **W**

wattpad books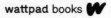

Copyright © 2019 Sky McClurkin. All rights reserved.

Published in Canada by Wattpad Books, a division of Wattpad Corp.
36 Wellington Street E., Toronto, ON M5E 1C7

www.wattpad.com

First Wattpad Books edition: October 2019

ISBN 978-0-99368-992-5 (Hardcover edition)
ISBN 978-1-98936-500-7 (eBook edition)

Library and Archives Canada Cataloguing in Publication information is available upon request.

Printed and bound in Canada
1 3 5 7 9 10 8 6 4 2

Cover designed by Michelle Wong
Images © igor_kell

A NOTE FROM THE PUBLISHER

This novel deals with themes like suicide and depression. If you or anyone you care about is having similar thoughts or experiences, please know that there is support available. The National Suicide Prevention Lifeline provides 24-hour assistance at 1-800-273-8255 or SuicidePreventionLifeline.org. For global resources, refer to w.tt/HelpPreventSuicide for international helplines.

To Marlee

For I wouldn't have known true friendship
if it weren't for you

POEM

Every time you cry, I feel it. My eyes swell with fat salty tears and my lungs deflate. My throat becomes dry and my heart twists in knots.
I feel every ounce of your pain.
And I'm so sorry.
I know what it's like to feel like you're just floating through life.
That you feel like you have no purpose.
That only if you died, people would understand your pain.
Do you realize that there are millions of people who understand exactly how you feel?
Depression houses millions of people.
It's tragic because you didn't choose to live there; it kidnapped you.
Please escape.
You don't have to give up. You can't see the world

*because depression blindfolded you, but life is truly
beautiful.*

It's so damn beautiful it brings tears to my eyes.

I didn't see it before.

*You don't know how much I wish I would have
dragged the blade upon depression's skin instead of my
own.*

*I look back and wonder why I added more pain to
myself. It doesn't sound logical.*

*I lived life with a lock on my lips. I was dying inside,
but no one knew it. The key sat hidden under my heart,
but I was oblivious.*

I believed that there was no saving me.

Please don't believe that.

Because you deserve to be happy.

*I looked at your smile before this mess happened,
and it was golden.*

Chin up, you're golden.

1

BEVERLY

It wasn't every day that you heard about the most popular guy in school attempting to end his life. It was actually the last thing I expected to hear this morning.

All summer I dreamed about this day. Working three jobs, you kind of can't help but dream. Lifeguarding was where I decided I should probably try out for cheerleading. Working concessions at Heinz Field was where I came up with the idea of trying out for the musical. Being at 21 Daisies Café reminded me that I couldn't sing or dance, but in reality all I wanted was to make my last year of high school memorable. Now, with the halls caving in from all the talk of suicide, I wished nothing more than to forget this day. The voices of the other students echoed through the halls. Although different they were all the same.

"Why are we even talking about him?"

"It's not like he actually died."

"Who would have known Everest would do this?"

"He probably tried to kill himself because he realized how much of a demon Cara was. If I was dating the devil's spawn, I would try to kill myself too."

* * *

As I walked on the freshly polished floors of the halls and digested the poisonous conversations I passed by, I subconsciously found myself heading toward the nurse's office. Everest Finley was the king of Shady Hills Academy, so it wasn't that surprising that rumors swirled around him. Once, I heard that he had an affair with the Mandarin teacher; later I realized our school didn't even teach the language. For a brief moment I allowed myself to believe that this was one of those ridiculous stories.

But on the way to the nurse, I noticed that even the teachers were huddled outside their classrooms, glancing around every so often as they whispered in heated conversations. Taking sips from their ceramic coffee mugs and nodding their heads, they engaged in their own whisper-fests. With each step grew this feeling—this terrible, dreadful monster of a feeling in the pit of my stomach.

I never made it to the nurse.

The school called an emergency assembly, and although there was no mention of the subject, we all knew what it was about. Mr. Sticks, our principal, who usually wore a permanent scowl on his stern face, shared a look of remorse as he broke the news. He was a large man, but on that stage he seemed really small. He ran a hand through his thinning gray hair and read off a paper he held with shaking hands.

"We take seriously the importance of a positive school climate and the safety and well being of our students and staff. Mental health professionals are available to anyone who is in need. It is important to talk to someone if you feel like giving up." He spoke solemnly.

The rest of the speech was a blur. My head spun as the auditorium buzzed.

I was stunned by how callous everyone was being—it seemed like no one even cared. These people had practically worshipped the ground Everest walked on for the past three years. Even from a distance, Everest seemed to be one of those people you couldn't help but like. One time, when the school band didn't raise enough money for their trip to Disney World, he paid the difference.

The best part was that he tried to make it anonymous. He was the quiet jock, and when he would talk, he sounded so polite, so well educated. He was ridiculously amazing on the football field, and was incredibly humble and modest about it. No, it couldn't be Everest. He was perfect.

Being the only black girl at a predominately white school made me stick out like a sore thumb. I didn't really fit in anywhere, so I was always kind of thrown off to the side. Everest, though, was undeniably admired by *everyone*. Shockingly, it seemed as though I was the only person who felt any sympathy. Just because his body wasn't dead didn't mean his soul wasn't barely living.

Sophomore year in biology, I remembered him picking up my book once. It was something that I'll never forget. He didn't even look at me as he handed it back. As I scrambled to gather my belongings, it had fallen, and as he was walking down the aisle to leave class, he bent down, picked it up, and laid it on my desk. It was such a simple thing for him to do, but I appreciated it anyway.

That was just about the only interaction I'd had with Everest Finley. After that day, though, I watched him. That sounds incredibly creepy, but I did.

I noticed how he tugged on his lush sandy-brown hair when he was thinking. I noticed how he was always polite and respectful, even when his friends were being stuck-up and rude. I noticed how his eyes weren't exactly blue or green, like the two colors were fighting for dominance, the azure in the lead most of the time. If one thing was for sure, Everest Finley had some breathtaking eyes. I couldn't help but see how he laughed a lot, and had one of those smiles that was perfect—rehearsed, even. Like there was something deeper, something different, behind it.

I wondered what made him want to die. Everest had the world at his feet, so why did he want to leave it?

* * *

Everest had been the topic all day today. By the time lunch rolled around, it was like hearing every conversation all at once. Each table had their own set of thoughts to share. Although different, they were all the same:

"Everest is so selfish."

"Seriously, he really failed his suicide attempt."

"His story is now on the news. Do you know how bad this makes our school look?"

"Imagine if he comes back. That would be so awkward."

"I don't care if he's crazy, I'll still blow him."

Cara, his girlfriend, sat at the usual table with the popular kids. A handful of cheerleaders and in-betweeners were at her side as she cried. Nash Spies, Everest's best friend, wrapped his arm around Cara in an attempt to calm her down. Martha, her best friend, stroked her hair.

"How could he do this to me? I can't handle this kind of stress."

The cafeteria was loud, but I was able to make out the words that passed through Cara's lips. Nash's face held no kind of emotion as he rubbed her back in a soothing manner.

I entered the line and quickly paid for a bottle of water. I was desperate to get away from all the chatter from the assembly. This year, one of the things I promised myself was that I would start eating in the cafeteria, but there was no way I could do that today. No words could explain how happy I was that I didn't have to stand in the line anymore. Every conversation was about the boy who tried to kill himself.

Walking past the popular table again, Cara was now laughing. Clutching my water tight, I made my way to my spot. The place where I could be alone and eat—the library. It wasn't like anyone noticed that I didn't eat lunch in the cafeteria. If someone needed a book, they'd use the new library in the west wing of the school. When it was built, it seemed as though everyone had forgotten the library in the east wing. It provided me with a space where I could be a true hermit. Sitting at one of the old oak tables, I pulled out my journal and started to draw. My pencil glided along the paper, a great sense of sorrow in the motion.

Alone. But that was how I was used to being anyway.

POEM

I don't even have to know you
To have the wisdom of knowing
That the world would suffer a great loss
If you weren't here

2

EVEREST

Words couldn't even come close to describing how I felt right now. I didn't know what was more sad: the fact that I tried to kill myself or how I failed.

I failed. I was still here. Why was I still here?

My mom was convinced I was crazy. Out of the five days I'd been in the hospital, my dad had come to visit me a total of two times—not to mention he was on his phone the whole time—my little sister was afraid of me, and none of my friends had come to visit or even called.

I had a feeling this was what it would be like if everyone knew just how messed up I was.

"I don't see why you are so against the Sunshine Valley Rehabilitation Center!" my mom whispered furiously at my father.

I could just imagine it now. My mom, tears brimming in her eyes for the hundredth time this week, looking up at my father—

who would have rather been back on his phone and putting this whole situation out of his mind—and pleading for her son to get thrown in some mental hospital because she was afraid to be alone with him.

"He needs some serious mental help," she continued, her voice cracking at the end.

That was the thing—I didn't want help. I wanted to be dead.

This week all I kept hearing was how I needed help. In stale rooms and cold leather chairs, I tried to look anywhere but into the burning gaze of Dr. Marinzel, whose eyes seemed to go right through me. Typically, I settled on this terrible drawing of a bear on the wall, or a cow—I could never make out exactly what the creature was, so I'd spend my sessions trying to figure it out. Marinzel, or Marty, who insisted we both be on a first name basis, was consistently trying to get me to talk—but I couldn't. I hated myself more for putting myself in this situation. I was embarrassed that everyone knew what I tried to do. I never wanted to disappear more. So I pretended that I wasn't there. I didn't talk for a full week.

"How are you feeling today?"

Silence.

"You don't have to talk until you're ready."

Silence.

"Everest, I believe you have major depression. You may feel a lot of negative emotions with this diagnosis, like shame? Or anger. That's normal. You don't need to come to terms with clinical depression right away. What's most important is that you know that you aren't alo—"

Silence.

I ignored Marty for so long that he stopped prodding me and

instead we spent our hour with him staring at me while I stared at the drawing, most likely in hopes that the silence would get too loud for me. Sometimes it did, but I never knew what to say when those moments came. Sometimes I'd lose myself in the whispering classical music he'd play. It wasn't exactly my style, but some music is better than no music. Thankfully, my parents saw that I wasn't getting any better and decided I didn't have to attend any more sessions. During our last session Marty decided to join my observation.

"What an odd-looking monkey," he remarked, and I turned my head to the angle he was viewing it from, and sure enough, the muddled picture finally made sense.

"All this time I thought it was a bear." I leaned back against the hard cushion seemingly satisfied, and it was then that I realized this was the first time I had talked since the attempt. Marty realized, too, because, for a brief moment, his face flashed with surprise before he concealed it.

* * *

My father's sharp voice shook my thoughts. I squeezed my eyes shut harder as I heard my parents' footsteps approach. "No son of mine is crazy. He will not attend that crazy house. I can't have that kind of baggage under our name."

Oh, I almost forgot the argument between my parents about attempting to send me away to a building filled with Martys trying to pick apart the darkest parts of my mind. Good thing my dad's pride would never allow such a thing. The only reason I was in therapy was because it was kind of mandatory after trying to kill yourself. Who would've thought?

I felt a hand laid on my forehead gently.

"I failed as a mother." Wetness invaded my cheeks as my mom sobbed. Her tears rolled down my cheeks and down my neck. I lay there, not daring to open my eyes.

"Go get yourself cleaned up. The nurses are going to come in soon to check his vitals. Your makeup is dripping," my father's deep voice commented, void of any emotion. He didn't even cry at his brother's funeral. I wasn't surprised he wouldn't have any emotion at a time like this. Sometimes I wondered if he had to charge himself at night.

"Okay," she replied, her voice broken. Her hand left my forehead, and I soon heard my mother's designer heels click out of the hospital room.

I felt my father's presence tower over me, watching me. I took deep breaths and let the oxygen pass through my nose, to make the idea of me sleeping more realistic.

The beats of my heart filled my ears in an almost a mocking tone. My chest moved up and down with each breath. Lungs expanded and deflated, one of the most disappointing rhythms I'd ever heard.

I didn't even realize my father was still in here until I heard his phone ringing.

"Hey, baby, I can't wait to see you tonight." He spoke in a hushed whisper. I didn't know why though, it wasn't like I didn't already know he was screwing his assistant.

While my mom had been here—afraid out of her mind— beside me, my dad had been seizing the opportunity to further his affair. I thought this one's name was Tanya. She was twenty-four-years old and was into men with wives and money.

I was sure my mom suspected it, but she'd rather ignore the situation. It was so painfully obvious, and I didn't understand how she could. Late nights in the office, business trips that weren't actually business, and an assistant who dressed like she was trying to satisfy every man's wet dream. She tried to come onto me once, but gold-digging vultures with more boobs than brains weren't really my type. My father chuckled deeply into the phone, which was actually a weird sound because my father never laughed . . . and because he sounded like a bald, eighty-year-old man who only wore wifebeaters with denim cutoff shorts.

The door opened and my mother's heels clicked toward where I lay and my father stood.

"Okay, remember to bring those forms to the meeting tonight. I'll see you later." He cleared his throat and spoke professionally before ending the call.

"Another meeting?" My mom sounded back to her regular self.

"Yeah, Sonya and I have some more business to discuss."

"Hadley's recital is tonight. Can you please stay with Everest so I can go to her event?"

My father cleared his throat, something he did when he didn't approve. "No, you have to stay. I have some important business I need to handle tonight at the office."

"Hadley has been with Susan all this week. I've barely seen my daughter. I must go to her recital. I'm sure she'd want her mom there rather than her nanny. I've been in this hospital all week, and I need to get out. This is your second visit—all I'm asking for is for you to put your work aside and watch him for one night."

She talked about me like I was unstable and would probably

murder the whole hospital if someone didn't have an eye on me.

"He doesn't need someone to watch him. Go to the recital and I'll go to work, and that's final."

Hours later and I was alone. But that was how I wanted to be anyway.

3

BEVERLY

She stumbled through the front door and removed her heels. Her hair was a wild mess and her eyes bled mascara. It was six in the morning, and the dried puke on my mother's jacket was a clear indicator that she'd enjoyed herself last night.

"Here, come on. Let's get you to bed," I said, making her jump slightly.

"Why are you still up?" she slurred slightly, chuckling a little.

"I'm about to leave for school. The bus will be here pretty soon. I have a big test first period and I was studying a few notes before you came." I grabbed her arm and led her to her room.

Her eyes instantly shut in comfort as she climbed into her bed.

"Who would have thought I would have given birth to a nerd," she cackled against her pillow as I pulled off her jacket.

She moaned and gripped her head. "Can you please hand me

the painkillers? This headache is killing me, and if you really love me, you'll make me some breakfast before you go."

I hated when she said that: *If you really love me you will.* I couldn't even remember the last time she told me she loved me, but yet it seemed like I had to constantly prove my love. "I have, like, seven minutes to make the bus, I don't have the time to . . ." I gripped my bag, glancing at the clock hanging above her bedroom door.

"You can't take seven minutes of your time to make your own mother some breakfast?" she spat, her eyes red and her breath bad.

I missed the bus.

I missed the test.

But my mom didn't miss breakfast.

I grabbed my books as the bell for third period rang. The halls filled quickly, and it wasn't long before we were packed like sardines in a can. The raging school of students flushed through and was about to dive into its classes. I tried to stay with the current until everyone stilled in a tight circle, staring at the scene that played before their eyes. I didn't care what they were seeing; I was just trying to make my way to my locker. I pushed and slid around the thick crowd, until I, too, became rooted to the spot.

Everest.

He murmured quickly to Cara, a gray hoodie covering his head. He was positioned at an angle that only gave away the profile of his face.

I felt like I was seeing a ghost. Even though I knew he didn't actually die, looking at him, I didn't think he'd ever come back. It had been two weeks since the first day of school, and the Everest drama had sort of died down since then.

But there he was. In the flesh.

Cara's features betrayed only disgust. "You have some nerve coming here." He tried to grab her arm but she yanked it back. "Don't touch me."

Everest glanced around the large crowd and I saw redness— sadness—brimming in his irises. He quickly whipped his head back toward Cara.

"Look, he's about to cry," someone laughed in the crowd, causing a few more chuckles to arise in the large group.

"Is this really how you're going to treat me?" I'd never seen Everest angry before.

Cara shrugged and grabbed some books from her locker, her blond hair shielding her face. Nash stood between them, his face a sleet of stone. "Get outta here, man. You don't belong here anymore."

His words struck me to the core, so I could only imagine how Everest felt. Head hung low, the gray hoodie shielding his head, strands of his bronze hair sticking from out of the top, he nodded slowly before turning on his heel and storming out of the high school.

Teachers came into the hall to break up the crowd, and for the second time, my heart broke for Everest.

4

EVEREST

"I never thought the day would come that *the* Everest Finley would ask for my services," Mikey rasped out in a deep chuckle before taking another hit from his blunt.

Never did I ever think I would come here. I dreamed of dying and never having to accept the reality of the world. But here I was, buying weed and beer, allowing myself to sit in this dirty basement and forget about everything.

Mikey Cosweld, school stoner and lowlife, allowed people to chill in his basement. The Basement was full of druggies and drinkers. You entered through the garage because his grandpap had the late shift and needed to rest. You smoked and drank, maybe even popped a few pills. But you never talked about your problems; this wasn't a shrink's office. After handing him a fifty-dollar bill, I grabbed the brown paper bag, the key to my oblivion.

"Whoa, dude, what's with the scars on your arm?" some guy from behind me asked.

"I . . . my . . . I have a crazy cat," I lied, hoping no one could sense my discomfort.

Mikey eyed me, and I knew I'd failed.

"I want a cat, *ha-ha-ha,* so cute and fat," some girl with purple hair on the old ratted couch giggled. She laughed and laughed, and I struggled to see what was so funny.

"I can cover that up." Mikey nodded toward my wrist.

He must have read my confused facial expression because he lifted his sleeve to reveal a new set of sleeves—ones that were obtained by ink.

I looked back at him and he shrugged. "I had a cat too."

After a few hits from my joint and a couple of beers, I looked like a different person. It didn't take much. The girl with purple hair, who I later learned was Aurora, asked to dye my hair from its sandy-brown color to the darkest level of black, and I didn't care to decline. My left arm was scattered in ink, a half-sleeve design that was pretty all right, even though I'd regret it later, but not now. I didn't care. I was getting sick of seeing the same person in the mirror anyway.

* * *

When I looked in the mirror the next morning, part of me absolutely hated it. It was the complete opposite of who I always was, and that was why the other part of me loved it. After getting ready for the day, I treaded down the stairs and was met by my mom and sister sitting at the large mahogany dining-room table.

"Good morning, Everest," Susan greeted me with a wry smile and wide eyes.

Hadley looked up from her breakfast and glanced at me before quickly glancing back down and chewing on her toast like it was the most interesting thing in the world.

My mother gasped. "What have you done?"

I was out all night and she didn't even care to know where I was.

No calls.

No texts.

Some people may find it weird that I wanted my mom to call me, but it would show that she'd care if I was gone. Ever since I came home from the hospital she'd avoided me at all costs. This was the first time she actually acknowledged me, and it was to scold my appearance. I ignored her and grabbed an apple from the dining table.

"Why would you do that to yourself? How will you go out in public now? Matter of fact, you will go nowhere until I call Dr. Marinzel."

So he can prod me with questions again just to offer lousy solutions?

"Fuck no," I laughed in response, as she let out another gasp.

I'd never cursed before. I felt that notion was completely unnecessary, but it was time for changes, and I was loving every bit of it.

"I don't know who you are anymore," my mother said to herself, a wild look of sorrow and bewilderment on her features.

I grabbed my hoodie and walked toward the front door. "You never did."

"Where are you going?!" my mother yelled after receiving my parting blow of words.

"To another place I don't belong," I answered, shutting the door behind me.

5

BEVERLY

Heading into school that morning, I walked right past a group of students vying for attention during school elections.

"Vote Nami Lynn for senior class president." The girl absentmindedly handed me a flyer and a lollipop.

There wasn't much diversity in this school, but Nami Lynn was among those small numbers. Being black and Asian didn't stop her from climbing up the social ladder. Her ethnicity didn't get in the way of the things she wanted. She was president of almost all of the clubs and her grades were impeccable. Nami Lynn was just one of those people who seemed to have their lives together.

I watched as she threw a lollipop at Nash's head. "Vote for me, bitch."

Nash rubbed at his head as Cara glared at Nami.

"You look tense. You should masturbate with a knife sometime,

I bet that will loosen you up, darling." Nami smiled sweetly at Cara's horrified expression before walking away.

I chuckled and slipped the lollipop and flyer into my bag. I was going to vote for her even though it wasn't like she was going to lose. She'd won for the past three years.

I gathered my belongings from my locker with a smile. I was seemingly in a good mood for no reason at all. Maybe because lunch was next period.

"Whoa, is that who is think it is?" I heard someone say, bringing my attention to the end of the hall.

Gray hoodie. Everest.

Instead of bronze hair sticking from out of the hood, the hair was now black. He dyed his hair? His head was covered as he put his bag into his locker.

"Hey, Everest." Martha Summers, one of the cheerleaders from Cara's entourage, swayed her hips toward Everest and threw him a flirty smile.

He turned and she gasped. "What's next? Black nail polish?"

I couldn't see from the angle where I was standing, but other people stood around with surprised looks on their faces. Cara's eyes practically bulged out of her head, and even Nash looked startled. I really wanted to see what they were seeing, but the lunch bell rang, and I was really hungry.

After waiting in line for about two minutes, I heard Nami's voice as she joined the end of the line.

". . . and he stuck his middle finger up, and asked her if black would be a cute color on that nail," she laughed along with her best friend, Tiffany.

Tiffany's laugh rang through the line. "That was so funny, her face turned, like, six shades of red. I never knew Everest could be capable of being rude to someone."

"Are you guys talking about Everest? Am I the only one who thinks his new bad-boy image is sexy?" Another female voice joined the conversation.

I couldn't believe what I was hearing. Everest sticking up his middle finger was such a taboo thought. Everest being bad? An even stranger thought.

Grabbing my water, I made my way to my dusty utopia. The sunlight barely peeked through the large windows—it was a beautiful autumn day. I couldn't help but smile. I sat at my usual table and pulled out my brown paper bag before something happened that I would never forget.

"Are you lost?"

The voice was dangerously husky, and I almost fell out of my chair. No one ever came to the library in the east wing, so randomly hearing a deep voice inside a badly lit library was enough to make me almost crap myself. I dropped my sandwich and hurried to the door before I saw Everest come out from behind a bookshelf. I stilled and zoned in on his face. He looked confused as I stared at his newly ebony hair.

He looked so different.

My throat itched as smoke filled my nose. I glanced down at the smoking object in Everest's hands.

Since when did he start smoking?

"Helloo?" he asked, slightly annoyed. He brought the smoking object to his lips and puffed. It was slightly beautiful—the image, I mean, not the potential risk of lung cancer.

"Smoking isn't good for you," I blurted, mentally slapping myself.

He stared at me weirdly for a second before chuckling. "Neither is trying to kill yourself, but that didn't stop me either."

Everest brought the butt back up to his mouth and the smoke

whizzed around him. His strong jawline flexed as the smoke floated in patterns before disappearing.

"Are *you* lost?" I asked.

"Huh?" He squinted his eyes at me, and his mouth gaped slightly open in a sideways fashion.

"You asked me if I was lost, but I've always been here. I'm not the lost one, you are."

Everest glanced down at the ground before looking back up at me. His piercing eyes met mine, making my skin tingle, before he chuckled a humorless laugh. "I guess I am the lost one."

And in that moment, I realized I was talking to *someone*. Not only someone, but Everest, the most popular guy in school. Everest, the boy who tried to kill himself; the boy with the sad eyes. I noticed the crinkles between his eyebrows and I wanted to do something about them.

"My name is Beverly, and we are going to be good friends."

I walked closer to him and held my hand out. My heart thumped in my ears as I waited for him to respond. The energy of the room stilled, and maybe I'd ruined whatever I'd tried to start. He stared down at my hand before returning the handshake.

"My name is Everest, and there is no chance in hell."

This is going to be a little harder than I thought.

6

EVEREST

The first thing I noticed about Beverly was the four freckles that sat on the bridge of her nose. I immediately felt bad at how quickly I dismissed her. She looked harmless. I watched as her big brown eyes filled with disappointment, and she released my hand before she smiled.

"Good thing we aren't in hell."

Is she for real?

"Are you hungry?" she asked randomly.

"Not really," I responded, quirking my left eyebrow at her. This girl was sort of strange.

"You sure? I don't mind splitting my sandwich, and plus smoking can't possibly be a filling lunch." She laughed quietly at her lame joke and looked down at her shoes before glancing back up at me.

This girl was too nice. I already felt like a jerk for being rude, and although I was going through some stuff right now, she hadn't done anything to me. I threw the cigarette on the ground and immediately crushed it under my boot. I took a deep breath while I bit down on my lip. "What kind of sandwich are we talking about here?"

I was hungrier than I realized and ended up eating my half and Beverly's. She saw me eyeing her half, and so she just gave it to me.

"Turkey and avocado is actually way better than what I thought it would taste like." I spoke into the silence.

"Told you," she said, and stared at me in almost an observing way, like she was the scientist and I was the specimen. Fidgeting in the oak chair, I looked away because, honestly, that was really weird.

"So, what do you like to do for fun?" she asked, her nose wrinkling slightly.

No one had ever asked me that question. The only instance was when we all had to fill out those random questionnaires on the first day of school so the teachers could get to know us better, but I was in the hospital this year, so I didn't exactly get the chance to read that question and jot down those same eight letters. Mostly because that was what I liked to do, and partly because that was the answer everyone expected me to put. I'd had a football glued to my hand for as long as I could remember. My dad played for this school back in his day, so I guessed he wanted to keep the legacy alive.

The game was fun for a while, but the pressure of winning wasn't. My dad got a call from the coach saying that I couldn't be quarterback this year because I missed too many practices while I was in the hospital, but I think we both knew it was because they didn't want a nutcase running the team. My dad's heated glare still followed me, and the mist of disappointment and disgust still hung in that room.

"I like to sing?" I said. I hadn't spoken this revelation out loud before, and not answering "football" for the first time was tripping me out a little bit.

Her eyes grew bigger and she smiled an open-mouthed smile, her chest raised as if she had something on the tip of her tongue but couldn't get it out.

"Really? I work at this café on Brisklin Street and we have a lot of underground artists and people who come and play their music. You should come over sometime."

She almost reminded me of a cartoon character, she was so animated. I stared at her for a minute, and for the life of me I couldn't understand why I'd just told her that.

"Maybe I will," I said before I heard the dismissal bell.

What just happened?

7

BEVERLY

I love the way rain sometimes falls sideways, and even the most beautiful things aren't straight edged. That was all I could think about as I sat in the passenger seat on the way to work.

"Hurry up, this rain is doing horrible things to my hair," my mom said.

I pulled my head from the clouds to see my mother's stormy expression. I wasn't sure why she was upset, though—she was under the protection of her Honda, and her hair looked fine. I gathered my bag and prepared to make my way out of the car and into the rain to cross the street to my job.

My mother worked at the local salon. She'd had me at a young age, when opportunities were limited. Becoming a new mom and losing the love of her life within the span of two years definitely bruised my mother in a way that I never figured out how to heal. The story was that my grandparents never approved of my parents' relationship, and when a pregnancy came into the mix, it only made matters worse. Her pregnancy rattled the already loose foundation of the nest, and so her parents decided it was time for her to fly away. They kicked her out but my dad was there to bring her in. My father was a miracle baby, conceived by surprise. My father's parents were well into middle age when he came around. He was spoiled rotten because they never expected to have any children. My mom said when she told my father she was pregnant, he laughed. He never took anything too seriously. For my mom, that was a breath of fresh air compared to the restricted background she was raised in, which was pretty much all I knew about my mother's side of the story because she never talked about it.

When my grandmother on my father's side passed away a few months into my development, my father turned up his reckless behavior. Things only got worse when his father passed away from a heart attack three weeks after my first birthday. Shortly after that, Sebastian "Bash" Remington was gone too. My mother, riddled with shock and overwhelming pain, moved as far away as she could. She wanted no traces of the boy she loved or the family that took her in. If you looked around our shabby apartment, you wouldn't find a single photo. But that was okay because I knew how much it hurt her even bringing up anything about him.

It was hard to miss something that you didn't remember. It was even harder missing something you *did* remember.

So I didn't complain or ask questions. I helped her with anything she needed. The pay at the salon wasn't the best—I couldn't even tell you how many times I'd scraped up anything I could find to make meals. Or the number of times there were more batteries in the fridge than food. So, when I turned fifteen, I started working at 21 Daisies Café. It was a win-win situation. I worked somewhere I loved, and I could help my mom out with the bills.

"You're going to pick me up right?" I asked, already knowing the answer.

"I have an appointment—Brazilian blowout. I need the gas to get back home," she lied, but I didn't say anything.

I nodded. Disappointment hit me hard, but I refused to show it. I smiled and pretended that she wasn't going to the bar with Aunt Macy. My mom didn't really get to have a childhood; she had to take care of me. So I couldn't be selfish and interrupt her plans. The walk home wasn't that bad anyway. It was just unnerving how effortlessly she could lie to me.

I watched as she drove off and the rain swished beneath her tires. God, I loved the rain. I could literally have stood out here forever—the way the rain was still dribbling from the sunny sky was so beautiful. If I didn't have work today, I probably would just stand out here.

"Hey, Betty," Felix, my bearded hippie co-worker, greeted me when I entered.

Poppy, Lily, and Rose all greeted me afterward. Their grandma, Daisy, owned the place. I asked them once what was with all the flowers, and they told me it was family tradition to name the girls after flowers. I didn't think the "flower triplets" or Felix cared to call me by my actual name. Trying to correct them was no use, because every time I'd come in, they'd call me Betty.

I greeted them with a smile.

"Hey, guys."

The café was just one of those places that gave you a relaxed vibe. Candles were placed on the tables, filling the place with an indescribable warmth. Poets lay in beanbags and wrote their works, and musicians sat in the back and strummed their guitars. An hour passed, and I was completely relaxed—not that many people came in, so I only occasionally had to actually use the register.

I read behind the counter until a customer came in to order coffee and a gluten-free cupcake. Some nights I sat on the edge of the counter and listened to an indie artist sing a song on the stage that sat in the back of the café.

No one really talked to me, but I didn't really mind.

I grabbed a cinnamon muffin from the glass case to eat. No lunch today meant my stomach was growling. I smiled a little to myself thinking about Everest eating my sandwich. I placed two dollars in the register to pay for the muffin, and watched as Felix hugged Lily from behind. I couldn't get over how the two of them were engaged. It was like I could still remember the first time Felix came in, with his fedora and long brown beard.

I was so engrossed in watching their embrace, I didn't even notice the bell above the door ring.

8

EVEREST

My mother was convinced I was a drug addict. I overheard her rambling on the phone, probably to one of her old cheer buddies, with great concern for my behavior.

"He's slipping through the cracks," she said. Pause. "He reeks of weed." Pause. "Yes, I went into his room today and confiscated it."

I sighed, slightly bothered by the fact she was in my room, and majorly frustrated to wake up to her complaining about me. I rolled out of bed and threw on an outfit from the clothes already scattered on the floor. It was wrinkled and worn but I didn't mind. The sun assured me that I didn't completely sleep the day away, and sure enough, my bong and bud were gone from my nightstand. I knew exactly where to find them, though. My mom hid everything under her bed.

Careful not to be seen or heard, I slipped into her room, not in the mood for questions. Thankfully, my mom was still on the phone listing how disappointing I was. Crouching down, I looked and saw nothing but junk under her bed: gifts for Hadley, a few boxes, my dad's favorite ugly yellow tie, and, boom, my things.

I bent down and pulled but instead of my weed, it was a photo. My mind blanked.

He was in his favorite sci-fi fan shirt, smiling the width of Texas. It had been a year and three days, but it felt longer. There wasn't a single day when I didn't think about him. It happened so swiftly. I could be tying my shoe, and suddenly, I remembered that my uncle died in a car crash. Something deep prickled the inside of my stomach. I could have cried, but I held it back.

I looked again and noticed that the photo came from one of the boxes. Inside, it only revealed an old pair of his glasses and a small black notebook. I always thought my dad wasn't affected by my uncle's death in the slightest, but why would he have these things if that was the case? The thought ran away as quickly as it came. I grabbed the notebook and flipped it open. The curiosity swallowed me whole. The first page was labeled *Confessions* in his familiar chicken-scratch handwriting.

February 20, 2005

I don't know if I have the heart to tell my wife I hate her cooking.

June 2, 2003

I genuinely hate receiving compliments.

October 11, 2007

Maybe I should start my own radio show, conversations with myself are too good to not be displayed.

May 6, 1990

My father is a terrible person but I can't help but love him.

Page after page was another date and another confession. I knew I should stop reading, but I couldn't. I gorged myself on the words. I was back with my uncle, in a way. He was right beside me, with his messy hair and cheesy smile, telling me all of his secrets. I read and read until I heard my mom's voice growing closer and closer. I stuffed my belongings in my pocket along with the small notebook and left.

* * *

I stopped by the Basement, but Mikey was leaving for his dad's house for the week. And now I was even stopping by Brisklin Street because I didn't know where else to go. I drove around the street three times before I finally decided to go to the café.

Whether or not Beverly had a shift today didn't even cross my mind as I approached the quaint coffee shop. The closer I got, the more the internal battle inside my head increased. She had invited me to come, but I didn't think she'd meant so soon. Walking across the wet pavement, I pulled open the door. The warmth instantly surrounded me as I took in the place. Surprisingly, I was in a good mood. The first thing that caught my eye was the girl sing-ing softly and playing her guitar on a stage. People were sitting at tables, either typing away alone on their laptops or having a cup of coffee with a friend. The place smelled like indescribable spices.

It was *calming*.

"Whoa, who's the cutie?" I turned my head to face two identical-looking girls. They both shared the gene of red hair, but it was obvi-ous that one shade was darker. The darker-haired one walked over to me and smiled slyly, like she was the fox and I was the chicken. "Hey. I'm Rose."

The lighter redhead stayed behind and threw me a smile and a wave, before turning and tapping a blond who shared the same distinct features as the other two. They were triplets. A guy with a long beard standing with her turned to look at me. The eyes and the stares bothered me. I felt as though I was being violated of the right of ever being viewed as a normal person. The change of the gazes from admiration to judging was astonishing.

"Everest."

I kept it simple and didn't even throw a fake smile like I usu-ally did. My lips remained in their thin line, and I was sure that my eyebrows tightened as well. A small gasp entered the room, but it was so discreet that if the room wasn't so quiet, there would be no way that I would have heard it.

"You came." I turned and saw Beverly smiling, her eyes bright-ening, and I couldn't understand why.

She walked from behind the counter and toward me, ventur-ing through the triplets and bearded guy, and wrapped her arms around my torso in a tight hug. I immediately tensed.

"You know this guy?" the fox asked. Such a perplexing ques-tion due to the fact that Beverly didn't actually know me.

"He goes to my school, and I invited him to come check the place out," she said after she released her arms from around me, her face a tad disappointed that I didn't hug her back.

The guy with the beard tapped her hard on the shoulder and chuckled loudly. "Good job, Betty! Keep bringing in customers."

Betty? Her face went slack, but I think I was the only one who noticed.

"Hey, weren't you on the news? For . . ." the light red-haired girl said, her eyes searching for recognition.

"Poppy! You can't just ask people stuff like that," Rose cut her off, giving me an apologetic look.

"Attempting to kill himself? Yes, that's me," I cut off the fox, my bluntness shocking even me.

Their mouths took the shape of circles, but Beverly just stared at me. I was starting to notice that she did that a lot. But it didn't really bother me as much as the other ones did; her eyes weren't judging, just curious.

"Wow, how did you do it? They didn't say on the news. Isn't your dad Frank Finley from Finley Corp? Dude, is there any way you could advertise our lil ol' place? It would really help . . ."

"Poppy!" The blond spoke for the first time. She turned toward me with a sad smile, and I wanted to shut my eyes so I wouldn't have to see it.

"Twenty-three years old and she still doesn't have a filter, I'm so sorry. You can order anything, it'll be on the house for whenever you're hungry." She tucked a strand of her blond hair behind her ear.

"Really, Lily? He's filthy rich and we are giving him free food? That makes no s—" Rose wrapped her fingers around Poppy's mouth.

"Shut up," Rose scolded her, and I looked over at Beverly, who was now staring at the stage. She must have felt my gaze because she turned back to me and nodded her head toward a table near the stage.

We sat at the small square table and she propped her head up, her chin upon her fist and her elbow grounded to the table. She did that weird staring thing again, and I directed my eyes toward the stage.

"Sorry about Poppy, she's kind of . . ."

"It's cool." I shrugged it off and looked back at the stage.

"No, it wasn't," she mumbled, and from the corner of my eye, I saw her take a bite from a muffin.

We sat in comfortable silence for a while, until she started staring at me again, her large brown eyes reading me.

"Did your mom ever tell you it's rude to stare?" I asked, turning to stare at her now.

"Nope," she answered innocently, sincerely.

"Well, it is," I said, slightly annoyed.

"Sorry," she apologized, oblivious to the little crumbs that had made a home on her cheeks. She even had bits of crumbs in her curly black hair. I wanted to remove them but I ignored that feeling. Now that I was looking at her hair, it was oddly distracting—the large spirals that covered her head were almost hypnotic.

"Did your mom ever tell you it's rude to stare?" she teased my words back at me.

"You have some crumbs . . ." I gestured to my cheek. She brushed them off, missing a spot, but I didn't say anything. I had already made myself look stupid, and thought it would be best if I didn't say anything else.

"You know what I've realized about you?" she asked, her eyes bright and full of knowing.

"What?"

"You've turned into, like, this dark cloud."

"Excuse me?"

"You're like this gloomy shadow, just floating around, ready to explode." She took another bite of her muffin.

"Sorry?" I didn't really know what else to say.

"No, don't be. Because without those clouds, we wouldn't have rain."

"But rain ruins," I added, thinking about the topic. We all seek shelter from the storm.

Beverly was interesting—weird, but no less intriguing. In less than twenty-four hours, she'd been nothing but nice to me even when everyone else wasn't. Even after I was a jerk. Even after knowing I tried to kill myself.

"You know what I realized?" I asked her. She looked at me curiously, her left eyebrow arching upward. "You are too positive."

"W-What?" She reeled from laughter; her large smile causing my lips to twitch slightly.

"You're just too much rainbow and butterflies. I could take a dump on this table right now and you'd call it art." She laughed louder this time, and I couldn't help the chuckle that escaped from my mouth.

"You can't be too positive," she giggled.

"You're too positive. It's nice to know destruction sometimes," I said.

"You hold too much destruction, it's good to have positivity too," she replied.

I eyed her half-eaten muffin, and she rolled her eyes before pushing it toward me. I bit into it while she stared at the performance taking place onstage.

"This muffin has made a positive impact on my taste buds."
I cracked a joke, and a feeling hit me right in the gut. I couldn't
even remember how long it was since I was genuinely amused.
She chuckled at my words, her eyes diverted away from the stage,
downward, and then finally meeting my eyes.

"Why don't you go home, Betty? We got it from here," Poppy
yelled across the café.

Beverly looked up. "You sure?"

"Yeah, go spend time with your boyfriend."

Beverly's eyes grew huge, and she fumbled over her words.
"We aren't together."

She looked at me, embarrassed. She got up, stumbling from
the chair, and made her way behind the counter to get her bag.
I followed her and stuck my hands in the pockets of my hoodie,
unsure of what to do next. She pulled on her jacket, and when she
turned to grab her bag, our eyes connected.

"Do you need a ride?" I asked, swinging my keys on my ring
finger.

* * *

"Nice car," she said as she climbed into the passenger seat of my
pride and joy.

I'd got this Ford Mustang on my sixteenth birthday. Nash had
spent the night when my parents "surprised" me first thing in
the morning. Only it wasn't a surprise at all—I'd been telling my
parents I wanted a '67 Mustang since my uncle bought himself
one when I was ten. No, the only thing surprising that day was
when I caught Nash kissing Jacob Riley, our rival team's quarterback. Nash was mortified but I didn't care. You love who you love.

He made me promise not to tell anyone and I hadn't broken that promise. I would never break it.

"Yeah, it's all right," I answered absentmindedly, my thoughts wandering.

The tension in the car was awkward. Beverly was sitting with her hands in her lap, staring out the window. I turned the music on and tapped my fingers on the wheel. It was some terrible pop song, but it would do for the silence.

"I live in the east end." She practically swallowed her words so quickly that I barely caught them.

The car ride consisted of awkward eye contact, September night air passing through our hair, and laughing at stupid random things. When we got to the edge of her neighborhood, she grew even more tense.

"You can drop me off right here," she said. I looked around and there weren't any houses.

"Live at a secret location?" I joked.

"Something like that. Bye, Ev."

I found myself kind of liking the nickname. Everyone always referred to my name formally. Now, after my attempt, it wasn't nicknames, but horrible names. And this was the first new nickname that I'd liked.

"Bye, Bev." I smiled as she climbed out of my car.

As I drove off, I realized that Beverly was the first person who'd treated me normally after my attempt.

9

BEVERLY

Have you ever woken up with the bright sun welcoming you, the birds outside chirping, and you didn't seem to mind? You lay there in bed thinking that you were happy just to be alive?

If you haven't, then I'm sorry, because on this particular morning, I was happy to be alive—to hear those birds and feel the warmth of the sun coming from the window. My thoughts were too big to fit in my twin bed. I was thinking about nothing at all, but everything. I knew that didn't make sense, but it did to me.

"Beverly!" the voice cut through my reverie. "Come on, get up and clean this place, it's a wreck."

The Friday morning feeling soon died. I checked the time and I had about an hour and some change to get ready for school. As I walked into the hall, I peeked into my mother's bedroom, where she was sound asleep. A burning smell came from the kitchen, and when I entered, my aunt, Macy, lit a cigarette.

She must have spent the night, because she was wearing clothes that were wrinkled, and her once heavy makeup was smeared.

"You shouldn't really smoke in here, it takes a while to get the smell out," I said, opening the fridge and pulling out some orange juice.

"Maybe, but some cleaning around here will get the smell out. It's a mess here. Your mom works hard. The least you can do is clean up," she lectured, taking another puff from her cigarette, her long hot-pink nails harboring the cancer stick.

I glanced around the kitchen and saw dishes piled high in the sink, a Chipotle bag on the floor, ashes from cigarettes laying around, garbage filled to capacity, and an empty wine bottle sitting on the stove. My mother told me she didn't have any gas to come and pick me up, but she had enough money for her little adult get-together last night.

I swallowed the frustration. I had nothing to do with this mess—I came straight home and went to sleep. Throwback music, smoke, and laughter filled the living room all last night, but I didn't mind. I just didn't understand why I had to clean up their mess.

"I'll clean it," I replied, gripping the glass of my orange juice tight.

My aunt Macy is like my second mother. She was there for my mom before I was even a thought. They'd been best friends since sixth grade. And when my mom and I left after my dad died, Macy came with us; they've always been two against the world.

"Yeah, you have to pick up your weight aroun—" Her obnoxious ringtone cut her off and she answered her phone.

I placed bread in the toaster and ate a banana while I waited for my toast.

"Seriously? . . . but . . . I can't . . . please," she argued into her phone as I sipped more of my orange juice.

She hung up, and her head drooped low, her long black hair covering her face. She pulled on the long stands and groaned. Sitting up, she took another puff from her cig. I tried to ignore her, but her constant groaning was an obvious sign that she wanted me to ask her what was wrong.

"What's wrong?" I asked cautiously.

"My job interview is at the same time I have to pick up Manny from school."

It wasn't not surprising that Macy would want to get a second job. The pay at the salon sucked.

"Didn't he just start at that new private school?" I asked, remembering that Manny was one of my favorite people in the entire world. He was eleven, but had a much older mentality. Manny was the brother I never had.

"Yeah, you know where Carnegie Pine is?" she asked.

"Right around the corner from Nesbits' bowling alley?"

The bowling alley was a mile from my school, and I heard people making plans to go there all the time, but I'd never been.

"Exactly! You'll pick him up? Thank you, Beverly, you're a lifesaver. You may have to watch him for a few hours until the interview is over."

My toast popped violently out of the toaster as she hugged me tightly, reeking of nicotine and cheap perfume. I didn't remember agreeing, but I'd pick him up. I hadn't seen Manny in a while. After getting ready for school, and after persuading my mom to let me take her car, I left. If I was going to be honest, I liked taking the bus rather than walking or driving because although nobody talked to me, I still valued their company. I could deal with solitude, but I didn't prefer it.

Walking into my high school, I felt like I carried a secret. I'd hung out with Everest Finley, and I would never forget it. When lunch rolled around, I wondered if Everest would be in the library. I, at least, hoped I would meet his Earthly eyes again. But when I entered my spot, he wasn't there. I felt kind of silly for thinking that he would come back.

* * *

School was the same old thing. It was as though yesterday never happened, like I dreamed it all up—that I believed that not only had I talked to someone, but that it was Everest. The day was quickly over and I drove to pick up Manny. With the window rolled down, as the colored leaves blew gently in midair, I wished I could take a picture because it was so pretty.

I turned up the radio slightly as Ed Sheeran eased out of the speakers. Out of the corner of my eye, I watched as a guy stumbled out of a house, clearly not in the right state of mind, but what caught my eye was the gray hoodie and black hair. Lots of people have gray hoodies and black hair, but it was just too coincidental—a guy of Everest's build leaving from a garage door and stumbling slightly.

Waiting at the red light, I watched as the guy climbed into a Mustang—a replica of the red Mustang that Everest had driven me home in.

It was Everest. And he was in no condition to drive.

At the next given opportunity, I made a U-turn. I was relieved to know that he hadn't started driving yet; actually, the car wasn't even on. When I climbed out of my vehicle, I looked into the window to see Everest sitting in the passenger seat stuffing his face with a hard-shell taco.

He didn't even notice me as he practically inhaled the taco. He looked crazy, with his eyes tinged with pink and the food enabling a satisfied look on his face. He even went to take a bite of his taco and missed a few times. I knocked on the window and he looked behind him.

Seriously?

"Who is it?" he laughed to no one in particular.

I knocked again. "Everest," I called.

He whipped his head around, and smiled. He looked like a giddy little kid with his goofy smile, remnants of his food around his lips. He rolled the window down and rested his chin on his arm.

"Are you stalking me?" he asked, his smile strangely comforting. It was like a glimpse of the old Everest, the one who smiled all the time.

"Are you okay?" I asked him as a slight, foul odor filled my nose.

"I'm just so pea-cc-hh-yy."

The fact that he could barely get the sentence out though his laugher was an indication that I had to get him home.

He started laughing randomly. "I want a cat."

"Why don't you let me take you home?" I asked him, treading lightly.

He stared at me for about a full thirty seconds before he stepped out of his car. I grabbed his keys and locked the car, then slid the keys into my pocket.

"Can we go to Taco Bell?" he asked as I strapped him into the passenger seat of my car.

"I don't have any money," I responded, and started the car. He wiggled in his seat and dug his hands deep into his left pocket.

A lazy smile formed on his lips as he found what he was looking for, and he slapped a hundred-dollar bill on the armrest. "A-ha."

"That's a lot of money for Taco Bell."

I found it strange how he could just throw money around. Glancing at him, he shrugged. "I'm starving."

Checking the time, I realized Manny got out of school soon. Ignoring Everest as he talked about things that didn't make sense, I pulled up to the school.

I turned to Everest right before I left the car. "Don't move."

"Yes, banana." He saluted me, and I couldn't help but chuckle.

I searched for the dark-haired boy with hazel eyes and the Batman book bag.

"Beverly!" a voice shouted.

When I saw Manny, I pulled him into a tight hug. "Hey, bud." I ruffled his hair.

He smacked my hand away and gave me a toothy grin. "Where's my mom?"

"She had some business to take care of," I explained, walking toward the car. He nodded. He was so adorable, but I didn't voice my opinion because he got annoyed when I told him.

I opened the back-seat door for him, and he instantly looked at me. "Who's this?"

"My friend Everest. We are going to drop him off at his house first," I explained as I climbed into the driver's seat.

"You have friends?!" Manny asked, and I ignored the feeling in my chest.

Shut up, Manny.

"Can we please go to Taco Bell?" Everest asked again. He was positioned as if he was napping, with the seat slightly reclined and his eyes shut. His bottom lip jutted out slightly.

"Taco Bell sounds nice right now," Manny added.

Everest perked up and turned toward Manny. He held out his fist and they fist-bumped. "See, even the kid knows what's up."

"Okay, fine," I agreed.

Everest ordered twenty tacos and bought Manny whatever he wanted. Of course, I had to place the order because Everest was not in his right state of mind. He told me I could get something if I wanted to, but I wasn't hungry. Finding Everest's house was not hard—everyone knew where the Finley mansion was; it was the best house in town. I parked the car and started gathering bags.

"We're going in?" Manny asked, taking a huge bite from his burrito.

"Sure, I want to make sure he gets inside okay," I said while Everest tried to balance a piece of lettuce on his ear.

"You have weird friends." Manny observed Everest. "But he bought me burritos, so I guess he's pretty cool."

I used Everest's key to open the door. The place was so grand and beautiful, and I just knew I'd made the right decision not showing him what my home looked like.

"Wow," Manny said, astonished.

Everest patted Manny's head. "Game room is the third door on the left."

Manny ran off and Everest made his way into the kitchen. I followed him, and watched as he ate yet another taco.

"So good," he mumbled.

"Where is your room?" I asked.

He placed a hand on his stomach, and his face twisted in discomfort. I quickly pushed him toward the kitchen sink, into which he emptied the contents of his stomach.

"Where do you sleep?" I asked him once he was finished heaving.

"Fifth door . . . right." His voice was hoarse and he suddenly looked weak. I followed his directions, and led him to the unmade bed.

I took off his shoes, found a facecloth, ran it under some cold water, and placed it on his forehead. Then I went into the kitchen and grabbed him a bottle of water. The soft glow of the sun came through his window, and I closed the blinds so it wouldn't interfere with his rest. I placed his keys on the messy desk sitting in the corner of the room. Watching him for a second, with the little wet strands of his hair on his forehead, long lashes that fell gently upon his cheeks, and his cheeks with a hint of pink, he looked so peaceful.

I opened the door to leave before he gently called out my name. "Want to know something?" His eyes were still shut, a small smile faintly on his lips.

"What?" I said.

"You're the first black girl I've seen with freckles."

His voice was so soft I could tell he was falling asleep.

"Want to know something?" I asked him back.

"Sure," he whispered.

"I've never seen a white boy eat that many tacos." His smile was translucent before he pulled his pillow over his head.

Grabbing Manny, I left his house. After all, I still had a kitchen to clean.

10

EVEREST

Confession: it's been a few weeks since my attempt and I don't know where to go from here.

That Saturday morning my mouth felt like cotton and my head pounded. I woke up aching and confused, eyes blurry, and throat dry. I groaned and rolled over. My hand cradled my head to ease the ache. A bottle of water next to my bed caught my eye, and I gulped it down. I lay back and stared up at my ceiling, collecting my thoughts.

Have you ever just lay in bed and thought about how you managed to make it? I'd had thoughts so absolutely horrid about myself, I literally tried to kill myself and I was still here. Why? I still couldn't figure it out.

The dark room corresponded to my dark thoughts. The sun tried to make its way through the shield of blinds, but it was no use. Light couldn't win with this darkness.

The night before yesterday, my dad came home, bringing my grandpa. My grandfather wasn't too different from my dad, both with stern faces and briefcases. I thought the reason my dad was the way he was now was because of his father. When I was younger, I thought that my grandfather was the coolest guy, with his cigars imported from Italy and his expensive suits.

One day you'll have it all, he used to tell me.

I was eight and I remembered being so determined to make sure I lived up to the family name. I was not yet eighteen and I'd failed.

The pressure and stress were too much. The lying awake thinking about how I could be better—to not let anyone down, to make my father finally proud of me. Anxiety filled me up with emotion—too much emotion. The tears and the blood, there was so much of it. But nothing compared to now, where absolutely nothing but disgust and disappointment came along with my name. My grandfather told me last night that he thought I was weak. He called my appearance a disgrace; my dad watched with his arms folded and eyebrows furrowed. When my grandfather punched me in the gut, my dad left the room. I bent forward and groaned, wrapping my hand around my stomach and coughing a few times.

I didn't want to have to do that . . . but your father needs to start toughening you up.

When Thursday rolled around, I didn't want to go to school. I took my car and went to the Basement, where I smoked until I couldn't even remember my name. I didn't remember how I got home; the last thing I remembered was Aurora bringing in tacos. The taste of tacos was still present in my mouth. My car wasn't in the garage, so I must have walked all the way home.

My weekend was pretty much uneventful. I stayed in my room and listened to music. When you had earbuds in and shut your eyes, you could kind of forget about the world. My family didn't come and check on me, so there were no interruptions. It was getting hard to tell if I was avoiding my family or if my family was avoiding me.

I decided to go to school today just to spite everyone—especially Nash, my supposed best friend, who hadn't talked to me in weeks.

"Hey, Everest!" I lifted my head from my desk and met the eyes of my former teammate, Gabe Brooks.

"How's it feel knowing that Nash stole your girlfriend and your quarterback position?" he asked, laughing, his blond bowl cut shaking slightly. It was funny how fast he forgot that I was the one he'd talked to when his girlfriend had cheated on him.

"How's it feel knowing that your hair is three Justin Biebers ago?" Nami told him, before sending me a sympathetic smile.

I looked away and put my head down. The teacher was collecting the work sheets that I hadn't done. When lunch came around, I entered the cafeteria out of habit. I eyed my old table, and Cara was there. Someone patted her shoulder and pointed at me, and our eyes met. Seeing Cara made me think of all the memories between us, and my stomach filled with a swarm of bees from the notion.

She looked away. I turned and left the cafeteria; I couldn't be there any longer. I found myself entering the east wing library. Beverly sat in her usual spot, and glanced at me before taking a bite from her sandwich. I was so caught up in my thoughts, I'd completely forgotten that she usually came in here.

"Hey," I greeted her, taking a seat.

"Hi." She smiled briefly at me before turning the page of a book. "How's your head?"

How did she know about my raging headache from this weekend?

"I drove you home," she explained, probably reading my confused facial expression.

Pieces of my memory came back to me. Image of tacos and a small Korean child surfaced in my brain. Flashes of Beverly taking care of me also surfaced and I didn't understand why she'd helped me.

"You helped me?" I asked, astonished.

She nodded before sipping her water.

". . . but why?"

"Because we're friends," she said.

"But we're not—" I didn't even know her, but then realized that she'd been more of a friend than anyone else I knew right now. "Tell me about yourself," I said.

She looked surprised. "What do you want to know?"

I shrugged.

"How about I tell you something about myself in exchange for something about you," she suggested, and I hesitantly nodded. I didn't mind as long as she didn't ask anything personal.

"What's your favorite food?"

"Pizza rolls all day," I said.

She laughed at my answer.

"What?"

"Nothing, you just answered that really fast and really serious." She chuckled more, causing me to smile a little.

"Pizza rolls are the best."

"I thought you were going to say something fancy, and then

you say pizza rolls." She attempted to imitate me saying pizza rolls, and I shook my head in amusement.

"I don't sound like that! Now how about you? What's your favorite food?"

She pondered for a moment. "Chicken parmesan. What's your favorite color?"

"Blue," I answered.

"Same," she smiled.

"What's your favorite movie?" This little game was kind of fun.

"That's a hard one. I think as of now it's *If I Stay*. It's so sad. Personally, I like the book better, but the movie was amazing nonetheless. How about you?" Her eyes brightened as she answered.

"I don't really have one, but as of right now I really like *The Purge*," I answered.

"*The Purge*?" she asked.

"Yeah, I wish they would have a real one," I told her, my lips twisted in an amused manner.

"I don't think that's a good idea—like, what would you even do?" Beverly asked.

"Rob a bank and then hide," I replied. She flashed a grin as if she was proud of my answer.

"What would you do with the money?" For a moment I noted that this felt like the start to every great heist.

"I would go straight to Sam's Club and get the big family pack of pizza rolls." And then she laughed, like really laughed.

"Is that really the first thing you would buy?"

"Hell, yeah."

The game continued until the bell rang and it was time to go to class. Before leaving, I realized that maybe it wouldn't be so bad if I had a friend.

11

BEVERLY

Later that day while I was at work, hour by hour, I couldn't get what happened at lunch out of my mind, and I couldn't even begin to explain what it felt like to have someone actually be interested in who I was. My brain tried to sort out the emotions, but I couldn't place my finger on them. He actually wanted to know me—Beverly Davis—the girl who usually sat in the shadows.

I learned a lot about Everest today. Among those things was that his favorite singer was John Mayer, his favorite number was three, his favorite animal was a lion, and he was afraid of cats. I had laughed at the irony while he'd done this side-smile.

I noticed how he side-smiled a lot, like he was restricting himself from fully smiling. I noticed how he chewed on his lip when he was slightly embarrassed, and I noticed how his laughs were never wild like mine, and his chuckles were also restricted.

All it took was one period, and those forty-five minutes left me wanting more. I wanted to know everything there was to possibly know about him.

"Hey, Betty, don't you just love open mic night?" Poppy hummed, breaking me out of my thoughts.

I couldn't help but agree. Open mic night was when the small café filled a little more than usual. People came to watch their friends make fools of themselves, or an upcoming artist came to play hoping to get their sound out. I remembered when I first starting working here, the place would be packed. It still filled up, but it wasn't what it used to be.

"Hey, Betty, could you be a doll and clean the chai tea that spilled?" Lily called from across the café. I glanced at the liquid dribbling from a nearby table and onto the floor.

"I'll do it," I said, and grabbed a nearby rag as I made my way to the liquid mess. But being the uncoordinated person that I was, I slipped on the mess and fell backward, landing flat on my back. The impact from me hitting my head caused me to groan in pain. I lay there for a second, eyes closed, as the ache increased.

"Really, Bev? Napping on the job? I expected more from you," a deep, teasing voice called from above me. My dirt eyes met his Earth. Everest really did have some beautiful eyes, with swirls of green drowning in the pools of blue. It was so cool how his eyes wouldn't make up their mind on what they wanted to be.

His lips were curled in that side-smile, and his eyes were slightly teasing.

"Oh goodness, Betty! Are you okay?" Lily asked, pushing Everest aside, Rose and Poppy standing by her.

"Yeah, I'm fine," I assured her, and even started to stand up. Though the ache in my head from hitting the ground increased, it was nothing.

Being up on my feet, the wetness on my back became uncomfortable. I rubbed a little at my shoulder blade, trying not to meet his eye.

"Go sit down for a second, that was a pretty nasty fall," Lily said. "I'll clean it."

I sat at a table and Everest sat across from me.

"Are you really okay?" he asked, slight amusement on his features.

I rubbed my head a little. "Yeah, my shirt kinda absorbed all of the mess when I took the fall, and that's bothering me more than anything."

"Here," Everest said as he pulled his hoodie off, "wear this."

The infamous gray hoodie was warm and smelled just like I imagined—of his natural scent with a slight undertone of nicotine. The hoodie was big, but that just made it all that more comforting. Everest wore a fitted short-sleeved black T-shirt underneath. His arms were lean but muscular. A tattoo caught my eye and I was shocked—I'd had no clue he had a tattoo.

"I didn't know you had tats," I chuckled, poking his arm.

He pulled his arm onto his lap. "I only have one."

"Anyway, I think it's cool," I responded, and he looked up from his lap, his eyes meeting mine and an unreadable expression on his face.

"You think anything is cool," he said, a ghost smile of a smile on his lips.

I scoffed. "No, I do not."

"You find the beauty in anything. It's like you're not real—unicorns and fairies come over your house on Saturdays and you have tea parties."

I threw a nearby sugar packet at him. He chuckled.

"Life is too short to live it recklessly. I can't do negative things, it's better to be positive, to be good. I need to be mature and see the world on its better side," I explained.

"You know, I never saw you until recently. Not at a party or a football game or anything. You don't even eat in the cafeteria, it's like you want to be invisible. You're a teenager, you're supposed to be reckless and stupid."

I took in his words as I stared at a nearby napkin dispenser. He talked a lot of game for someone who didn't even want to continue his life. And that was when an idea struck me.

The words came out before I could stop them. "Okay, let's make a deal. You teach me to be a bit reckless and I'll teach you to see the beauty."

I whipped my hand out for him to shake. His large sleeve slid down my arm and covered my hand, and I pushed it up to my elbow. It was no doubt the strangest thing I had ever said, and I hoped that I hadn't ruined whatever we had with my silly proposal.

By now I realized that he was still staring at my outstretched hand, probably thinking of an excuse to never talk to me again, before taking me by surprise and gripping the handshake. "You got yourself a deal."

I felt a wave of victory crash over me—I was going to have a chance to convince him that this world was worth staying on.

"Welcome to open mic night, would anyone like to go first?" Rose announced, and I nudged Everest.

"Hell, no," Everest mouthed back at me, as if I'd asked him to suck my right toe.

"Remember the deal," I whispered, before standing up. "Everest will."

His eyes grew big and he shook his head vigorously. I pulled him by his arm to make him stand up, and he looked around the semicrowded café. His eyes flickered to each corner and each person, and he gulped visibly.

"I don't have my guitar or anything," he announced, trying to get out of performing.

I felt a bit guilty for putting him in this situation, but there were only about fifteen people in here. He should explore interests other than football. And even if he was bad, he'd learn that this wasn't for him. Singing wasn't the only thing in the music industry.

"That's all right, come on up. We have an extra one, you can use it."

Poppy pushed Everest toward the stage, and he looked helplessly back at me. He climbed up, and blocked his eyes from the overhanging lights. Rose nudged him closer to the band. "Tell us what you're going to sing," she encouraged, before exiting the stage.

He awkwardly tuned the guitar as he stood in front of the mic.

"Hi, my name is Everest. For the first time, I'm going to cover 'Mad World.'"

The slow melody carried through the café, and from the first haunting note that passed through his lips, he captured the attention of everyone there. I couldn't tell a lie, as that note crawled from the soles of my feet and engulfed me whole, it was so disturbingly beautiful, and it didn't make sense but it made sense.

That moment made sense.

When he first sang into the mic, it was like everything disappeared and it was just him and his emotions.

People looked up from their laptops, and conversations stopped—all attention was on him.

I did not know he could sing like that. The runs and riffs were perfectly imperfect, something that couldn't be rehearsed. The raw emotion that spilled from his diaphragm and passed his lips knocked everyone off their feet. I felt like I was someplace different. His tone was raspy, his face contorted in pain—the emotional kind.

I wanted to cry, because, my God, that was too perfect.

When he finished, the room was dead silent. We were all in shock. He gripped the mic like he was afraid it was going to leave him. His head hung low, and his chest expanded as he took deep breaths. It was like he didn't know we were there, like he'd completely forgotten that people were watching him.

Poppy was the first to clap. She jumped up from her chair and hooted. The rest of the room followed, clapping loudly and whistling, but I still couldn't move.

He slowly looked up, and watched as people cheered for him. There were only fifteen people, but it felt like more. I felt so incredibly proud of him. I watched his features as they grew into a breathtaking smile. His smile was like living poetry. His gaze met mine, and it seemed as though his eyes were smiling. I thought the rain was beautiful, but nothing compared to this— watching someone broken finally getting a glimpse of happiness after so long.

12

EVEREST

*Confession: sometimes I wonder if I'm playing this
whole life-game all wrong.*

—CF, April 29, 2002

Looking at my uncle's notebook the other day made me feel
like I wasn't the only one who felt off in this family. You'd never
have known it by looking at him, but my uncle struggled. We
were more alike than I thought. Like him, I knew firsthand that
it wasn't as good as it seemed to have everyone adore you. At
first, it was great, knowing that people put you in the limelight.
But all that praise was just in their minds; that made-up idea that
something and/or someone was close to perfection. And I was for
damn sure not perfect.

My tears, blood, scars, and toxic mind were proof of that.

People expected so much from you. You weren't supposed to

screw up because in their minds you weren't a screw-up. Being up on the stage took me back—too far back. In the fields, halls, and practically everywhere that I went, people looked at me like they wanted more. Admiring faces and loving gazes. Being up on that stage took me to a time when I was in everyone's good graces. You would think that all that praise would have led my dad to start being proud of me, but no. He strove for perfection, and no matter what I did, I was always doing something wrong in his mind.

I didn't know why I needed my dad to be proud of me. I guessed I wanted him to show up to my games and not criticize me afterward. I guessed I wanted him to look at me one time and say "Son, I'm proud of you," or "You did a good job," or even "How was your day?"

When he didn't approve, I beat myself up. He drove me to become this perfectionist, and I hated it. I was trying to teach myself not to care about the same things that mattered to him, but no matter how much I lied to myself, I still cared.

How did anyone not know that my depression was still here, if not stronger than ever? I was suffocating. And the people who at least acted like they once cared were now turning their backs.

It wasn't just my dad's disapproving eyes anymore. It was everyone who knew me and everyone who didn't know me. Everyone had joined his team and I was sick of pretending that I didn't notice.

I wanted people to like me so badly; *I* wanted to like *me*. But I always found something that I didn't like, and now I'd given up.

Being on stage at first made me feel like I was worth something. When I was singing, I kind of blanked out. I was happy, but then I realized that the gazes of admiration would soon change to disgust. And that sucked because it felt good. It felt *so* good to momentarily be happy. But happiness wasn't meant for people like me, because it would always crash and burn.

Fire. Ashes. Smoke.

I couldn't breathe.

I exited the stage in a rush, people patting me on the back and smiling to my face, and I was sure my smile lacked the enthusiasm it once had. I had to get out of here, because my thoughts were clawing at my skin from the inside out.

* * *

The September night air was chilled with the upcoming October and swallowed me whole. My hands gripped my keys so tightly that I swore the scent of my blood would soon start to fill my senses.

"Everest!"

"Everest!"

"Are you all right?"

I turned my head to see Lily, Poppy, Rose, and Beverly in the doorway.

I turned my head and rubbed roughly at my jaw, before murmuring a curse and turning back toward them.

"Sure, I'm . . . not feeling too well. I think I'm catching a cold."

Poppy and Rose told me to take a minute and then went back into the café. Lily reluctantly nodded, whispered quickly to Beverly, and then followed her sisters.

Beverly didn't say anything as she stared at me. Her large brown eyes zoned in on mine, and I hated how hers knew mine were lying. She was too observant for her own good.

"I'm fine," I assured her as the depression zoomed, bolted, and leaped through my veins, begging to be cut and released.

She took a step closer to me. "No, you're not."

I stared at her, shocked by how much I wanted someone to say that to me. I found it hard to accept how much she cared about me. One half of me believed that I was just too damaged to even be around someone like her. But the other part of me selfishly wanted her around. And I didn't know why. Maybe it was because I was lonely. And maybe it was because I found it sad how she was always alone.

But either way, this friendship could end badly, and I wanted to put the embers out before they caught fire.

"I have to show you something," I said, hoping that maybe I could scare her away.

* * *

The entire drive, I was anxious. Beverly sat in the passenger seat and I could practically smell the unspoken questions she desperately wanted to ask. My mocking heartbeat filled my ears with its rhythm, and I wanted to claw the sound out. Finally, we arrived, and I felt like I was going back in time. I looked at Beverly and her expression was one of confusion.

"It's this way," I said, leading the way to the back of the building. Through the door and up trillions of steps, I led us to the top of the building. I jiggled the knob like I had a hundred times before, and it swung open.

Holding the door, I glanced back at Beverly.

"This isn't the part where you kill me right?" she half joked.

I chuckled as she walked through the door. "No promises."

Being on the rooftop made all the swimming memories float past me. I walked toward the ledge.

"When I was figuring out how I wanted to kill myself, I would sit up here . . ."

Beverly stayed silent. I looked over the edge and watched the cars drive by.

"I contemplated just getting it over with and jumping off this building. But I just couldn't do it. I didn't want to fail and be paralyzed for the rest of my life. Every day I would think about how I should do it," I said. "It's crazy how many ideas I came up with. Everywhere I was at, I thought about it. I convinced myself that the reason I hadn't done it yet was because I hadn't picked the right way, but I was actually just waiting. I was waiting for someone—anyone, really—to notice, to notice that I was drowning while watching everyone take a breath."

I looked up at her, my unshed tears betraying me with their presence. Clearing my throat, I turned away from her. It used to be so easy hiding my emotions, but my emotions had gained strength, and my resistance was weakening.

Suddenly, her presence came at arm's length from behind me. "Do . . . do you still think you want to die?" she asked me, and I turned around to face her.

Think?

"I want to die," I told her, straightening my back. She needed to leave me alone now. She needed to come to her senses and just leave me alone.

"No, you don't." She spoke with confidence and assurance. "Tell me this: why haven't you tried again? If you really wanted to die, then you would have done anything to get the deed done."

She looked up at the night sky and sighed. Then her eyes met mine and she smiled gently. "You don't want to die. You just need to figure out how to start living."

And in that moment I realized that she was going to be someone that I would never forget.

13

BEVERLY

We sat up on the roof for a while until Everest noticed I was getting really cold. He led me back downstairs through the industrial hallway, and into the parking lot, which was so quiet and still.

"What was that place anyway?" I asked Everest once we were back in his car.

"It's one of my dad's hotels. You didn't see the sign on the way in?"

He jerked his head at a sign once we passed the lot. The sign was forest green with gold lettering. *The Finley Inn.*

I hadn't noticed, but I knew that his family owned a bunch of establishments in the city. I remembered when they first moved here—the Finleys. They moved in the summer before ninth grade, and when they came, they knocked down half the east side with them, rebuilding it from the ground up. The place I grew up in was no longer corner stores on every block and abandoned buildings; now it had superconvienience stores, coffee shops, and luxury hotels.

Everest's name was a big hit before he even started his first day of school. His family practically owned a portion of Pittsburgh—bars, restaurants, the aforementioned hotels. The first day of ninth grade, everyone was talking about the new kid—the new *rich* kid, his football legacy, the handsome son of a handsome father. The perfect family. The gold standard.

I didn't really remember what it was like before Everest came. It was funny to know so much about someone and have them know nothing about you.

Everest turned the steering wheel, his jaw slightly clenched.

"You honestly think I'm going to get better?" he whispered, eyes still set on the road.

"I *know* you will," I said.

He stopped at a red light. "Are you going to tell me where you live now?"

I didn't want him to know where I lived. Not because I didn't trust him or anything, but because I was embarrassed. I lived in a run-down apartment with two bedrooms. It couldn't compare with his mansion. Our kitchen faucet didn't even work sometimes, while he had a beautiful sculptured fountain in front of his house.

I mumbled incoherently. I looked out the window and concentrated on the sky. It was a mix of purplish blue tonight.

"Come on, Bev."

I hid my oncoming smile at the use of his nickname for me. Maybe it was the way he called me Bev, or maybe it was because he was doing that side-smile, I didn't know. All I knew was that I caved. I told him my address and hoped I hadn't made the wrong decision.

"This it?" he asked when he pulled into the parking lot. He glanced around the area and I expected him to snort, but he didn't say anything. His eyes scanned all around, to the shoes hanging above on the telephone wire to the plastic bag slowly dragged against its will by the gentle wind. I wanted to get out of the car before he thought poorly of me. I opened the door in a rush, but a not-too-obvious rush.

"Bye, Ev," I chirped quickly, but as soon as my feet hit the concrete, he grabbed my arm.

I guessed it was pretty obvious.

"Hold up Speedy Gonzales—do you want me to walk you up?"

I chuckled. "No, I'm fine."

I watched as he unclipped his seat belt, turned off the car, and pulled out his keys out of the ignition. What was he doing?

He climbed out of the car and shut the door behind him. The sound of his heavy footsteps came around the car and in my direction.

"What are you doing?" I asked slowly.

"I'm walking you up," he said like it was the most obvious thing in the world.

"But I just said—"

"I know."

"So, basically you asked me . . . but I really had no say in the matter?" I asked, confused.

"Basically. But I wanted you to feel like you had a choice." There went that smirk. "Lead the way, Ms. Davis," he laughed softly. I wondered what his real laugh sounded like—the one that he was constantly fighting.

I walked up the ancient concrete steps, the paint chipped from age. Everest walked behind me, his Doc Martens practically slamming down with each step.

As we approached my door, I turned to face Everest. "I want you to know that you were absolutely amazing tonight. I had no clue." Everest's big blue-green eyes stared at me intently, and a half smile hung from his lips. "Lily said you're welcome to play anytime you'd like."

"Seriously?" he asked incredulously.

"Yeah, she wanted me to tell you." I smiled, watching his reaction. It would be great if Everest was at 21 Daisies—to have my only friend there.

Just then his smiled dropped. "I'll think about it."

I wondered why his mood changed so quickly. "Just give it some thought," I said quickly. "You made everyone feel something tonight. You sang from your soul, and that was just about the coolest thing I've ever seen."

He stared at me for a second and then chuckled. "You need to get out more."

"Laugh all you want, but I know it felt good to get your emotions out that way," I told him. "I saw your smile, Everest. I don't know. It was . . . s-something special. I know you were happy in that moment."

He looked at the floor outside my door.

"When was the last time you were really happy?" I asked curiously.

"You're going to think it's stupid."

"No I won't, Scout's honor." I twisted my fingers.

"Were you even a Scout?" he asked.

"No," I answered with a chuckle.

"Okay, I was ten. I was over at my grandma's house, and she made this fort with me. It was the craziest fort too—it stretched from one end of the hall and into the living room. My gram even put Christmas lights all through the tunnels of blankets, so it was easier to see. She baked brownies and watched Disney movies with me that night." The faint dimple in his left cheek made an appearance.

"That's actually really cute."

"Yeah," he mumbled, snapping out of his daze. "Good night, Bev."

He abruptly turned to leave, but I didn't miss the boyish smile on his face.

* * *

The next day at school, I didn't expect Everest to approach me at my locker. I actually didn't expect him to acknowledge me with the exception of the library or outside of school. He wore a beanie today, and I thought it looked really nice.

"Can I come over your apartment today?" he asked me, completely oblivious to everyone staring at us.

His voice echoed in the background, and eyes zoned in us. I'd been in the shadows for so long, but I'd imagined what it would feel like to have all the attention on me. The feeling was surreal.

"Bev?" Everest said, waving his hand in front of my face, trying to gain my attention.

"Everyone is staring," I whispered. He turned his head to look at the curious eyes before he shrugged.

"So?" he said nonchalantly. But he was used to the stares; I wasn't.

He stood in front of me, blocking the eyes and hushed whispers. "Do you think I could come over today?" he asked again.

I was a little caught off guard—why my apartment? It didn't have arcades or a home theater. "Sure . . ."

"Give me your phone. I'll text you when I'm coming." He reached into his back pocket and pulled out the latest iPhone. I groaned inwardly—of course Everest would have the most high-tech gadget.

I dug in my bag, fighting my embarrassment, and pulled out my phone. It wasn't even a touch screen. I had put a butterfly sticker over the low-budget logo, but it was still pretty obvious. Even though I had a job, I'd been saving up for college. And it wasn't like I had any friends to talk to, so a top-notch phone wasn't high on my priorities.

When I handed him my phone, his bottom lip instantly pulled into his mouth.

"I know. It's bad," I said.

"No, no, it's not bad." He held it between his fingers, examining it, his lips fighting against an amused expression. "Does it still work?"

"Ha, ha, ha," I said sarcastically, and grabbed the phone out of his grasp. "And for the record, it works like a charm."

He laughed louder than he usually did, but still not to his full potential. "I like the butterfly sticker."

"I'll see you later," I said as I pushed passed him playfully, scurrying to class, hoping not to be late.

* * *

I took my usual seat in French class and pulled out my notes, waiting for the teacher to begin.

"So, are you new?" Martha, a cheerleader from Cara's clique, asked as she approached my desk.

I couldn't find any words—the answer was on the tip of my

tongue but wasn't strong enough to pull through with the message.

"N-No," I stuttered.

She flicked her glossy brown hair over her shoulder, a snarky, sly look on her face. "Really? I know everyone, and yet I don't know you."

I looked around the room for some form of help, but everyone just watched. The teacher, busy checking email, hadn't even looked up from her screen. "Yeah . . ." I responded, feeling uncomfortable.

"Hey, Martha! Your extension fell out," Nami shouted across the room, and Martha immediately looked at the ground.

"Made you look," Nami laughed, and Tiffany, on her opposite side, was also cackling. People started to join in, and I was relieved the attention was off of me. That wasn't the kind of attention I wanted.

Martha huffed away, her manicured nail flicking off Nami. Today was the first day I was acknowledged by someone other than Everest.

14

EVEREST

Confession: I worry too much about there not being enough time that I end up wasting it.

—*CF, November 22, 1998*

I was starting to run out of cigarettes so I stopped by the Basement. Mikey offered me a blunt, but I didn't want it. The last time I smoked weed, I couldn't even remember my name.

"I saw you talking to that black girl today," Aurora said, attempting to start a conversation.

"You go to school?" I asked, dodging the question.

"Only when Mikey goes," she laughed.

"You guys are a thing?" I asked, taking a quick shot of vodka. Only one shot, though, because I was going over to Beverly's today.

Mikey took a seat next to me on the couch. The long part of his dark-brown hair was thrown up in a small man bun.

"We hooked up a few times, but we aren't, like, exclusive," he explained nonchalantly, shoulders shrugging.

Aurora's face was pure disappointment, but when she saw that I noticed, she picked up a beer bottle and drank.

"Did you and Cara break up? Or are you guys taking a break? Because I hate to be the one to break it to you, bro, but she and Nash are getting pretty close." It didn't matter if the two of them were getting close—Nash was gay. But of course, I wouldn't tell anyone that. I shrugged.

"I don't care."

Mikey nodded his head and puffed on the joint.

* * *

On the drive to Beverly's, I thought about Cara, wondering if she ever thought of me, or if she missed me at all. Did Nash feel guilty for unfriending me when I needed a friend the most?

I wasn't going to sit here and lie. It sucked knowing that my suspicions were true; that Nash and Cara never really cared about me.

I pulled into Bev's lot and realized I hadn't sent her a text that I was coming. Sitting in my car, I typed the note quickly, giving her time to do whatever. My vehicle was starting to smell like Beverly, and I honestly didn't know how I felt about that.

Ten minutes later she replied with an okay. I didn't know if she was just busy or if her phone signal sucked. I was going to go with the latter because her phone had been around since prehistoric times. I waited for a bit longer before I made my way to her door and knocked once. She opened it in a hurry.

Beverly's demeanor was flustered, her hair shaking from her quick movement, and her eyes slightly wide.

"Hi." She smiled, and her voice breathy.

I couldn't help but chuckle a little at her frazzled look. "Hey."

The warmth from her apartment crept upon my chilled face. A whiff of something sweet filled my nose, and I wanted to find out what it was. Beverly stared at me intently, my gray hoodie still keeping her body warm. I'd kind of forgotten about it. I should get it from her later today.

"So, you going to let me in?" I asked, amused.

"Oh yeah, sorry." She pulled the door open wider.

A tunnel. Tunnels made of blankets. I looked at Beverly, speechless.

"W-What is this?" I asked, breaking the silence.

"It's a fort so epic that it wraps all around my apartment," she said excitedly. "I had to hurry up since you came so early, and the cookies are still in the oven. So if we want them to watch with our movies, you are going to have to crawl through the tunnel to get them."

I couldn't. My brain refused to form coherent thoughts. Why would someone do all this just to see me happy? She'd re-created my happiest moment, and I didn't know how to take it.

Too many emotions ran through me, and all I could do was laugh. I must have looked crazy, but I didn't worry about that anymore. Because I was crazy. I laughed and laughed, and Beverly just stood there.

"You all right?" She raised an eyebrow.

I pinched the bridge of my nose and tried to contain myself, but I couldn't. All the holding it in, it was now coming out, like a broken dam gushing water.

"I'm going to go and check on the cookies, since you can't stop laughing," she teased, then disappeared under the blankets.

Tears hit my cheeks and I wanted to punch something. I really needed to pull myself together because I was freaking myself out. Laughing and crying? Really, dude? I literally laughed so hard I cried.

"Get a grip." I said it two more times.

Straightening myself up, I climbed under. There were Christmas lights lining the fort just like I had told her. I touched them gently, and smiled.

"In here!" she called from the opposite direction from what I would imagine would be her living room.

This fort was huge. It wasn't too low or too high—it was perfect. Beverly lay on a pile of pillows surrounded by a laptop and DVD cases. There were bowls of popcorn and the plate of chocolate chip cookies. I turned my head to follow the smell coming from a plate of pizza rolls sitting on a pillow.

"C'mon, do you want to watch *Toy Story* or *Finding Nemo* first?"

I crawled closer and glanced around. The lights, the movies, the snacks. "Why did you do this for me?"

She sat up on her elbows and said: "You've been sad for too long. I wanted to do something and show you that it's okay to be happy, so this is your reminder. Now shut up and enjoy it."

"Thank you, Bev, this is . . . this is great." I meant every word.

This wasn't just great; this was amazing. She was amazing.

"It was really nothing," Beverly said. "Now sit back and enjoy it, my friend."

I really didn't want to watch *The Little Mermaid*, but Beverly told me it was one of her favorites so we put it on, and it actually was pretty good.

Suddenly, I was ten again and my grandmother had cheeks

budding like roses, and her hair was a towering mess of gray and blond. The same color of rose on her lips left a print on my forehead for my mom to scrub off later.

I glanced at my phone and it was only eight thirty. Beverly didn't have work today so I knew she didn't have to go in, but I did wonder where her family was.

"When do your parents come home?" I asked. The last thing I wanted was for her parents to catch me under the blankets with their daughter.

She picked up the plates and bowls, and said, "My mom won't be home for a long time and my dad won't be coming at all because he died when I was small."

"Hey, I'm sorry." I bit my lip nervously. "So, what do you want to do now? Want to put in another movie?"

"It's okay, it's been a long time. Let's take a little movie break," she suggested as she crawled away toward the kitchen.

While she was gone, I lay on my back and stared at the star-hemmed blanket at the top. I smiled knowing that Beverly had strategically put it there.

"That's my favorite," Beverly said, and I didn't even know she had already come back.

"It's a nice blanket," I said.

She crawled closer to me, then lay on her back and stared at it, side by side with me. Her swirls of hair tickled the side of my arm.

"When I was younger, I used to think the moon followed me." She tugged on one of her curls. "I remember thinking that I was special because something so beautiful and bright wanted to be with me. It could have gone anywhere it wanted, but it was with me."

She continued, "I wanted to follow the moon, I actually wanted to be it . . . I know I'm sounding looney."

I knew what it was like to be in awe. "When I was around six or seven, I was obsessed with my dad. I used to put on his shoes and his ties the best way I could, and pretend I was him," I told her, but don't ask me why because I honestly didn't even know anymore.

"That's cute," she said, laughing, but I thought otherwise. My dad had paid me no attention, but even then I wanted him to notice me.

"I have very faint memories of my father. Just a few flashes but they don't really mean anything," she said, a hint of sadness in her voice. "I think I liked him, though."

I looked at her and instantly felt bad.

"What happened?" Maybe I was stepping beyond boundaries here, but the question came out as a thought.

"Car crash when I was four. My parents were young—way too young to have a child on their hands. My mom told me she met my dad at a party, and he was the most charismatic person she knew. He loved to party, and their relationship moved so fast. But they were in love. So I guess that kinda makes up for the speed at which they went. She wanted him to slow down when I was born, but he was a free spirit, and I guess there's no slowing down a free spirit. Car racing at a party went wrong and he was gone."

I stared at her, and now I understood why she hid. She didn't want to be reckless and young, because of the risks. She'd rather sit in a library behind a book than go to a party. She needed to get out of her shell, and I was going to be the one to help her do it.

"I think we should watch *Monsters, Inc.* now," I said.

"I'll pop more popcorn." Beverly rolled over to get up.

"Can you make pizza rolls too?" I asked as she was crawling away.

Her head turned toward me, an amused expression playing upon her features. "You have an unhealthy obsession, Ev. Another plate of pizza rolls coming right up."

I had a lot of problems, but pizza rolls were certainly not one.

15

BEVERLY

The sound of my phone ringing jolted me awake. We must have fallen asleep during the last movie. Rubbing my eyes, I tried figure out where I was. Groping blindly in the direction of the ringing, I answered.

"Hello?" My vocal cords were dry from sleep.

"Finally! I've be-eee-nn-nnn . . . I've calling you for the past ten minutes. I called Burger Hut six times thinking it was your number." My mother's laughter cackled into the phone, and I held it away from my ear.

I struggled to fully open my eyes, yawned, and returned the phone to my ear.

"I'm calling to tell you that I'm all right, I'm just over Macy's house. We were celebrating that she got that new job." Just then I heard Aunt Macy shout in victory, but it resembled more of the scream of a banshee. My mother laughed while Aunt Macy screamed, and I really wanted to hang up the phone. It was pretty evident that they had been drinking. I could practically smell that cheap box-wine smell through the receiver of my phone.

I glanced at the time and it read midnight.

"I'm coming home now," my mom said.

My eyes snapped open and I was suddenly awake. "No! Stay the night over at her house. I don't think you should be driving anyway . . ."

"I haven't had that much to drink, Beverly," she tried to assure me, but I wasn't having it.

"Nope, I still don't feel comfortable. Just stay there."

"Okay, Ms. Mom," she laughed. "I'll be there in the morning."

I hung up the phone and lay back. My head thumped on something warm and hard. My neck couldn't get comfortable, as the pillow wasn't shaping to fit it. I squirmed and wiggled but it wasn't getting any better. I reached back to fluff it, but my hand grabbed what felt like a shirt. I gripped the shirt material and felt hard muscle.

Suddenly, I sat up and turned around to look at what I was feeling, and almost screamed. I was basically feeling up Everest's stomach. Luckily, he was fast asleep, so I could face this embarrassment in private.

My hand flew up to my mouth. I'd completely forgotten he was even here.

I stared down at the sleeping Everest and noticed how he looked grumpy, but, then again, he almost always looked grumpy. Those stubborn wrinkles between his eyebrows looked like they'd made a permanent home.

Without thinking, I reached over and used my thumb to smooth out a wrinkle. His skin was warm, projecting heat as if attempting to release his frustrations. When I removed my thumb, the wrinkle was gone.

I observed his face. I noticed how Everest was really attractive when he wasn't grouchy. I noticed how he had a bit of pizza sauce at the corner of his mouth, and, unthinking, went to wipe it off. Just as my finger touched the corner of his mouth, his eyes fluttered open in confusion. I quickly jumped back.

"We . . . we must have fallen asleep," I stuttered, completely embarrassed and trying to move the subject away from the fact that I was being a weirdo.

Everest sat up and rubbed at his jaw. "I should get going," he said, his voice thick with sleep.

My eyes were still on the floor. I was unable to look at him as he started to move around. When he stood up, the fort broke, and the blankets engulfed me whole. I didn't even mind, because I wanted to curl up in a ball anyway.

He murmured a curse. "I kind of forgot we were in a fort."

I moved the blankets from above my head and resurfaced, and watched as Everest did the same, a small smirk playing at his lips.

"Thank you for tonight, Bev. I haven't felt like this in a while," he said.

I looked at him and noticed how his eyes now looked more green than blue.

"You're welcome." My voice was high pitched, nervous.

He stood and walked toward the door. "Bye, Bev."

"Bye, Ev."

When he shut the door, I pulled a nearby pillow over my head and released a breath of relief that he hadn't noticed me being weird.

* * *

Everest wasn't at school today, but he was there to pick me up when I got out. He wore a green sweater that probably cost more than this month's rent.

"What time do you have to be at work today?" he asked.

"Six thirty. Why?"

"I was thinking we can hang out?"

I thought for a second. "Your house?"

"You sure you can't think of anything different?"

"Your house has a home movie theater and an arcade. Plus, you were over at my apartment yesterday and now it's your turn."

"Fine," he groaned.

His house awed me just as much as it had when I had first seen it. If I lived somewhere that looked like this, I would never leave. The carpet was so white, I felt like I soiled it just from staring too long.

"*Hola*, Miranda. *¿Cómo estás?*" Everest greeted a woman standing by the sink rinsing produce. "This is Beverly."

"*Muy bien, mijo*," Miranda said. Our eyes met and for a moment her features betrayed a flash of surprise before a gentle smile replaced it. "Hungry? Thirsty?"

"No, thank you, I'm fine," I said without even thinking.

"You sure? Miranda makes the best grilled cheese." He stared up at the ceiling, reliving the taste. "I'll actually take two and a chocolate milk, please."

"Of course," she piped, and went straight to the fridge. "I'll bring it to you in a moment."

We left the kitchen and wandered into the giant game room, which was filled with classic arcade games and a huge screen for watching movies. Everest lay back in a reclining chair and threw his hands behind his head. When he felt me staring at him, he turned his head. "What?"

"Does she do that every day?" I blurted.

"What?" Everest asked.

"Never mind." I turned back to face the screen, and now it was his turn to burn a hole in my head. As if on cue, Miranda came into the room with a tray holding the things he desired. Something about it felt all wrong to me.

"You let me know if you change your mind about anything, Beverly," she said warmly.

Everest took a bite of his sandwich before turning to stare at me again. "Were you talking about Miranda?"

Busted.

"Yeah," I responded, trying not to meet his eye.

"She makes other things too. I don't know a better cook. Taught me everything there is to know about cooking."

"Then why couldn't you make your own grilled cheese?" I should shut up.

"Two reasons." He held up his fingers in a peace-sign formation. "One, I can't make it like her." He dropped one of his fingers. "And two, my dad pays her for a reason. It's her job." He dropped the other finger. "I've known Miranda basically all my life. She's family."

I nodded my head and bit my lip, because of course what he said made sense, but it still felt wrong. I didn't want to get into an argument with Everest about it, through, so I dropped the subject.

"It bothers you, doesn't it?" he asked after a moment.

"That's a privilege that I'll probably never understand." I hoped that my words didn't sound harsh.

He nodded in response. "It's my family, it's not me. And Miranda takes good care of me. It's not always the warmest environment around here."

"Where's the bathroom?" I asked through the awkward silence.

"The closest one is upstairs to the left, third door on the right."

I walked out of the arcade and up the grand steps. The sun came in from the large windows surrounding the hallway and reflected off the marble floor. Everything about his house was grand—it reminded me more of a museum than a house.

Once I reached the top, I took the left and immediately forgot which door. I opened the first door on the right, which looked to be a closet. Then I tried the first door on the left, and that was an office. No luck with the second door on the right; it was locked. When I went to open the second door on the left, I was met with a pale-pink room and shocked little girl looking back at me.

She was sitting on her bed in front of a mirror and had a brush in her hand. Her large green eyes widened and her small mouth formed an O shape. This was clearly Everest's little sister.

"I'm so sorry. I was just looking for the bathroom," I said, faced by her mix of curiosity and confusion.

She stayed silent, too shocked and confused to say anything.

"I can help you with that, you know?" I smiled, and gestured to the braid she was trying to do. "My mother is a hairdresser. She taught me a few things," I added.

Looking down at her attempt to make a braid, she nodded slowly. I walked into her room, and noticed that one side of her room had a large mirror with a long bar alongside of it, and there were trophies on shelves everywhere.

"You must be Everest's sister. I'm Beverly, a friend of your brother's," I said, sitting down on the bed beside her.

"Hel-lo," she said.

"What's your name?" I asked.

"Hadley," she responded politely.

I pointed to the wall with the medals. "What's all that for?"

She turned her head and looked at the wall. "I'm a dancer."

"You must be really amazing if you have all of those trophies," I said.

She tried to hide her smile but failed. "I'm all right."

"What kind of dance do you do?"

"I do jazz, ballet, and tap, but my specialty is contemporary. I actually have a competition this Saturday, and in my solo I'm supposed to be, like, this warrior-ninja-princess, and I can't fit my hair into a cool braid."

I looked at her as if asking for permission before getting up and sitting behind her and gripping her hair. I thought a fishtail braid would be the cool braid that she was looking for. I took the soft, long strands in my hands and put them in that style.

"How do you know Everest?" she asked quietly.

"He goes to my school." I said, "Although he's really grouchy sometimes, your brother is pretty special."

"He's special all right," she spoke slyly.

"C'mon, he's still your brother. Imagine if people treated you the way they treat him now," I spoke softly but reassuringly.

"He doesn't care about me anyway." She looked down at her lap.

"I don't think that's true. He may act like he doesn't care about anything, but I know he does. He cares a whole lot."

She stayed quiet while I braided her hair.

"All done," I said.

"That's so cool!" she said, astonished, lightly touching the braid. "How did you do that?"

"Like I said, my mom's a hairdresser."

"That would explain your hair. It's really pretty," Hadley said.

I smiled. "Thank you, Hadley. I think you're really pretty."

"You think so?"

"I know so. You're going to be a heartbreaker. I can help you anytime with your hair if you'd like," I offered as I stood up from her bed, remembering that Everest was probably wondering if I'd fallen in the toilet.

"I'd like that," she said as I walked out of her room and closed the door behind me. "Wait, Beverly!"

I reopened her door. "Yeah?"

"The bathroom is the third door on the right," she laughed.

"Thanks."

I'd almost forgotten I had to pee.

16

EVEREST

Confession: I am still learning to be the best man I can be and that's okay.

—*EF, August 26, 2010*

I sat on the stool and flicked through the small laminated booklet for the rehab center. People on their backs lying on grass and smiling at the sun—the sunshine miraculously not burning their eyes; pages filled with large smiles and flowers everywhere.

It all seemed so generic and fake, and I was so sick of being around fake. I wanted real. The people who have always been around me always wanted something—me to throw a football, or for my connections. They never wanted to just know me.

The front door opened, and my family came back from Hadley's event. My father was talking on his phone and my mother had her arm around Hadley, who was grinning ear to ear, holding a large trophy in her hand.

"Look, Everest, your sister won first place overall." My mother's grin was almost bigger than Hadley's.

"It's about time someone brought another trophy into this house," my father said under his breath. He couldn't help himself.

They all entered the kitchen and I slowly put the pamphlet in my pocket. "It's Saturday night, are you not going to go out?" my mother asked.

I shrugged. I didn't feel like going anywhere tonight. Because I'd been out so much, I thought my mom would be happy that I was staying in, but she actually looked disappointed.

"Your hair is starting to mess up and it looked so pretty tonight," my mother said to Hadley, grabbing her by the arm and trying to fix it. "How did you even do it?"

My mom tried to make sense of the intricate braid.

I wasn't really close with my sister, but from the moment she arrived, I always felt the need to protect her from the bad in this world. It was unfortunate that I ended up turning into the bad. When my mom told me she was pregnant, I was so happy. My young mind of seven realized that I wasn't going to be alone anymore—that the adults won't just shove a toy in my face and tell me to go in my room. But when she came, she looked so pretty and fragile that I was afraid to even breathe hard around her. After Hadley came, the already small amount of attention my family gave me diminished almost completely. I didn't resent her, but I would be lying if I said I wasn't jealous.

The more I stared into her eyes, the more I felt ashamed of myself.

"Someone did it for me." Hadley looked at me when she said

that—she never looked at me; every time we made eye contact, she looked away.

"Who?" my mother asked, looking confused.

"Beverly," her soft voice stated, and I immediately popped my head up.

I hadn't talked to Beverly since she came over my house. She'd been busy with work and I simply didn't want to go to school. I texted her last night, but she only responded by saying she'd text me back, but she hadn't. I'd been trying not to think about it, but now her name was even coming out of the mouth of my little sister.

"Who's that?" My mother stared down at Hadley with a bit of scrutiny.

I was just as weary as my mother was, sure this might be some kind of coincidence, but something told me that it wasn't. I silently hoped that we weren't talking about my Beverly. My family wasn't something that I would connote with happiness and light—Beverly was nothing but good vibes, and my family was nothing but negative vibes. I couldn't have those two come together.

"Everest's friend?" Her voice wavered.

My father straightened his tie. "I don't remember a Beverly."

As if he showed enough interest in my personal life to notice who was in it and who wasn't.

"Everest, you should invite her to dinner tomorrow," my mother suggested, and I wanted to sink farther and farther down into the stool.

Sunday dinners hadn't been the same for a long time. The only things that came from that dining room now were the pangs of metal meeting glass, judgmental eyes, and blueberry pie.

"We aren't really friends, and plus I don't think she would be able to make it," I lied, praying they'd believe me.

"That's a shame."

My mom seemed to believe the fib.

"Yeah, I figured you wouldn't have any friends left." My father spoke under his breath, pouring himself a cup of coffee.

Something inside of me snapped. He pushed and pushed, always knowing the effect his words had on me. I saw he was making an effort to not make his snide comments so loudly, but just because he didn't say them loudly didn't mean I didn't hear them.

"Actually," I began as my inner self shouted for me to stay quiet, "we aren't just friends, we're actually best friends. I just remembered that she's off work tomorrow, so she should be able to come."

"Best friends?" My father quirked his eyebrow up at me.

"She's been there for me more than anyone else has, so she qualifies as the best," I shot back, the pamphlet crumpling in my pocket.

* * *

The next day I drove to over Beverly's apartment. I probably should have called, but she hadn't been responding. I'd been acting pretty impulsively lately; maybe it was because thinking too much killed. It killed hopes, it killed dreams, it even almost killed me.

I knocked on her door, not even sure if I was doing the right thing. I hadn't heard from her since Friday, and I wasn't going to lie and say that it sat well with me. Beverly had made her way into my life. It was kind of too late for her to try and leave now.

"What are you doing here?" she asked when she opened the door. That really wasn't the reaction I was expecting, but I didn't let my face show it.

"Hello to you too," I said sarcastically. Her extremely curly hair was piled high into a bun, and she wore my gray hoodie. She looked embarrassed before awkwardly staring at my shoes. I looked at the ground, focusing on the dead plants in the ceramic pot by her front door.

"So are you going to let me in?" I mumbled to the plants.

"Am I supposed to?" An ant climbed through the ruins of the dead plant.

"Yes. I mean . . . it's up to you." I finally looked into the brown eyes staring back at me.

Beverly closed the door behind us, and I made my way to her room and sat on her purple comforter, staring at the many posters on her bedroom wall.

"It's been a while . . ." she drew out, sitting on top of a desk.

"Yeah, why is that?" I asked.

She looked out the window and shrugged. "I'm new to this whole friend thing. I've lived here my whole life, and the closest thing I've gotten to friendship is playing with Manny. I don't want to mess this up, you know? I don't want you to get sick of me, so I gave you space." She fidgeted with the strings on my hoodie. I'd been meaning to get that thing back.

"You don't have to give me space, Bev." I threw a pillow at her.

"Why, did you miss me?" she teased, tossing it back.

I made a big show of pretending I was thinking. "Well . . ."

She laughed. "I missed you too."

I thought about the dinner and how I should ask her. I felt

such a need to prove my dad wrong that now I was stuck in this situation. Who said she would even say yes? I wasn't even sure why I was so nervous about asking her.

"I actually have something to ask you."

"No, I won't marry you," she stated seriously before starting to laugh.

I was a bit taken aback by her joke, being that it wasn't what I expected to come out of her mouth. It was like hearing your teacher curse.

"What's up?" she said.

"Meet my parents?" I blurted impulsively.

Her eyes grew big and she looked confused. "Are you joking?"

"Nope."

Maybe I shouldn't have just come out and said it like that.

"Okay . . . sure?"

A bit of weight lift off my chest.

"When?" she asked like she still couldn't believe I'd just asked her like that.

I scratched the back of my head and stared at the wall before looking back at her.

"Now."

"Now? Like, when?"

I looked up at her frazzled expression and glanced at my watch. "Like, right now."

17

BEVERLY

The way I was getting ready was like that scene from *The Princess Diaries*, when Mia changed in the back of the limo. I tugged on the strands of my hair, trying to make it somewhat presentable, thinking about Everest's house and what a Sunday dinner must be like in that huge dining room. When you thought of elegant, you thought of straight and defined, which my hair was definitely not. As he drove, I tried to fix my bun, so it at least wasn't so messy.

"How do you know Hadley?" Everest asked me from the driver's seat, once we hit a red light.

"I'm kind of busy right now," I said, pulling on the cream cashmere sweater that my mom bought herself for Christmas last year.

"I just don't understand how you guys would have met."

"Remember, I got lost and couldn't find the bathroom?" I said, pulling out a tube of lip gloss.

Just as I was about to use the wand and apply it to my lips, the light turned green. He accelerated and the lip gloss landed on my cheek.

"Sure," he answered.

"I walked into her room by accident and we talked for a bit," I explained.

Everest nodded, deep in thought, before pulling into his driveway. He parked and then turned to look at me. "My parents don't mean to be assholes. I don't think they can help it."

I nodded, his words making the reality of what was about to happen even more realistic.

"C'mon." He grabbed my hand once I climbed out of the car. The grip wasn't romantic, but it did feel intimate. The warmth from his large hand gave me comfort. I glanced down at our linked fingers and felt peace. Like yin and yang. We walked through the doors of his house, and I wondered when his grip would go limp. But his grip was strong and firm, yet gentle—like he needed his hand held too.

"Everest is that you?" a voice asked.

"Yes, Mother, it's me." He squeezed my hand.

"Remember, don't let them get to you," he whispered into my ear before using his thumb to slowly wipe off some of the gloss I hadn't got. I had to remember how to breathe when we were this close. My tongue felt heavy in my mouth. Was that normal? I repeated that it wasn't a big deal over and over in my head.

The first thing that I noticed was the food. It was displayed on the large dining table, silverware and plates perfectly assembled. I glanced around the full table and noticed that it was staring back at me. I released my grip in Everest's hand and immediately combined my hands together.

"Oh, well, who is this? Is Cara not coming?" A beautiful middle-aged women with long dark-brown hair and green eyes asked. The jewels around her neck probably cost more than what I was worth. The large diamond on her finger flashed in the setting sun.

Everest's back stiffened, but I thought I was the only one who noticed. "No, Mom, remember? This is Beverly."

The room was so silent I swore somewhere off in the distance I could hear an ant tiptoeing. I felt eyes everywhere. Watching me, judging me. I could feel their thoughts, but I couldn't hear them, their words crawling upon my skin.

"Beverly!" A young voice broke the silence, and I smiled as Hadley got up from her chair and hugged me.

"Hadley!" Everest's mom said. "Sit down. Actually, all of you should take a seat. This dinner is already behind schedule."

We took our seats. I sat between Hadley and Everest's great aunt, Sherma. Everest sat directly across from me. The table had many empty seats.

"We will begin with the blue cheese and pear tartlet hors d'oeuvres," his mother stated, and I glanced at Everest, confused, while he tried to hide his amusement.

What on earth was a *blue cheese and pear tartlet*?

"Here you go." His mother placed one on my plate and stared at me expectantly.

I placed it in my mouth and fought the urge to gag. The blue cheese with the pear just wasn't a good idea to begin with, but I kept chewing like it was the most delicious thing I'd had.

"Good, right?" His mother smiled before taking a bite out of hers. Everest popped his in his mouth and then discreetly spat it out in a napkin.

"Sorry I'm late. I got held up in the office again." A man with a deep baritone voice, light-blue eyes, salt and pepper hair, and an expensive-looking suit spoke. He took off his suit jacket and loosened his tie as he took his seat at the head of the table. He twisted the large ring on his finger. His very presence was intimidating.

"This must be Beverly," he spoke again, and I felt myself start to get nervous.

"Hello." I smiled and wanted to pat myself on the back for not stuttering or anything.

"I didn't expect you to be black," his father added, before taking a sip from his glass.

I was not expecting him to say *that*. Sure, I knew it was sitting on everyone's mind, but I didn't think anyone would *say it out loud*. There weren't that many black people in this town, so I knew it was surprising to see one. Everyone kind of stilled like they, too, were unsure how to react to Mr. Finley's words.

"Well, I am." I spoke easily, my smile unwavering.

"Good thing I suggested we have chicken for dinner tonight," his father laughed to himself. "You do like chicken, right?" He looked at me pointedly.

I wasn't sure if he was trying to be a jerk or not. Everest's jaw clenched and his unease wasn't helping my nerves.

"Chicken is fine," I responded, unfazed. My voice was clear, light, and easy.

"So, Beverly . . ." His mother blinked at me, clearly uncomfortable with her husband's choice of words. "Where did you meet Everest?"

"In the library." I smiled at the memory, and my heart rate slowed.

"Really? Everest in a library? That's good news." She laughed, but no one followed suit.

So awkward. Why am I here? repeated on and on in my head, like a broken record.

"I hear you have a job," Mr. Finley said.

"Yes, I work at a coffee shop in town, 21 Daisies, do you know it?" I replied, as the meal was passed around.

"You work a lot?" he asked, cutting into his chicken.

I was confused about why he was asking these questions, but I tried not to think about it as I answered. "I do. It's nice to make my own money and help my mom out along the way."

"That's admirable." Everest's aunt Sherma smiled at me.

"What's your mother's profession?" his mother asked me.

"She's a hairdresser," I answered warily. The question seemed harmless but something about it didn't rub me the right way.

"Oh." She pursed her lips, the word falling dead on her lips.

"What does your father do?" Everest's dad asked.

"That's enough," Everest said, his tone harsh.

"I wasn't talking to you, boy."

Everest briefly shut his eyes, as if to control himself. He reopened his eyes and stared at me. "You don't have to answer."

He fought to say more, but I'd seen all of the unspoken words floating in his eyes.

"I don't see why it's such a big deal," his mother added.

"Because . . ." Everest began but trailed off.

"Because what? According to statistics lots of people from her background don't have their father's support," Mr. Finley said.

Have you ever just sat frozen because you couldn't put together what your ears heard? It was like I couldn't react because I simply couldn't believe it.

I stared at Everest. He gave his father the most confused and disgusted look. I watched it all unfold—the way he fought to keep his mouth shut and keep it all in before finally letting it gush out.

"You know what? Fuck your statistics bullshit." Everest stopped and took a deep breath, his fingers clenching the bridge of his nose. He looked back up with a cold yet vulnerable stare. "Her father is dead and physically can't be there for her. You're alive and choose not to support me on anything. According to my stats, you can be any race and not be supportive."

And with that, he stood up from his chair and walked away from the table. His heavy footsteps were followed by the slamming of his bedroom door. The dining room grew quiet. His father took a sip of wine from his glass, seemingly unaffected, but I saw a glint in his eyes—a glint of something real, but it only lasted for a second.

"It was about time he opened his mouth." Sherma gave a small proud smile, and began eating her chicken.

"If you would excuse me." I finally found my voice. I got up from the table and followed the direction in which Everest had gone.

* * *

He lay on his bed, his pale-yellow designer button-down shirt no longer on his body and the muscles from years of playing football on full display. I sat on the edge of his bed, unsure of what to do or say.

"You okay?" I asked him, and watched his eyelids, waiting for them to open. "Don't let them get to you, remember?"

His messy black hair stuck up in different directions, and he opened his eyes with a smirk.

"Are you really okay?"

"I'm just tired." His voice was different, almost as if there was an underlying message.

"Go to sleep, and then wake up. Tomorrow is a new day," I told him with a small smile.

He looked at me for a long second before pulling me into a hug. I was so surprised that I fell stiffly into him. Everest pulled me down beside him, spooning me.

"Hey, Bev?" he asked softly.

"Yeah, Ev?" I responded, my cheek snuggling into his pillow.

"I bet your dad misses you, and that he didn't mean to die."

My heart warmed as I closed my eyes.

18

EVEREST

Confession: sometimes I hurt myself to spare the feelings of others.

—CF, October 11, 2000

Moments after waking up, I spent a good amount of time in my head. I lay in bed and stared up at the ceiling, and I dreamed, deep in my subconscious, where all my denial made art. It was so colorful nowadays, and my soul that once hid from the colors now embraced them whole and my blood was no longer just red. I dreamed about making things better with my dad.

Yellow.

I dreamed about my mom finding someone worthy of her heart.

White.

I dreamed about my sister never ending up like me.

Pink.

I dreamed about Nash finding peace with himself and me for-giving him.

Green.

I dreamed that Cara woke up and realized that perfection didn't exist.

Blue.

I dreamed that I got all my shit together.

Orange.

As rain thumped against my window, my chest thumped with it. I sat up and flicked on my lamp; my alarm read eleven forty. School had already started. Beverly was gone. I looked over the side of my bed to see if my shoes were there, grabbed my phone, and noticed I had a new message.

I took the bus home

Why hadn't Beverly just woken me up so I could take her home? Maybe she wanted distance from me. I understood why. My parents weren't the best hosts. She handled it well though— her smile never faltered or showed signs of weakness.

Grabbing a camo sweatshirt, I decided I owed it to Beverly to go to school today.

* * *

I entered the halls, tugging slightly on the longest strands of my black hair. I hadn't even bothered to comb it today; neat hair seemed pointless when my mind was a mess. Teachers didn't say anything to me as I wandered the halls out of fear that they would trigger the suicidal kid.

Suicidal kid. That sounded like either a tortured superhero or a blissful villain. I wondered which one I was.

I hadn't thought about death in a while. Well, I wasn't going to lie. I'd read the Sunshine Valley pamphlet about five times front and back, but I didn't think that counted as thinking. I thought about life more now than ever, if anything. I thought about all the different ways my life could pan out. Reading my uncle's confession book had become a ritual every morning. It was comforting, knowing someone else felt the way I did.

The school was decorated top to bottom in red and gold, and I could just feel it, everyone's spirits and high hopes for a win on Friday. Even though I got kicked off the team, I still had the need to win filling my veins. You didn't stop bleeding red and gold.

You had to put in blood, sweat, and tears for the gold of the trophy. I caught the eye of my coach while he was chatting with one of the lunch ladies, probably sweet-talking her into giving him extra fries for lunch. He always told me how he thought the staff was stingy with the food. Standing frozen for a second, I contemplated running back in the direction I'd come from. I hadn't seen the coach in a long time, since before my attempt, actually.

The last thing he said to me directly was, "It's okay to lose sometimes, champ."

It was right after our last game of the previous season. He was joking around at the time, patting me on my back with a light and easy smile. Our team was on a winning streak. He never called me anything but champ. I couldn't believe I'd managed to avoid him for this long.

The lunch bell rang, and I turned to flee to the library. I wanted to try and get there before Beverly. While zooming through the halls, I caught sight of my old group of friends standing by the usual meet-up spot—the stairwell beside the gym. We usually waited for the rest of the guys to finish up so we could all head to the cafeteria together. Sometimes Nash would convince us to get burgers a few blocks away. When the weather was nice we'd eat on the bleachers. It felt wrong to pass the stairwell. Everything in me was saying that I was going the wrong way, but this was my life now. I wondered if I'd ever get used to feeling like this.

"What a coward."

I didn't need to turn around to know that it was Nash who said that. It hit me in such a way that I had to concentrate on not bumping into anyone. With my head down, I walked faster, every step bringing me closer to the library. When I opened the door, I saw Beverly sitting there—so much for getting there before her. She was sitting crossed-legged on the ledge of one of the large, bright windows, scribbling away at something in her notebook. Her hair was no longer in a fury all over her head, but was straight instead. That image alone caused me to stop for a second. Between her and the sun, I couldn't tell which was glowing more.

She looked up from her lunch and smiled. "Everest?"

"I want to apologize again for last night." I paused, a cold, dead feeling hitting the pit of my stomach. The night's events played over in my mind. It was one thing for my family to disrespect me, but for them to make a guest of mine uncomfortable was not only embarrassing but disappointing. I knew I shouldn't have invited her. She didn't deserve any of that.

"Hey, no worries." She waved me off, and it was then that I realized that I hadn't even finished my apology. "Do you guys eat tartlets at every dinner?" Her voice dropped and her eyebrows were furrowed in concern.

"Only when my mom is feeling really fancy," I scoffed.

When she laughed her hair shook with the notion. Her hair was longer than I originally thought it was.

"Your hair." I pointed like I had no more than two brain cells.

"Oh yeah, I was trying something different," she explained, tugging on the ends before stopping herself and pulling out her lunch.

Not only was her hair different, but her clothes were too. She was wearing a yellow shirt with red bracelets. Our school colors. She didn't strike me as the type to be involved in such antics.

"Oh wow, check out the school spirit," I teased.

She looked down at her outfit and shrugged her shoulders before pulling out a bag of chips. "I've never even been to a game before, so I guess I'm an imposter."

"You've never been to a game?"

This blew my mind and even broke my teeny black heart of coal a little. She shook her head and played it off as if it was nothing.

"We're going Friday," I said. She was going to a game, even if I had to drag her kicking and screaming. It was a part of the high school experience.

Her eyes grew big and she quickly tucked a strand of hair behind her ear. "What?"

I chuckled. "I'll take you to the game."

"I don't want to go." She shook her head.

I grabbed the bag of chips from her and leaned back, throwing my boot-covered feet on the table. "Not an option. We have a deal, remember?"

I winked at her then tossed a chip in my mouth.

19

BEVERLY

I couldn't believe that the week flew by that fast, and now I was face to face with Everest, as he concentrated—so seriously—on my face.

"Quit moving," Everest said as he put eye black on my cheek.

"Is all of this really necessary?"

"It's your first game, you have to go big or go home."

"Can I go home?"

"Nope, nice try though." He tapped me on the head with the eye-black container. We were sitting in the parking lot of the school, ten minutes before the game was to start.

He stared at me curiously, fingers gripping his chin. "What?" I asked, uncomfortable with the scrutiny.

"Something is missing," he said, kind of dazed, and stared at my face like the answer was written there in tiny letters. I'd put effort into my outfit tonight, making sure that I looked like someone who'd be attending a high school football game. Everest had been talking about tonight all week, asking me if I was excited for it every time I saw him, and I didn't know if I said yes because it was actually something on my senior-year bucket list or because I liked the way his eyes lit up when I did.

His face brightened like he had a brilliant idea, and he climbed into the back seat, digging for something. Jersey in hand, he said, "An authentic school jersey would complete your school spirit look."

He smiled and held it toward me. I took the dark-red mesh between my fingers. I flipped it over, and the yellow numbers read *11*.

"Wait, is this y—" The words caught in my throat.

"Yes, it's my jersey. I found an old one in my room," he said quickly, as if he'd practiced what he was going to say. "Don't worry, I washed it."

"I can't wear this . . ."

"Sure you can." His tone was matter of fact.

I looked down at the jersey, and then stared back into his mask of an expression. "I know how much this jersey meant to you at some point, how hard you worked with this mesh on your back, and the pressure that it came with . . ."—I shook my head and held the jersey back out to him—"it doesn't feel right."

He grabbed my fist clutching the jersey and softly pushed it back. "Just wear it, please."

To make him quit looking at me like that, I threw the jersey on, the oversized material engulfing me like the sea.

"So, can we actually go to the game now?" I asked.

* * *

The first thing that hit me when we entered the stadium was the mass of people all gathered together wearing two colors. Everest wore a black jacket, and I wasn't surprised that he'd be the only one not wearing the school's colors.

The next thing that I noticed was the smell. The sizzle of hot dogs and butter and the combustion of popcorn kernels. The cotton candy that looked like plausible clouds—colorful, edible clouds. The bands from both schools tinkering with their instruments. Cheerleaders sitting on the ground, pom-poms in hand, ponytails pulled high. Shirtless guys who were overly dedicated, painting their abdomens gold and red. Girls taking selfies and parents picking a good seat.

I looked up at Everest and noticed him taking everything in. "You know, this is the first time I'm in the stands watching the game."

"Are you okay?" I asked gently.

He looked down at me and smirked. "C'mon, let's get some snacks."

One look at the line and I instantly wanted to retreat. "It's fine, I don't want anything."

"You sure?"

The scent of freshly-made pretzels filled my senses. A girl walked past me with a batch of cheese fries that hit the back of my throat, but then another look at the line persuaded me.

"No, I'm not hungry." My stomach made a desperate plea for food.

"Looks like your stomach disagrees." A smug know-it-all expression played on his face. "It won't be that long."

As we entered the line, we ended up standing behind a group of girls who were arguing about what color they were going to wear for homecoming. I was so deep into their conversation that

I barely realized that Everest had grown incredibly quiet. I stared up at him and his face screamed that he was lost in his thoughts. For a moment I thought he looked sad, but the emotion flashed by so quickly I couldn't tell if I actually saw it or not.

Nami walked past the line and spoke into her phone. "Tiffany, I'm here."

She angrily ended her call and stuffed her phone into her pocket. Undoubtedly, she must have felt my stare because she looked straight into my eyes and approached us.

"Hey." Her black hair looked almost blue in the fading sunlight.

I was stunned that she was actually talking to me; we had never really spoken before. "Hi." I tried my best to keep my voice from wavering.

"Nice to meet you. I'm Nami Lynn." Her smile was that of a politician.

"I'm Bev—"

"Beverly Davis, senior, seventeen, works at a café right on Brisklin Street. Resides in the east end of town."

I was speechless.

"Don't be so freaked out. Nami knows everything about everyone," Everest assured me.

"Not everything . . . are you guys a couple?"

I blinked in response to Nami's bluntness.

"Geez, Nami, you don't waste any time," Everest said, his laugh forced.

"Sorry, but it's the thing that has been on everyone's mind. And now you're wearing his jersey. You didn't even let Cara wear your jersey. But I'm being rude." Nami grabbed our hands in one brisk movement and led us to the front of the line. "Presidential advances, order whatever you like, free of charge."

We ordered just about everything on the menu. I was just going to get some popcorn but Nami urged me to get more.

"You should sit with us," I said without a second thought. I'd never been the type to be outspoken, but this year I'd been talking without thinking. Although it came out accidentally, I meant what I'd said. It seemed like the right thing to say despite Everest turning stiff and Nami giving me an apprehensive smile.

She shook her head. "I couldn't possibly impose."

"Sure you can," I said, and then remembered she was talking on the phone, most likely to someone she was meeting. "I'm sorry, you probably already have plans."

"I'm actually usually at these things alone or behind someone's very sweet but highly overtalkative grandparents until my friend is finished playing the drums terribly." She must be talking about Tiffany.

"Don't want to keep the grandparents waiting, do you?" Everest asked, looking bored while walking up the ramp leading to the bleachers.

"On second thought, I think I will sit with you guys."

Nami sat down right between us. It was clear she was comfortable when she dug her hand in my popcorn and took a sip of my soda.

"Your hair is different, it's really pretty," Nami complimented me.

"Thank you." Nami was get-signed-by-a-model-agency-at-a-car-wash type of pretty, and here she was complimenting my looks.

"What's taking this game so long?" Everest said after we'd been sitting for a while.

Nami groaned. "They are trying to convince someone to sing the anthem." She looked at us and shrugged.

An idea struck me. "They are looking for someone to sing?"

I didn't even have to look at Everest to know he was giving me the death glare. Nami tucked a strand of hair behind her ear and popped her left eyebrow upward.

"Yes. It was supposed to be Taylor, you know, from Glee Club, but she lost her voice this morning. Do you have any ideas?"

"I do, actually." I smiled at Everest, relieved that looks couldn't kill. "Everest."

"Everest can sing?" Nami said in disbelief.

"He's amazing."

"They don't have, like, a track or something?" Everest asked, annoyed. "Like, why do they need a singer? Just type in a performance online and play it through the whole stadium."

"I'm going to pretend you never said that," Nami replied. "Could you please sing?"

"No." His answer was immediate and his tone was clipped.

"Please sing. You're so good. Show them how amazing you are. You're not just football, Everest. You are so much more." I grabbed his arm gently. "And last time I checked, we had a deal."

He clenched his jaw before drawing in a deep breath. "Okay, okay, where is the mic?"

Nami's eyes grew big before she gave him directions. She turned to me with a look of disbelief on her face.

"Are you blackmailing him?" she asked as she took a seat next to me. I couldn't help but laugh as I shook my head.

The bleachers were cold so I snuggled deeper into the jersey. The cold wind blew on my cheeks and my teeth chattered. Everest's figure appeared on the field and I instantly smiled. He looked so comfortable out there—even without his football gear.

There were confused gazes all around as Everest climbed up on the black stand with the mic. He gripped it confidently, but when he took his bottom lip between his teeth, I knew he was nervous.

His eyes searched the crowd, and I wondered what he was looking for until they landed on me. He looked at me as if he was asking for permission, and I nodded. With the movement of my head, he visibly took a deep breath and glanced around the large crowd again.

"Please rise for 'The Star-Spangled Banner.'"

His voice didn't waver.

People around me chuckled and stood. They had no clue for what they were about to hear.

"What is this fuckery?" someone laughed behind me. Immediately, the whispers of people already beginning to talk about him rose up around us.

"O say can you see . . ."

He began and the crowd's reaction was priceless. The girl to my left placed a hand over her mouth, completely taken away. Everest loosened up, a beautiful smirk on his lips as if he liked the reactions, liked knowing that he'd tricked people.

"And the rocket's red glare . . ."

The elevation, the crescendo, it was simply beautiful.

"Where was he hiding this talent?" Nami laughed.

Everest finished the song and smiled. People in the stands went crazy—absolutely nuts. They roared. They screamed. They were proud.

His smile was wide as people patted him on the back and screamed for his attention. He continued to run up the wet bleachers and I feared he would fall. He stopped and scoped out the crowd until he saw me and ran in my direction. Cara caught my eyes, and I immediately looked away.

When he approached me, he was out of breath. He bent forward to catch it before coming back up with a full smile. His chest moved rapidly up and down.

"Beverly Davis, will you do me the honor of accompanying me to that shitty event they call homecoming?" he asked.

I almost choked—this was so abrupt and so spontaneous that I quickly tried to come to grips with my new reality. Nami couldn't stop squealing next to me. I looked like a fish as my mouth gaped open and shut. I'd never been to homecoming. The thought I'd ever go never crossed my mind, let alone go with Everest Finley.

Everest noticed my discomfort and bent down to whisper in my ear, "After what you just made me do, it's only fair you have to accept my challenge, Ms. Davis. Don't live your life wondering what-if."

"Y-Yes," I choked out, still surprised that he'd even asked. He went with Cara each year, and I couldn't help but realize that I was breaking that pattern.

"Do you solemnly swear to eat their horribly catered food and do the electric slide like it's our last time?"

The curious gazes that followed Everest to his seat had gone back to the game. It felt like Everest and I were the only ones in the world.

"Yes," I laughed.

The rest of the game was a blur. Tiffany joined us at some

point, and like almost everyone, she complimented Everest on his performance.

"You never fail to keep all of us on our toes," she said. Her drumsticks were stuck in the base of her ponytail. She was all smiles and even hugged me when she met us on the bleachers. Everest's eyes smiled for him, and it was then I noticed that the green in his eyes had finally defeated the blue.

"Everest, you have full permission to sing me to sleep every night," Nami joked, and we all laughed.

All I could think about was how incredibly brave Everest was, and how he asked me to homecoming. I knew it was a part of our bet, but why wouldn't my heart stop thumping out of my chest?

20

EVEREST

Confession: How can I trust someone when I can barely trust myself? I genuinely care about this girl and, honestly, that scares me.

—EF, October 7, 2018

My sweatshirt was suddenly too dark and too hot as I climbed out of my car in the parking lot of Beverly's apartment complex. I ignored the voice in my head telling me that this was all wrong. I had spent the weekend trapped by my thoughts, going back and forth before settling on the fact that I was going to attempt to be happy. I didn't know if it would work but I'd decided to try.

"Hey, you." I couldn't help but grin seeing Beverly there on her balcony.

She turned around quickly, a fast smile settling on her lips. Had I ever mentioned how much I was fascinated with her smile?

I swore Beverly had the kind of smile that made flowers grow. I'd never known anyone as genuinely happy. She never faked anything, and was an open book with bold lettering. Her heart covered everything in a five-mile radius, forget the sleeve. She wore a faded navy-blue sweater that swallowed her whole, her hair spiraling in every direction, and her signature beat-up high-top sneakers. Unlike the girls I used to hang around, she never talked about her appearance. It was like she didn't care if every hair was out of place.

"What are you doing here?" she asked, leaning slightly over the chipped railing.

"I . . . w-was wondering if you needed a ride . . . to school?" The words I'd rehearsed in my head didn't come out as smoothly as I'd hoped.

"Oh, I've got my mom's car," she said, holding up the keys. I knew this was all pretty random. I wasn't usually up this early, and it wasn't normal for me to show up to her place unannounced. The only time she saw me was in the afternoon or the evening, but that was about to change—a few things were about to change.

"I was thinking we could carpool, being that we are going to the same place and all." The words flew out freely now. I turned to display my backpack.

"Tell me this isn't a joke," she squealed.

Everything on her lit up, like she was reminding the sun to rise and display itself to the world. She scurried down the steps, approaching me with plenty of momentum. I was caught off guard when she dropped her bag and keys and jumped on me, wrapping her legs around my waist and fastening her arms around my neck.

"Whoa." I stumbled back a little bit then caught my balance. A swarm of bees appeared in my gut from our closeness.

Her scent invaded my senses as she held me tight. Her hair tickled my neck, and not laughing at her excitement was impossible. Pushing every doubt and menacing thought away, I wrapped my arms around her.

She lifted her head up and focused her eyes on mine. "I'm so excited you're going back to school."

"Oh really? I can't tell."

"Sorry," she said sheepishly, and climbed out of my grasp. I already missed the comfort of her embrace. Somehow thinking it could wipe out the feeling, I cleared my throat. I even took a step back.

"What made you want to start going again?" she asked while picking up her book bag.

"You're there." I shrugged. "Shall we go?"

"Indeed we shall," she said and hopped into the passenger seat.

After the game and all through the weekend, my phone was flooded with messages from people I hadn't heard from since before my attempt. I guessed I shouldn't have been that surprised. Nothing was going according to my original plan—not being here. Now I was pretty much winging everything, especially after my performance at the game. I lay in bed thinking about all the different ways the rest of my life could pan out, and I still hadn't got a clue. I was still floating, but it was different this time. Hope was my sidekick in this adventure for the first time, and it was in the form of a deal with a loner girl who had the brightest smile and the dirtiest sneakers.

"Hey, you okay?" Beverly asked from the passenger seat, and I nodded casually and grinned for her sake.

* * *

I forced myself to believe I was doing the right thing as I threw my arm around her shoulder and walked into the school. Eyes zoomed in on us instantly, but no one approached us, they just called out greetings. I walked Beverly to her locker and all the way up to her first class, before heading to mine.

The first class of the day was just as boring as I remembered it to be. I'd worked hard all weekend finishing off the stack of papers that had collected on my desk. Luckily, they weren't hard—I'd always done pretty well at school. Just because my mind was sick didn't mean that I didn't know the difference between an anion and a cation.

My dad had always been pretty strict with me about my education. *Anything less than an A is not okay*. I hated when he said that—like he had any right to give criticism or judgment. He cheated and lied; where was his integrity?

I knew he wanted me to take over the company, but business had never been my interest. Now that I was older, I no longer found myself wanting to be just like my father—I hadn't for a while. I didn't need his shoes; I had my own.

Cara walked into the classroom and this broke me out of my thoughts, and right then I remembered how much she hated history. It didn't matter where in the world or the time period; it was all pointless because to her they were dead people. Maybe she saw me the same way. I made sure not to look at her while she took a seat. I focused on my notes and bit my tongue as she took the seat right behind me.

"Hey." Her voice stiffened every bone in my back.

"Are you ever going to talk to me again?" she continued. It

wasn't until she poked me in the back with her pen that I turned around.

I didn't say anything. I stared at her, at that face I'd seen so many times but that was now just too unfamiliar. Her crystal-blue eyes were so clear I could see right through her. They said your eyes were the gateway to your soul, and Cara's were so translucent, I had her figured out within ten minutes of knowing her. Pretty face, she'd do anything to fit in. She strove for perfection, and my parents loved her for it. Heck, even I'd loved her for it.

"Is anyone alive up there?" she said.

What a wonderful choice of words.

She smiled like she was next up on stage, her manicured finger pointing to my head. I didn't know why she was acting like nothing happened—had she forgotten what she did to me? Because I hadn't. I turned back around and finished copying the notes on the board.

"You've changed. I don't even know who you are anymore," she whispered. And I feared I'd break my pencil from gripping it so tightly. There were only fifteen minutes left of class, so I decided I'd just walk around the school until next period; I couldn't be in here any longer. I quickly raised my hand. Mr. Evans gave me the evil eye through the space between the bridge of his nose and his glasses. I always wanted to pause his lessons and push his glasses up because they annoyed the crap out of me, but I ignored all of that today.

"Yes, Mr. Finley?"

Everyone turned to look at me.

"Can I use the restroom?"

"I don't know, can you?" he shot back.

My face instantly went slack. Man, I'd forgotten how lame

teachers were. Without thinking, I got up from my desk and kneeled on the floor and began to speak in an old-time British accent. "Forgive me. If it pleases you, sir, may I obtain your gracious permission to proceed to the toilet facilities of this establishment, so that I may, with haste, urinate, and thus relieve the unbearable pressure building in my bladder, lest I develop an infection, or, heaven forbid, soil my garments?"

Laughter rose from the class, and Mr. Evans looked like he was fighting a smile. "Oh, what joy for you to be back. Come get the pass, you smartass."

Everyone, including me, was surprised to hear him swear. He was one of the strictest, most boring teachers known to man, and he seemed to be joking around.

I grabbed the pass sheepishly. I would have never done that before my attempt. I always showed respect to adults; I always had respect for anyone. I looked at class clowns and would feel guilty if I laughed at their jokes. But now I was open to not giving too much thought to things. My brain seriously needed the space.

Entering the hall, I let my feet take me wherever. I walked into the bathroom to find Mikey sitting on the trash can under the window smoking what looked to be a blunt.

Idiot.

"Dude, seriously?" I asked, amused.

"Aye. You wanna want a hit?" He smirked.

"Maybe after school?"

"Still a goody-two-shit, I see. What are you even doing here, anyway? By the amount of booze you bought from me, I figured you'd be passed out somewhere for another month or so."

"Goody-two-shoes. The phrase is *goody-two-shoes*, and I

could be asking you the same thing. Aren't you supposed to be in prison or something?"

I eyed him and he eyed me, until we both started laughing.

"I'm too pretty for prison," he chuckled, taking another hit.

"Really, man, what are you doing here?" I asked.

He stared at the blunt before dropping and then stepping on it.

"I was hoping to bump into Nami." He looked up at me and grinned.

"Nami? Who *hopes* to bump into her?" I countered.

"Are you slow? I just said I did," he replied while picking up the smashed blunt and walking toward one of the urinals.

"I know what you said. I just don't understand why. She's a no-filter firecracker who knows everything about everyone. She is the kind of girl who could get you kicked out of school, so why do you want to be around her? She could get you expelled in three-two-one." I snapped my fingers as I counted.

"Word on the street is that she so wants this . . ." He held his arms out and glanced up and down his own body, and then flushed the joint down the drain.

He was definitely nuts. Nami Lynn would never go with a guy like him. "Doubt it, she's too smart to want you."

"We'll see," he laughed.

Just then I heard the bell ring, and I tightened my hand on my backpack. "See you later."

"The phrase is *See you later, alligator.*"

* * *

I walked into the hall shaking my head. Never in a million years would I have thought that Mikey Cosweld was pretty cool—an idiot, but still, pretty cool. The rest of my classes weren't as boring as I expected. I had eyes on me, but I didn't care. I was nice to everyone who approached me throughout my classes. I knew my appearance could be intimidating but I didn't want to be known for being a jerk. My old teammates didn't say anything to me, which was probably a good idea.

I went to English class and was surprised to see Beverly sitting in the far-right corner. I hadn't known that we had any classes together. I smiled and approached her desk, where she had her head stuck in her bag, digging for something.

"You're in my seat." I made my voice as deep as possible, and she jerked her head back so quickly that she hit her head on the wall.

"Ow." She clutched the back of head and dropped what looked to be a pencil from her hand while I chuckled.

"Geez, no need to be bouncing off of walls. We are in a respectable learning establishment, not a bouncy house." I handed her pencil back to her.

"You aren't funny." She tried not to smile but failed.

"Is this seat taken?" I asked, pointing to the desk next to hers.

"Yes," she responded.

"Aw, sucks for them." I maneuvered around her desk and sat right next to her.

"Everest, no, you can't just take someone's seat." Even when she scolded me it sounded sweet.

"I'm sure they will understand."

"I'd slap you, but shit stains." Nami appeared, her expression annoyed. She shoved my desk then purposely stepped hard on my shoe. She scurried away and sat a few places over, burning me with her glare.

"Hey, Mikey C.'s looking for you," I said teasingly. "You know, I've got his number if you need it . . ."

"Oh. My. God. Finley," Nami shushed me. "Shut your mouth!"

"I'm guessing this is Nami's seat." I looked at Beverly, who was trying not to laugh.

Class started and I was fascinated by how Beverly was so inclined to pay attention to the lesson. She wrote quickly, with superneat handwriting. It was like she forgot I was there. Her eyebrows furrowed together as our teacher taught, her teeth sometimes absentmindedly chewing on the back of her pencil. She was in a learning trance, and it was kind of funny. I poked her side and she jumped—her eyes grew big and a small sound of surprise escaped her lips. When she turned to look at me, I quickly turned my head to the board, as if I was paying attention the whole time. When she turned to look back at the board, I bit my lip to keep from laughing. I felt like an elementary kid who got a kick out of distracting their friend from paying attention.

After a few minutes, I poked her side again. She jerked and made an even louder yelp, causing a few heads to turn. She pointed at the ceiling and whispered, "Sorry, there's a bee."

The class looked up at the ceiling and tried to figure out where the imaginary bee was, and by this time, it was taking everything in me not to let this laugh out. When the class faced the board again, Beverly turned to me with annoyed amusement.

"Please stop," she whispered.

I shrugged and pretended to look confused. "Stop what, exactly?"

"Ev—"

"Ms. Smith, Beverly is being very disruptive and it's very hard for me to keep up," Cara said, and I hadn't even noticed her before now. We used to sit together every period we had; now I'd forgotten completely she was even in this class.

"Yeah, she and Everest haven't stopped talking this whole time," Martha chimed in, and before I could say anything, Nami cut in.

"Are you sure *that's* the reason you can't keep up?" Nami deadpanned, causing a few snickers to arise from the class.

"Drink bleach . . ." Martha seethed.

"Girls, girls." Our elderly teacher tried to contain the class.

Nami stood up from her desk and Tiffany held her back. "If I wanted to kill myself I'd climb your ego and jump in a pool the size of your IQ. You do realize that makeup isn't going to fix your stupidity, right?"

"Girls!" the teacher yelled, cutting off the argument.

"Beverly and Everest, save all conversations after class." Then she turned to the board and resumed talking about *Macbeth*.

Class soon ended and I had a bone to pick. Beverly started to walk out of class before realizing I wasn't following her. "You coming to the library?"

I walked over to her and grabbed her books. "Yeah, I'll meet you there. I have to ask Ms. Smith a question. I'm stocked on homework."

"I'm glad you're back even though you got us in trouble." She nudged me playfully. "I really hope you stay."

I went back into the classroom, spotting Cara. Storming over, I grabbed her hand and dragged her out of the class and into an empty classroom. "Leave Nami and Bev alone."

I was about to walk out again when she grabbed my arm, which I immediately yanked back.

"On one condition . . ."

I walked out of the room before I even heard her proposition; this wasn't up for debate.

* * *

"You hungry?" I asked Beverly, who was staring out of the window of my car. School had let out, and no matter how much I ate at lunch, I was always hungry afterward. I could honestly say I was drained at the end of the day.

"We had lunch, like, two hours ago."

"So? That's a long time for me."

"How are you not fat by now?" she laughed, poking my stomach.

I laughed. "I don't know."

"You and me both." She turned back toward the window.

I said, "I'm just going to go to 21 Daisies. I could go for a muffin."

She turned to look at me with a chuckle. "Do we have to? My shift doesn't start for another hour. We can hang at the park for a little before I have to go in. I don't think anyone would mind if I was a little late. I heard there are some new performers, so they'll be busy with that."

"That sounds nice and all, but then I'll be late for my set."

She froze and slowly turned to me. "Your what?"

I could see the excitement bubbling up inside of her.

"What do you mean 'what'?" I acted playfully confused.

"Repeat what you said." Her brown eyes sparkled.

"I'm just going to go to 21 Daisies. I could go for a muffin."

"No, Ev, repeat what you just said." She hit my arm.

"Okay, okay, so violent. I said I'll be late for my gig—"

I couldn't even finish before she squealed. "Tell me this isn't a joke."

"This isn't a joke." I smiled at her.

21

BEVERLY

Later that afternoon, while I was laying out baked goods in the showcase, Poppy asked, "How come you've never performed for open mic night?"

I'd always thought about doing it, but singing wasn't my thing. I'd rather doodle the faces of strangers or build a world on a canvas. I was more of a behind-the-curtain kind of girl—so it was a little funny that my best friend was a center-stage kind of guy. Everest could pretend that he didn't like all the attention that he got but everyone knew that he was a natural-born star.

"I like to watch," I replied simply, popping back on my stool once I'd placed the spider cookie inside. We'd been doing up the place with Halloween decorations. All the while, I tried not to let the crunchy leaves stress me about school, about how much time had passed. I'd applied to seven colleges. I worked three jobs over the summer just to pay for the application fees, and yet I hadn't heard back from a single one.

As I sat comfortably behind the register, the bell sounded, and I smiled. Everest had dropped me off earlier, and I'd been glancing every so often at the clock, watching the hours tick by until he appeared.

Facing the door, I was confused by the sight of Nash and a few other recognizable faces from the football team. Since I'd been working here, never once had I seen them here. I wouldn't imagine that it would be their kind of scene.

Lily greeted the boys and sat them at a table in the hidden corner. I stood still, unsure of how I should react. I walked farther down the counter to get a better look at the table and met Nash's smug expression, him lying back in the chair like he owned the place. He had a gold plastic crown on his head. I assumed it signified his homecoming king nomination. He was probably going to win this year. I couldn't imagine anyone else but Everest beating him off the ballot. But Everest wasn't even nominated this year.

Poppy nudged my shoulder. "Earth to Betty? Go on and take that order."

Suddenly, I was brought back from the stare Nash and I shared, and I didn't want to go anywhere near that table. Poppy's eyes widened and looked at me as if I was impaired.

"Well, go on," she urged. Everyone was busy today—the café was always busy on the open mic nights, but this was the fullest I'd ever seen it. I wished I was in the kitchen or sweeping up backstage; anywhere but here, about to take an order from those guys, but duty called.

I straightened my back, took a deep breath, and strolled to the table with a smile, like I'd do with any other customer. I clutched my notepad so tightly that the paper crumpled beneath my fingers.

"Hi, is there anything I can get you guys?" My smile was laid on thick and my voice was straight sugar.

The guys around the table had broad shoulders and arrogant expressions, and made me feel as if I were prey. Chuckles sounded around the table, and the thought of them as hyenas fit perfectly—those vicious scavengers with sly, sneaky intentions. Nash was the leader of the pack, and I'd never been this close to him. He was very attractive, but almost all of the guys around the table were. It wasn't so much a cliché as it was a statistic. Too often than not, rich attractive people went for rich attractive people, and then they make a breed of future rich and attractive people.

"So, you're Everest's girl? I didn't know chocolate was his choice of flavor." A guy with dark-brown hair and gray eyes spoke, his varsity jacket outlining his broad shoulders. I cringed inside, but on the outside I remained unfazed.

A chubby guy with red hair laughed. "She's, like, the only black girl in school. Everest is always getting something that no one else can have."

"Any drinks for you guys tonight? Or would you like to hear the specials?" I didn't acknowledge any of their comments, and did exactly what I was sent over here to do.

"Cute *and* determined," one of the guys said, but I was focused on staring at my notepad, so I didn't see who it was.

"I'll have a burger, no pickles," Nash said. I stared at his crown, confused by its placement. He looked like he was already bored.

I took the remaining orders and walked back to the kitchen. I handed Felix the order and stayed there until all of the food was ready. I knew I was being a punk, and I felt disappointed in myself. The guys hadn't even done anything to me—I just felt overwhelmed. All of the eyes and snarky looks were just too much for me.

Once the food was finished, I asked Poppy if she could serve it, but she was too busy helping set up the equipment for the band. I glanced at the clock and wondered if Everest had forgotten. A part of me was glad he wasn't here. He didn't need to deal with this.

"It's about time," one of the guys grumbled, and the others joined in on the complaint. I apologized and handed each of them their marked meals. This was a café, not a full-on restaurant. We had a menu for meals, but no one really came here for that. Felix was a great cook but the point of 21 Daisies was to relax and listen to music.

I was just about to walk away when Nash grabbed the sleeve of my sweater. "There are tomatoes on this burger."

I stared at the burger confused. "Cool?"

His jaw ticked and just like an order, the eyes of the guys around the table went dark. "I said no tomatoes."

I shook my head softly and furrowed my eyebrows. "You said no pickles."

I went to pick up the receipt to show him, and he snatched it from my fingers, his eyes still on me. "Are you telling me that I'm wrong?"

I didn't know what game they were playing, but it wasn't fun.

"Hey, Tim? What's that saying about customers?" Nash asked one of the guys from the table.

The one with blue eyes and blond hair answered, "The customer is always right."

My ears were heating up, and I could feel myself getting flustered. "If you would just take a look at the receipt, you'll see the order."

I silently praised myself for not letting my voice waver.

"This receipt means nothing," he said before ripping the receipt to pieces and tossing them on the floor.

I wanted to take the burger and smash it on top of his head. I wanted to take the tomatoes and push them down his throat—that was what my mother would have done. But I wasn't like that, and even thinking that way made me feel bad, so instead I smiled politely. "I'm sorry, would you like me to get you a new one?"

The boys, one by one, took turns being confused. I guessed that wasn't the reaction they were expecting. They never spoke to me at school or messed with me in any kind of way, so why now? Nash looked angry, and it didn't surprise me when he pushed the plate off of the table. It broke and the contents of the burger went in every direction.

"Of course, I want a new one. I can't eat one that you knocked on the floor, now can I?"

I did not knock his plate down, nor did I do anything wrong. He knew it and I knew it. I felt bad for him, having a soul so dark that he had to bring everyone down with him. I hope it got better, because he couldn't possibly be happy acting like this.

I forced myself to chuckle. "I guess not. A pickle-less, tomato-less burger, right, coming up."

I turned on my heel and quickly placed his order before returning to clean up the mess. As soon as I thought I was done, the boys would throw food under the table so I had more to clean. I felt stuck but willed myself to stay strong—these were guys with money and power, tons of it. If I did anything wrong, they could ruin my life. They'd chew me up and spit me out, and there would be nothing that anyone could do. After a while, it was just food falling from Nash's end. I looked around for help from my co-workers, but they were all scrambling from the surplus of musicians and customers. The boys taunted me every step of the way, saying abominable things about how much I must like being on all fours, and I was disgusted.

I was just about to place a piece of wilted lettuce on Nash's head when I heard the faintest bell ring above the door. My eyes met Everest's. He looked confused, then angry. None of the football guys noticed he was here, thankfully. He pushed through the minicrowd, and the chanting came to a quick stop.

Nash was still teasing me, completely oblivious to Everest coming up behind him. I felt frozen, and it wasn't until Everest's fingers snatched the plastic crown from Nash's head that I finally found my voice. The café was dead silent.

"Everest," I said softly. I had no clue what was going to happen next.

He grabbed me and gently pushed me behind him.

Nash's face was unreadable, as if this wasn't a part of his plan. He wasn't smug or arrogant, just unreadable. His teammates looked unsure as well. Everyone was at a standstill, waiting for Everest to make a move.

He twirled the crown in his fingers, in a way showing how the crown had no power. "Nice seeing you all here. It's been more than a while."

No one said anything.

"I'm actually glad you're here, I was just about to sing. I hope you don't mind if I borrow this." He placed the crown on his head and grinned. His voice was polite, but I knew he was fuming. I was just glad he hadn't resorted to fighting.

He climbed on the stage and stood behind the mic, tuning the guitar. I was just as curious as everyone else; we watched his every move. "Check, check, this thing on?"

How did he suck in everyone's attention? I guessed we would never know.

"I'm thinking of going freestyle tonight; you guys just gave me inspiration." He grabbed the stool. He winked at Nash and tilted the crown in his direction, as if he was tipping a greeting.

I'm getting tired of your disrespect.

Everest began, and it was so menacing that even I felt scrutinized. His face was centered straight on Nash's, and every lyric was out for Nash. Everest was angry and everyone knew it, and although it was a dangerous song, it was still raw and insanely good. We were all engrossed in his madness, captivated by the realness. This wasn't a teeny-bopper pop song, this was live, and it was something that I never would have imagined would sound good.

Aren't you getting tired?
just put it to rest.

Everest stood up from the stool and walked closer to edge of the stage, near where Nash and the others sat. This was all so intense, and I'd never heard Everest sing this way—rugged, exploding with feeling. The guitar was sweet and his voice was sweeter, but the words. Those words had enough fire to kill a dragon.

Don't forget I made you who you are
I'm the sole reason you made it this far

I was lost in the music, it all just poured out. Whenever Everest performed, he never left his emotions off the stage, and this time was no different. Who knew the last time Everest had talked to his ex–best friend? He was getting all of his feelings out—all of the hurt, all of the tears and sadness that he had to go through all alone. And even though he was mad, I could feel his pain. He was using anger to make it all better. The lights hit the crown on his head and his stone-cold face, and it was clearer than ever that he was one of the strongest people I'd ever known. He was a king in his own right. The outro was the most intense part of the song. Everest was standing, lungs taking all of the air in the room, to sing everything out. I could barely breathe, and everyone was drop-a-pin silent. He hit all kind of runs and high notes before quitting strumming the guitar.

Nash quickly stood up, telling the guys to leave. "He isn't worth it, he isn't worth anything."

The guys left the table, some staring at Everest hesitantly before walking out of the door.

"Wait, Nash—here's your crown." Everest smirked, jumped from the stage, and then placed it on Nash's head. Nash's jaw ticked. I feared he was going to swing and hit Everest but instead he pushed Everest back roughly and stormed out of the café.

The café was quiet for a split second before it broke out in applause. Poppy ran up to Everest and threw her arms around him. "Wow, you are so kick ass."

Other musicians shook hands with him and complimented him. I watched from afar and cleared off Nash's table. Lily came over to help me and saw the large mess.

She searched my eyes. "Hey? You okay? Did those guys give you any trouble tonight?"

I shook my head no, feeling completely drained. I could tell Lily wanted to say more, but she thought better of it, and silently helped me clean everything up. Glancing at the clock, I noticed my shift was over, and once I finished, I grabbed my jacket. Going home and reading a good book with a mug of tea sounded good right now. I opened the door and welcomed the cool night air. Then I felt a tug on the back of my jacket.

"Where do you think you're going?" I knew who the voice belonged to before I even turned around.

"Home," I said.

Everest turned me around to face him. "Without saying good-bye? That's not like you."

"I'm sorry, Ev, I'm just tired." I scratched the back of my head, flustered.

He looked at me with unreadable eyes, and gathered me into a hug. "Don't apologize. It's my fault that they were even here tonight. I should have been here earlier, but I was so nervous, I sat in my car forever. I know I have a habit of letting people down, but I don't mean to. You're the last person I want to let down." He kissed my forehead. "How long were they there for?"

If I told him the full story, then I knew that he'd do something dangerous, something to set him back after he'd been doing so well. "About ten minutes before you came," I fibbed. "They weren't there that long."

He looked at me with one eyebrow raised, then his face

remained soft. "Okay, good, good. Look, since I messed up today, I'll make it up to you."

"How?" The smile came before I could stop it.

"Patience, young grasshopper. Now come on, let's get you home."

22

EVEREST

I didn't *exactly* forget that homecoming was today, but I did lose track of time. I pulled out my black tux from deep in my closet last night. I hadn't touched that thing for so long that the shoulders were covered in a layer of dust. It was crazy how routine life could get. The world spun and didn't stop for anyone. When I put the tux on, I couldn't help but think it would have been the suit they'd have put me in if I had died. But as I looked in the mirror, turning this way and that, feeling the cut of the suit on my skin, I pushed that thought right out of my mind. Instead, I remembered the last time I had the suit on.

"Nash, I love you, man." I was sloppy even before he passed me the bottle of whiskey we'd stolen from his dad's liquor cabinet.

"You're my best fucking friend," he grumbled after I took another swig. We'd been drinking the whole night. His dad was so embarrassed that Nash was making an ass out of himself at his wedding that he'd locked the both of us in his study, regrettably forgetting that his liquor stash was located in the second drawer on the left of his desk.

"Yeah, and you're mine." Heat surrounded me and the room spun like the planets. I was no longer on Earth. Nash was just as messed up as I was. The whole day I didn't know how I could console him. I'd be pissed, too, if I had a stepmom who was four years older than me.

"You're the only family I ever need, man." He laid his head back against the bookshelf behind us. I could still remember how he abruptly started crying, and how those tears seeped into the shoulder of my suit, and I just sat there with my arm around him. "It hasn't even been six months."

That was the last time I'd had this suit on—that day when we were in his dad's study, sharing that bottle of whiskey. Nash had been so upset that day, and we never talked about the real reason behind it, but it was written all over his face. His dad was marrying again, and I guessed he wasn't in the mood for the party, especially since his mother had died not even a year ago.

A knock on my door brought me out of my thoughts. "Everest?"

I opened the door and revealed my little sister. "Yeah?"

"Beverly's here." Hadley came in and sat on my bed, watching me. She spoke to me as if we talked all the time, like she didn't usually avoid me at all costs. "How are you going to do your hair?"

I stared at her strangely before looking in the mirror. "What's wrong with my hair?"

"Nothing—it's just . . . don't you want this night to be amazing for Beverly?"

Of course I did. I nodded slowly.

"Then I think you should put more effort into your hair tonight," she replied before standing up and leaving.

I didn't know what that interaction was, but I was glad it happened. I went back to my mirror and stared at my hair. The black was growing out, but it was still such a dark look on me. It was as if I were a different person, and perhaps I was. It took a long moment of convincing myself before I grabbed a jar of gel and started laying down my messy locks.

As soon I stepped downstairs, I saw my mother, sister, and Beverly seated on the couch, engaged in conversation. Hadley was the first to see me, and the apples of her cheeks hit just beneath her eyes because she smiled so bright. She quickly tapped Beverly's shoulder, and she then turned to look at me.

But that wasn't the weirdest bit—my mom had a smile on her face. She was staring directly at Beverly, and it wasn't like an evil grin either—it was a genuinely happy smile. My mother actually looked human.

"Oh," my mother exclaimed.

Do you know how in every cheesy romance when the guy looked at the girl all done up, and his heart sped up and time slowed down, and he looked close to a panic attack? Well, for me it was the exact opposite. I felt calm. My mind was usually in jumbles, and I thought too much. But in this moment everything was clear, and all I could think about was how much like a goddess Beverly looked. Time didn't slow down; it sped up. Life didn't wait for me to come to grips on how pretty she looked.

Before I knew it, she was already in the passenger seat of my car, grumbling about how hungry she was.

"Ev?" she asked.

"Yes?" My throat suddenly felt dry.

"Your hair looks nice." She smiled through the side of my skull. I really hoped the gel held up.

"Thanks, Bev," I said. I glanced quickly at the gold-leaf crown on her head. "What are you even supposed to be?"

I hadn't put much thought into my outfit for this themed superhero dance. I actually hadn't put any thought into it.

She quickly sat up and looked at me, but I focused my attention on the road. "You didn't get it yet?"

"Are you supposed to be a goddess?" I asked her, wondering why my chest heated up when I said that.

She laughed. "Close. I'm Mother Nature."

"That's not a superhero," I observed.

"Mother Nature is a bit of both—she's a villain and a hero. She brings life but she also destroys it. Tornados, floods, volcanic eruptions, tsunamis, and just about any natural disaster. She gives light and darkness; thus my dress."

The gold and black dress fit that description perfectly. A mumbled "Oh" was all I could say.

I pulled into the school, which had decorations scattered all over the front of it. It took a while to find a parking space due to the high number of cars already in the lot, but eventually I found a space to park in.

"You ready?" I asked Beverly as we approached the school.

"I'm as ready as I could ever be." She smiled brightly, and all I could think about was how pretty a picture that would be.

"Almost forgot." I ran back to the car and grabbed the corsage of black flowers I had in my glove box. "Here you go, Mother Nature."

She laughed again. "It's perfect."

And with that, I grabbed her hand and led us into the school.

23

BEVERLY

Overwhelming was the only word running through my mind right now.

I, Beverly Davis, was attending homecoming with the most talked-about person in town. His calloused hand was linked in mine, pulling me through the clumps of people. I found it funny how it wasn't that long ago that I watched Everest from afar. He whisked me into a spotlight that I didn't quite understand. People at school now knew my name, and honestly, that scared me.

I was a nobody, and now I felt like I was starting to be somebody. I knew that didn't make much sense, but the shadows were my home, and Everest was like the sun, exposing me. That was weird, that I just compared him to the sun, because it could be *so* cold—those days in the winter when it was sunny but not warm? Maybe his parents jinxed him when they gave him the name

Everest, like he was almost destined to be cold and unreachable—
the tallest mountain in the world.

I looked up at him and something told me otherwise about
his fate. He had a good heart and a killer smile, but he locked it
up. He only showed you what he wanted you to see. He had his
moments, but no matter how much I tried to lie to myself, he still
hadn't fully opened up to me. I was patient though.

"The decorations are pretty shit," he mumbled, the sound somehow making its way to my ears through the blasting pop music.

His words took me away from my thoughts, and I actually
took in the dance: bright popping colors, capes, masks, and light-
ning bolts filled the area. The decorations weren't that bad—but
it was pretty obvious that the school hadn't put out a bunch of
money for them.

Everest pushed through some of the people, trying to find us a
table, but our classmates stopped him every few minutes.

Once Everest somehow found us a lone table, we both took a
seat. He pulled out a chair for me and then sat across the table.
We stared at each other through the glowing green crystal used as
a light on every single table. "Sorry about that," he finally spoke.

"About what?" I asked him, confused.

He pulled on his necktie. "You know, the constant stopping.
It's like everyone just remembered that I exist."

"Don't apologize," I chuckled. "It's what I'd expect when the
man of the hour makes an appearance."

I watched his features as they loosened up. His glowing eyes
narrowed in on me and a stupid smile fell on his lips. "That's your
fault, you know?"

I placed my chin on the palm of my hand and stared at him.
"I'm pretty sure that was all you."

He leaned forward with a grin. "Can you keep a secret?"

I nodded.

"I hate dances." He exhaled.

"Everest! Then why are we here then? I'd never have agreed to come if I'd known you'd hate it!"

"I'm showing you destruction," he said with a blank face.

I laughed. "At a dance?"

"Look around. You are surrounded by destruction whether you believe me or not. It's a space where teens and all their shit come together to create a shit storm. Virginities will be lost to people they will regret sleeping with. People will fall in 'love' with people who don't deserve it. Some gym teacher fifteen years from now will reminisce about the good old days, and mention this dance any chance he gets; he knows he peaked then but he won't admit it. They will drink and drink until it's too much to stomach and ruin dresses or ties they never planned on wearing again."

"Okay, that was dark," I said through the blaring music between us.

"I don't make the rules." He shrugged.

Just as he finished speaking, I saw Martha come toward the table. "Nice dress, Leah. Where did you get it from?"

From the tone of her voice, I could tell she was up to no good. "Beverly. My name is Beverly; and I actually borrowed it from my Aunt M—"

"That's cool. So, Everest, you should come and sit with us."

Cara watched from the popular kids' table, observing me, and I quickly turned my head. Everest stared blankly at Martha for a second before scoffing, "And why the hell should I do that?"

Martha seemed a little taken aback and adjusted her posture.

"Everyone told me to come over here and get you so we could all catch up. Cara has something to tell you, apparently."

His smug arrogance dropped and an unreadable expression fell upon his features before a mask of stone came back. "That would be a really good reason, if I actually gave a crap."

"I think this would be the part where you scamper away." Nami's comment came from behind us.

I couldn't help but chuckle and stood up to wrap my arms around her. I knew she was going to be here, but I also knew that she was going to be busy—presidential duties and all of that.

"You look beautiful," I heard for the first time tonight.

"Oh please," I responded to her, chuckling.

"Nami. Always a pleasure," Martha forced out of her mouth.

"I wish I could say the same for you," Nami laughed.

Martha rolled her eyes and leaned over to whisper in Everest's ear before walking back to her original table.

A beeping tone randomly came from Nami's boob, and she grabbed her phone.

"Tiffany spotted Mikey and the gang trying to make an appearance here, completely ignoring the fact that they aren't allowed to come to any more social events. Sorry, Beverly, but I've got to handle this."

"You're fine. Go."

"So, only us, huh?" I glanced at Everest, who was talking to some random kids who'd approached him, and realized he didn't hear me at all. "Guess not."

A different group of people approached him, and he chatted with them politely. I decided to go and get some food in hopes that by the time I was done he would be, too, but I wasn't so lucky.

I thought that the conversation was going to be short and quick, but it was still going. The pasta on my plate was growing more and more cold.

I glanced over at Everest, who coincidentally just happened to look at me. "Sorry that I'm being the worst date."

"It's fine. If this is the price to pay to hang out with you, then I'd wait hours," I said, trying to not make him feel bad.

"Stop, you'll make me blush," he joked, and I laughed.

"What were you talking about anyway?" I asked curiously.

"I was just catching up with people I haven't spoken to in a long time," he explained.

I looked around and saw Cara walking in our direction. We hadn't even been here for thirty minutes, and people had been swarming to talk to him the entire time. I couldn't feel any kind of way because Everest didn't belong to me. They were invested in him long before I was—so if anything, I was the intruder. The newbie to his fan club.

"Looks like you're gonna be catching up with a bunch of people tonight . . ." I tried to sound optimistic, but I knew it came out sounding awkward.

Everest looked to see what I was talking about, and his eyes quickly returned to mine. "No, this wasn't supposed to be how your night went." He took my hand and stood up. "Come on."

I looked up at him confused. "What?"

He laughed. "No time to explain. Come on, let's go—she's getting closer."

I didn't ask any more questions and followed his lead out of the dance. I felt the rush of running in my dress, and laughed along with him. Suddenly, we were outside. I didn't know where we were going, and I didn't care. The night air whooshed past us, and the only sound it made was the dance our laughter made as it intertwined with the sky.

24

EVEREST

Confession: is it wrong that a large part of me wanted to sit with Cara and Nash?

—EF, October 13, 2018

It felt so weird being at the dance and not being with them. Nothing made sense anymore. I didn't know who I was. I used to know exactly who I was—Everest Finley, the only son of the great Frank Finley. But now I was just a lost guy who'd befriended a ghost girl whose soul shone so bright, I sometimes believed that she wasn't human.

I glanced at Beverly and her face was a mix of confusion and amusement as she clutched her dress so she wouldn't trip over it. "Need some help?" I asked, slightly amused by the way she was running.

She quickly glanced at me, and I noticed the bright smile as she turned her head away. "Nope."

Just as quickly as she protested, I had to hold her steady so she wouldn't face-plant on the broken pieces of asphalt. A crack and a stumble were the only result. One hand on her waist and the other on her arm was the only thing keeping her balanced.

I couldn't help my slightly amused expression. "You sure?"

Her face was a mix of annoyance and laughter. "I think I broke my heel."

She backed away from my hold and held her foot out to look at it. Sure enough, the left heel was hanging and close to falling completely off.

"Well, this didn't go as smoothly as I planned," I laughed. We were only a few feet away from my car.

Beverly looked at me with a ghost smile. "This isn't funny. These aren't even my shoes. I borrowed them from Nami."

"No big deal. I'll buy her new ones. Are you okay, though?" I asked, observing her small foot for any casualties.

"Yeah, I'm fine, although walking might be difficult." She looked back down at the peg-legged heel, and huffed.

"Well, don't completely rule out running. Let me see you try with the broken shoe. I think you'll have a wicked cool limp—" I didn't even get to finish before she took off the shoe and playfully hit me on the shoulder with it.

"How about I give you a limp?" she threatened.

"Oh yeah?" I smirked, taking a step closer. I wasn't sure what was going on here, but it felt fun.

"What? You don't think I could take you, Finley?"

She surprised me with her words, and it looked like she even shocked herself.

"You said it, not me," I said with a grin.

She walked closer and rested the broken heel loosely in her hand, like she had an agenda with it. "So, you *do* think I can take you?"

Instantly, my mind went to a thought about what it would be like to kiss her, but it left as quickly as it came. I shook my head and quickly threw her frame over my shoulder. We were friends. I needed to keep telling myself that; only friends. "Just because I didn't say it doesn't mean I wasn't thinking it."

"Your butt is in my face," was her only response.

I laughed and realized that we were still in the school parking lot. "If it makes you feel any better, your butt is pretty up close and personal for me too."

"No, that does not soothe my concerns. Certainly does not make me feel any better whatsoever."

I laughed again for what felt like the millionth time tonight. I switched her body around so that I could carry her bridal-style.

"Better?" I asked.

Her eyes were so dark, but sometimes there were moments that seized them with light and made them glow. Like right now, for instance, the moonlight was hitting her irises and emphasizing her goddess-Mother Earth persona. Her lashes were short, but personally I liked it a lot because everyone could get the full effect of her big brown eyes. Her nose was petite and peppered with little dots and her lips were full and plump. Physically, Beverly was dark, but her spirit was so full of light. Physically I was light, but my spirit was torn in shreds and blacker than coal. Life was full of contradictions.

"My hero," she deadpanned.

Something about the way she said it hit me in the gut. I carried her to my car.

"Where are we going?" she asked once I placed her in the passenger seat.

"To get you some food."

I drove to Squirrel Hill to take her to get the best pizza in Pittsburgh. The restaurant was a place where the smell greeted you before you even pulled onto the street. We were overdressed and probably looked like a couple of idiots, but that was half of the fun of it all.

"Do you like it?" I asked when she had a mouthful of pizza.

She nodded her head while she chewed. "It's all right."

"Only all right, huh?" I grinned.

She wiped her mouth. "It's so good. How'd you know about this place?"

"How can you be born here and not know about this place? Shame. It's one of my special spots," I explained.

"You have a lot of special spots," she observed.

"If your family basically bought a town and you didn't know anyone in it, then you'd have lot of spots too." I leaned back against the booth.

"Did you have lots of friends before high school?" she asked.

"Honestly, no. I moved too much to form solid friendships."

I looked across the table at Beverly. How was it that she didn't have friends? I, for the life of me, didn't understand why I'd never noticed her.

"What about you? Were you Miss Popular in the preteen days?" I joked, but was actually really curious.

"I was homeschooled all the way up to eighth grade, and I've never been involved in any sports or activities. By the time I went to public school, everyone was already friends with everyone. I didn't fit in anywhere, and it seemed as though I was invisible."

That seemed like the opposite of what I'd had to go through as the new kid in my ninth-grade year. I was exposed—everyone seemed to have already me figured out before I walked through the building.

"Why were you doing homeschooling?"

"My mother didn't want me to leave. When all the other kids were leaving for kindergarten, she couldn't drop me off. I guess she was afraid of losing me."

I looked at her and her face was unreadable. "What's your mom like?"

She looked surprised that I asked her that question, which spiked my curiosity more.

"My mother? She's gorgeous. She used to compete in beauty pageants. She was amazing at them, too, won every single one she competed in. She's very sarcastic and has that dry humor that you kind of have to get used to. She's blunt and . . . stuff."

I cracked a smile. "And stuff? Care to elaborate?"

"She's a good person, and I love her, but sometimes she feels more like a roommate than a mother."

I guessed Beverly and I had the parent-drama thing in common.

"I saw you talking to my mom tonight," I said. "What were you guys talking about?"

"You," she responded simply.

I froze for a second. "What about?"

"About how you're getting better."

I wasn't exactly sure how I felt about that. Sometimes her encouragement was too much for me. I didn't deserve the hope she put into me. The future wasn't granted. There was no future for me—for us. She was going to get married, pop out some kids, and be the best freaking mom that there had ever been, and I'd be six feet under. Thankful that I was granted the opportunity to witness an angel on Earth.

I fought to keep this all in my mouth and squeezed out a simple response. "Oh."

She leaned forward. "Why the face?"

"Nothing. Are you done eating?"

We drove around a little bit after that, burning gas and time. Neither of us really wanted the night to come to an end. We were driving around the city for probably over an hour. The drive was silent, but the silence wasn't loud. I lost myself in the comfort of it. Beverly's head leaned against the window. I didn't know what I'd done to deserve her friendship, but I was grateful I had it. She was just so understanding. I often thought to myself that if she ever talked to the stars, they'd talk back.

"Bev."

"Hm?" she sighed.

"I'm sorry that homecoming didn't go as planned."

"Don't apologize. Believe it or not, I've actually had a good time. I never got to dance, but that just means that you'll make up for it, right?" She nudged me playfully.

"Whatever you want." I glanced at her and didn't miss her sweet smile.

"I want to know another special spot."

"Next time."

25

BEVERLY

"Hey, Betty." Everest hopped on the glass counter, which I was currently standing behind. He had a playful grin on his face as he looked at me.

"Not you too," I laughed while placing cake pops on display.

He immediately grabbed a fresh cake pop and swallowed it as quickly as he'd grabbed it.

"What's the story behind them calling you that?" Licking his lips free of icing, he waited for my answer.

"No story. I'm guessing they actually think that's my name," I answered, forcing a laugh.

The faint dimple in his left cheek popped out and his eyes widened a fraction. "No way."

"Way." I placed the tray on the cart behind me. Many times I would correct them, but it seemed as they always resorted back to calling me Betty.

"So, you mean to tell me that you've been working here for over two years and they still don't know your name?" He was getting a kick out of this.

"That's exactly what I'm telling you. Why else do you think they call me that?"

"I don't even know," he laughed, glancing up at the stage.

"Are you about to go on?"

"Yeah, break's over." He strolled through people before he turned around and jogged back over to me. "We're hanging out after work. I got another place to show you."

"New secret place?" I smiled, excited.

"Old to me, new to you," he answered before jogging back to the stage.

"He's amazing, isn't he?" Rose asked without looking for an answer. She gazed up at Everest on the stage, wooing the crowd like he had been for the past weeks. The café was getting fuller and fuller by the day, mostly with kids from our school. Everest had turned into a little-town rock star.

"Order at table three," Felix shouted and tapped the bell, signaling me to get back to work. Work had been more vigorous due to the increasing number of customers. I wasn't complaining; it kept me around people. I used to be always alone—that was probably why I enjoyed the company of others so much. It was just a bonus that my paycheck had increased.

I handed the plate of chicken fingers to table three: a guy with tattoos and messy brown hair and a girl with purple hair and lots of piercings. I'd never seen them in here before, but I needed to get used to not expecting to see my usual customers.

The guy looked mischievous but his eyes were warm. The girl looked bored.

"Here ya go." I smiled at them both, but only the boy returned it.

"Hello, Beverly, this seems to be the first time we have come in contact. I'm Michelangelo Cosweld, but to avoid getting their asses kicked, smart people call me Mikey." I laughed, and remembered hearing his name many times. He was the local delinquent, and apparently went through girls like they were underwear. This was the first time I was able to put a face to that name, and beneath the bad-boy look he had going on right now, he looked playfully innocent. He looked like he could persuade anyone to do anything, and that was probably what made him so dangerous.

"Hello," I responded softly, almost kicking myself for waving awkwardly.

Mikey rolled up the sleeves of his flannel shirt and nudged the girl before grabbing a chicken finger.

"Introduce yourself," he said.

She slowly turned to look at me, and her eyes looked so pretty, yet so sad. My heart clenched at her somber look before her face hardened and she forced a smile with clenched teeth.

"Aurora."

She offered nothing more and turned her attention to the stage, the same bored look present on her features. I said my good-bye and headed back to my station.

"Any requests?" Everest spoke into the mic, his white T-shirt damp from sweat and his growing-out, messy hair glossy in the lights.

He'd been singing for about an hour. The café was filled with the sounds of his voice—songs ranging from old to new, from originals to covers. His voice was timeless. I couldn't help but notice how happy and contented he looked, joking around on the stage and pouring his soul into the room. I couldn't even fathom how different my life would have been if he had succeeded in his attempt.

A slow melody carried through the café as his fingers began to work the strings. My heart rattled wildly in my chest. His eyes were closed and his lips parted, and from the first haunting note, he captured the attention of everyone in the café.

I couldn't tell a lie, that note crawled from the soles of my feet and engulfed me whole. It was like his pain took over his diaphragm. It was so beautiful.

> *Trapped on an island of my mind . . .*
> *quickly running out of time.*
> *Tell me I'll be fine . . .*

People looked up from their laptops and conversations stopped—all of the attention was on him. His runs and riffs blended perfectly with the lyrics, something that couldn't be faked.

> *Can you hear me scream?*
> *Lie to me,*
> *Lie to me,*
> *Lie to me,*
> *Tell me the last thing I see*
> *Won't be this blue sea . . .*

For just an instant, I wasn't at the café. I was someplace else, listening to his raspy tone, and watching his face contorted by emotion.

Lie to me, please . . .

Everest's head hung low and his chest expanded as applause shook the room.

"You okay?" a passing customer asked me. I stared at her, confused, before I felt a tear drop on my hand. Straightening my back, I was surprised when I touched my damp cheek. I hadn't even realized I was crying; I quickly wiped my eyes with the sleeve of my sweater and told the girl it was just allergies.

Well, that was embarrassing.

I cleaned until Everest's set was over. He chatted with everyone before heading in my direction.

"I'm just going to grab my jacket from the back room then we can be on our way," he said to me without stopping, heading straight into the break room.

"So . . . are you and Everest a thing?" Rose asked. Her question was so low that I barely heard it. I hadn't even noticed her approach me, but I did notice that she knew his name. He had only been working here for a few weeks and she knew his name. I could actually have cried again.

"No . . . we're friends."

She'd caught me completely off guard. I got asked this question every day so it wasn't the question, but her—why would she want to know?

Her cheeks tinted to the color of her name. "Sorry. You guys just look cute together, so I just thought—now that I know the truth, I don't feel bad anymore for having a crush."

"You like Ev?" I asked quietly, taking a step closer to her so no one could hear us.

"How could I not?" She smiled, dazed, like the very image of

Everest was sitting on her mind. She looked at me and laughed before walking away with a smile on her face.

"Wow," I muttered, unsure about how I felt about her confession.

"Ready?" Everest asked when he returned.

"Night, Everest," Rose said. He smiled in return.

"As I'll ever be," I sighed.

* * *

"So, what's the plan?" I asked as we pulled into a gas station.

"First things first, we have to get food, and this is the only place open." He opened my door for me and flashed me a side-smile.

It was late; the sky was superdark with no stars. The only light was from the full moon and the bright, obnoxious sign from the gas station. It didn't matter how many times I'd been out late, it always felt like the first time.

Everest must have had the munchies, because he had so many treats. He told me to get whatever I wanted, and the only thing I picked up were a few candy bars and a bag of chips. When we reached the counter, I saw just how much junk he'd got. The counter was full of sweet and salty snacks. He even took it upon himself to get some food from the hot section.

"Geez, Everest."

I stared at all the food the cashier was ringing up. He was lanky with greasy hair and a face that screamed that he hated his job. He said, "That'll be forty-three and forty-three cents. Cash or credit?"

Everest stared at him for a moment before slapping a crisp bill on the counter. "Cash."

The cashier's eyes grew to the size of saucers, and I saw that Everest had given him a hundred-dollar bill. Everest gathered the bags nonchalantly and headed to the door, holding it open with his back, not even waiting for his change.

"C'mon, Bev." Everest nudged his head toward his car outside, and I hadn't realized I was still standing in the same place.

"Wait, sir, you gave me too much." The lanky cashier's back straightened and he held the change out to Everest.

"Keep it," was all Everest said before we both left the gas station. I wondered what it must feel like to have financial freedom. Two of those bills would have been a single paycheck at 21 Daisies. I knew that I probably would never get to that level of life. College was my only option. I needed to get accepted. I'd spent all summer working—working on my art submissions and saving as much money as I could so I could be more. So I could *do* more.

"How long till we get there?"

The longer we drove, the deeper I dove into my thoughts. We had been driving forever but I didn't mind. Late night drives were good for the soul. I couldn't really explain why, because even with all the words I could have used to describe it, I'd never come close. The wind, the dark, that feeling of escape. Tranquility and peace followed you around like a lost puppy. Going somewhere all while going nowhere—man, there was nothing like it. It was almost like you were free and like some cool adventurer, not belonging to any city and nothing owning you. I didn't know; I couldn't really explain it well.

"Pa—"

"If you say patience one more time."

He laughed. "I wasn't!!"

"You're such a liar." I snorted amid my words.

"Nah, I was joking. It's right around this corner." I looked through the car window at an unfamiliar setting—this wasn't our town. Having never been out of town before, I'd have been lying if I said I wasn't exhilarated.

We pulled up to a large building. "Where are we?"

"You'll see." He hopped out of the car and grabbed the bags. I followed his lead to a building that looked closed, like everything else. Everest pulled a set of keys out of his back pocket, fit one in the lock, and twisted it.

His eyebrows furrowed as he set the bags down and tried the lock again—with no luck.

"Seems like someone changed the lock . . ."

"We drove all the way out here and I won't be able to see what this place is. Darn. I guess we're going back home then . . ."

Everest turned to look at me with a "what" expression.

"No, that just means we have to break in," he said, like it was the most obvious thing in the world.

My eyes grew big and I started to back up. "No."

"Bev, relax. You'll never be in danger if you're with me," Everest reassured me with a side-smile.

This was bad.

"It'll be fine. I promise," he told me, grabbing my hand.

"I'm scared," I said, letting the truth be told.

"Think about it. If I had a key to this place, is it really breaking in? Trust me. I was scared when you made me sing in front of everyone for the first time, but I trusted you and look at me now. Sometimes the things that scare you can actually be beautiful."

We jogged behind the building to a back door. It was locked and so were all of the in-reach windows.

"Wait, look, that window is open," he said, but we couldn't reach it, so that wouldn't work. "Here, give me your foot, I'll give you a boost."

Wait, what.

I calmed myself down and trusted Everest. I took a deep breath and put my foot into his hands. He lifted me up as if I weighed nothing, and then I was eye level with the window. I pushed it open farther and climbed through, knowing that what I was doing was absolutely crazy. Luckily, my foot landed on what seemed to be a filing cabinet. I jumped down and landed on the floor in a dark room.

I couldn't see anything, but something told me I was far from alone. I felt along the wall, my hands shaking from adrenaline. I felt a switch and flicked it, surprised to find myself in an office. Walking over to the desk, I picked up a frame. The picture was of a man with dirty-blond hair and piercing eyes. He wore a stethoscope around his neck and two little boys held on to his legs. A banging made me drop the picture back on the desk just as I was about to look at it again.

My heart pumped heavily as I walked to the door. Realizing that it was just Everest, I unlocked the door for him.

"Wow." He spoke more to himself with a smile. "C'mon, let me show you your prize."

I followed him as we walked up a flight of steps, and I couldn't believe what I saw. The puppies woke up almost immediately and wagged their tails in excitement. The little barks seem to awaken the entire room—birds chirped, kittens peeked curiously from out of their box, and a little piglet awakened in a pen. I walked past the cages and saw tiny bunnies nestled together.

"Ev, where are we?" I asked, laughing as the puppies ran over and attacked my legs with kisses.

I turned to look at him. He had a bright-blue bird on his shoulder. "We are in the CFE Animal Health Clinic. Currently, we're in the nursery."

A Siberian husky puppy was getting toppled by all the other puppies, so I picked it up in my arms and reveled in its pure cuteness.

I watched as Everest put the bird back on its perch and walked over to me.

"I see you met my baby, Tundra." He took the puppy from my arms and she went nuts, wagging her little tail and giving him all kinds of kisses.

"You missed me, babygirl?" He held her close and I couldn't help but laugh. This was adorable.

He didn't even care that I saw him baby this dog. "We should keep moving before we wake up Violet."

"Who's Violet?" I asked, looking around.

"The fattest, meanest cat you will ever meet." Everest chuckled before putting Tundra down.

I said my good-byes to the adorable cuties and followed Everest through the door and down the hall. Where could we possibly be going and why did Everest have a key to an animal rescue?

He opened a door and my breath was literally taken away. The walls were glass filled with water and colorful fish and other aquatic organisms. The ceiling was glass as well, displaying the now star-filled sky. I was literally in an aquarium with a planetarium ceiling, and it had to have been the most beautiful place I'd ever seen.

"Do you like it?" he asked while grabbing a blanket from one of the drawers and laying it down on the ground.

"I love it," I answered while placing my hand on the glass.

"Sit down." Everest smiled, and I saw he had all of the food laid out on the blanket.

I sat on the blanket and grabbed a donut. "How do you even know this place?"

Everest sprayed cheese on some beef jerky and took a huge bite. He chewed his concoction while I waited for his answer. "It belonged to my uncle, Charles."

"He doesn't own it anymore?" I asked, growing worried.

"He's dead . . . he died in a car accident a bit ago. Technically, my aunt owns this place. She runs it." Oh, so this place belonged to the Finley family—I was sort of surprised, sort of not.

"Does your uncle have blond hair? And a striking resemblance to Paul Walker?" I asked, remembering the picture.

A grin popped on his lips. "Yes, that's crazy you said that."

"I saw his picture in the office."

Everest nodded. "My uncle was a nerd. He was in love with science—hard core, apparently. He's the one who named me."

"Your uncle seems different from your dad."

"Night and day. My aunt Sherma told me stories about how my uncle was a little angel, always caring and loving toward anything. He took after my grandma. My dad was all about profit and probably never loved a thing in his life—my grandfather's mini."

He got up and grabbed a guitar from one of the closets. "My uncle was into music too."

"You guys sound a lot alike."

"Yeah, we were really close. I miss him. I miss him a whole lot. He would've liked you." He looked at me and smiled, and his eyes looked as blue as the aquarium water. "I actually think about him every day. Recently, I found a . . . book of his and I swear, it brings me a kind of peace I've never known."

I watched as he strummed the guitar, with the water and the stars around him.

"What's in it?"

"A series of confessions. I started writing my own, too, and it feels good. Sometimes I forget I'm depressed." His dark joke made neither of us laugh. He quickly glanced at me before focusing back on the guitar.

"What's it like to be depressed?" The question flew past my lips, swarming so fast that I couldn't have stopped it even if I'd tried.

His fingers halted and he looked up with a confused expression. "Do you actually want to know?"

"I do," I said.

"So, depression is like . . . it's like feeling so much pain that you feel nothing at all. You are completely empty. You're a hostage to the patterns distorting your mind, and nothing else matters. You just want the empty to go away. I don't wish being empty on my worst enemy."

He stared ahead at the aquarium, deep in thought.

". . . so, you feel nothing?" I asked, eventually, hating how each letter sounded.

When his head turned to face me, I couldn't miss the harsh look in his eyes. "No, Bev," he whispered while shaking his head. "I feel *everything*."

I put my hand over his and he swiftly moved his from under mine to keep his tears at bay. One sniffle, two sniffles, and he was fake smiling again. I knew he was only doing so to make me feel better. I realized in that moment that he'd never really got over it.

The pain. Sure, he may not always feel the hurt, but there was a hole in him that lingered. The memory of the destruction that it caused on his mentality would probably never go away. It didn't matter how much better he seemed or how many smiles were added up. You couldn't erase a hole.

"How do you deal with all those feelings?" I should have stopped. This was none of my business. My mouth was moving faster than my mind.

"You know, after my attempt, the hospital made me meet with a therapist for an hour each day. It felt like one poor attempt to save me." He stopped and stood up while strumming the guitar a few times. "I'm sure he was a good guy with the right intentions, but he wasn't going to be the one to save me. You can't save someone who doesn't want to save themselves. At the end of the day, I know that only I can save me."

"How do you plan to do that?" I could hear the tension in his voice.

"I don't know. One day at a time, I guess. Surrounding myself with things that make me feel like myself. Music, black coffee, clay-animation movies, late-night drives, good company, pizza rolls, and you." He attempted to laugh me off, but it was forced. "Bev, seriously, I'm okay."

I wrapped my arms around him. "It's okay not to be."

We stayed like that for a while. I'd never fully understand how Everest felt, but I did know that he was trying. I learned a valuable lesson from Everest that night—you couldn't erase a hole. You could only fill it.

26

EVEREST

Confession: my mind paints pictures of her in ways that I shouldn't see. I don't like Beverly like that. So why, when the night takes my consciousness, is she all that I think about?

—*EF, October 23, 2018*

Just as I was about to leave, my mom called me back inside. When she walked up with a grin, I was extremely confused. My mother never came up to me with a grin on her face; she usually wore a look of disappointment or guilt. Guilt was my favorite—instead of her being hard on me, she was hard on herself.

"Yes?" I asked, warily.

I didn't have time to react; she gently grabbed each side of my face and kissed my forehead.

"You need to stop leaving without saying good-bye."

I stared at her. Life was growing weirder and weirder as the days passed, and I constantly felt like I was in *The Twilight Zone*. I didn't even remember the last time I'd said good-bye to my mother. I came and went as I pleased, and it made her happy when I went—it was sort of an unspoken system we had.

"Bye." I took a step back and exited quickly.

Clenching the steering wheel, I wondered what the heck just happened. Confusion was my new symptom nowadays, and I was in desperate need of a prescription for sanity. I rushed to 21 Daisies, knowing that Beverly would most likely be disappointed if I was late. I didn't know what her disappointed face looked like, and I had no intention of finding out.

Once I pulled into the parking lot, I texted Beverly to tell her I was just about there. Glancing around, I saw that there weren't that many cars. My favorite slot to perform was on Friday night, because that was when it filled up the most. The morning slots weren't the most exciting, but at least I got to chill and talk to Beverly a bit more.

"Look who decided to show up," Lincoln Bricks said when I entered the café.

I was convinced he was the best guitarist in the city. He played like he breathed. It was second nature for him and for his brother, Lucky. Their dad was a dentist and their mother was a musician. For a while after she left their dad, they tried to avoid music at all costs. Lucky told me that music was just in their blood, and Lincoln said that when he went to smash his mom's guitar, he ended up messing around with it for hours and couldn't help but fall in love. We'd become kind of friends since I started playing. They were only a couple of years older, so it was easy for us to talk. It also helped that it was fun to be around them.

Lincoln was the brain of the two, and Lucky was the heart. Anyone could tell that in the first few seconds of meeting them—the classic case of the optimist and the realist.

"You need to stay off Tumblr, bro, everything is becoming poetic to you. You want to be Doctor Seuss so bad." Lincoln shook his head while I laughed.

I did a few songs and couldn't help but realize that I hadn't seen Beverly. At first, I thought that maybe she was in the break room or bathroom, but after time passed and she hadn't shown up, I knew something was up.

Lily was wiping down tables when I asked, "Hey, have you seen Beverly?"

"Oh, yeah, she called in sick today."

"She's sick?"

Lily ran a hand through her blond hair and her eyes filled with knowing. "Betty has never been the best liar."

Her eyes told me all that they needed to, and I knew that Beverly wasn't sick. I went over to my bag and checked my phone to see no new messages from her.

On my break I didn't waste any time zooming over to her place. Why wouldn't she come in to work today? I'd started this because of her, and now she wasn't going to show up? I let the memories of last night flow past me and tried my best to make sense of this situation. So far, I had nothing. I hoped that I hadn't scared her away last night.

I pulled into her parking lot and saw that her car was still there. Just then, realization dawned on me, telling me how impulsively weird I was being. I sat in the seat for a moment, wondering if I should go in, until three little knocks tapped on my window. Jumping a bit, I rolled the window down to see a flustered Beverly.

"He—" I started.

"What are you doing here?" she whispered, even though no one could possibly hear us.

"I came to see if you were all right," I said, confused. Usually, she would be flashing her teeth and jumping in my arms. "I texted you first, but you didn't reply, and then you didn't show up to work."

She huffed and her curly hair shook with the movement. "You shouldn't be here."

When I heard that sentence, it felt like a kick to the gut. What had happened over the course of those hours after I'd dropped her off? I thought everything was fine.

Her eyes widened like she realized what she just said, and her lips parted. "I didn't mean it like that."

She stared at me dead on, and in that moment I knew that I was incredibly attracted to her, and that realization caused me to freeze.

"I have to help my mom."

"Oh . . . okay," I stuttered, then coughed to hide the stutter, but failed.

"Yes, that's why you shouldn't be here."

I didn't know if my mind was playing tricks on me, but she looked sad. She moved her hand and crossed her arms, and I released the breath I didn't even know I was holding. But then my perverted mind didn't miss how it made her chest come more into my view, and I wanted to just succumb to the urge to just drive away. This was wrong, and I really needed help. This shouldn't be happening; I should not be thinking like this. I quickly turned to look out the passenger-side window, in hopes it would give a blank canvas back to my brain. I turned back to look at her, and thankfully her arms had returned to her sides.

"Is everything okay?" I asked as I felt the heat from my neck start to cool.

She nodded.

"Do you need my help?" I began to unfasten my seat belt.

Beverly grabbed my shoulder to stop me. "She's actually asleep right now, so that won't be necessary. Thank you, though, Ev. I should probably get back before she notices that I'm gone."

Her smile was sad as she took a step back. Whatever feeling that I felt right now, I hated it.

"So, wait, that means we don't get to hang out today?"

She shook her head, like she couldn't bear to say the words, and that was the knife that dug the wound deeper.

"What are you going to do today?" she asked, but I could tell she didn't really want to know.

"Probably hang with Mikey." I shrugged.

"He sure is a character."

I nodded, but I was only focused on one thing. She smiled but bit her lip to stop. "I don't want you to go."

"Yeah, me neither. You should just hop in my car," I joked to lighten the situation. Her eyes lowered and she cocked her head to the side, like she was deep in thought.

"Not now. Come tonight at nine. My mother won't be here."

"Are you serious?" I asked as she grinned mischievously.

"As a heart attack." Her big brown eyes smiled as she turned on her heel and jogged back to her apartment. "Bye, Ev."

"Bye, Bev."

* * *

Back at 21 Daisies, the place had filled up with more people. I had been watching the clock constantly while entertaining the crowd. I realized that I really loved entertaining people—when I saw people dancing to my voice or singing along, the feeling was indescribable. It was surreal because not even a two months ago, I was freaked out by performing in front of fifteen people. I sang until I smelled like a distant relative of Bigfoot, and I decided to freshen up before I left.

"Everest? Is that you, man?" I turned to see Jacob Riley come up behind me, and I almost dropped the towel I was using to wipe the sweat I'd worked up.

Jacob Riley, the secret boyfriend of Nash. I never had any bad experiences with Jacob—the only time we got aggressive was on the field—but we used to always bump into each other at parties, and he seemed like a pretty okay guy. He played on the same team as my cousin, Toby, so we would always see a lot of each other.

"Hey," I spoke, unsure of what to say to him. Nash probably fed him BS about me, and I was in no mood to deal with BS.

"I didn't know you could sing. You look good up there."

I thanked him, and then when a girl came out of the bathroom calling him "Babe," I raised an eyebrow.

She kissed him on the cheek, and I didn't know what to think. Did Nash and Jacob break up? Or was he cheating on Nash? I listened to my inner self telling me not to care. I ventured back to the stage before I realized my set was over. I ordered takeout from Felix and chilled with the remaining customers.

"Can you sign this?" a girl who looked to be around fourteen asked me as she held out her phone. I always thought it was silly to be signing other's belongings, like it was going to have any value, but I still did it for the heck of it.

"What's your name?"

"Andrea. Can you actually write *I love you, Andrea*?" Her cheeks tinted pink.

"Of course. Here you go."

"Oh my gosh, thanks." She smiled brightly before returning to a table with a bunch of girls around the same age range.

A few others had me sign things, and I was nice to each one of them. A girl came up to me with glossy black hair and a sultry smile.

"Call me?" she whispered and tucked something in my back pocket.

When she moved away, I couldn't help but laugh. Incidents like this kept happening more and more often, and it just never got old.

* * *

By the time I got to my order, the food was lukewarm. I still ate it in my car, though. I ended up getting ketchup on my white shirt since I was eating in the dark, but whatever. The night air massaged my hair thoroughly, and I knew it was going to be a mess. It was like fate didn't want my hair to have order. Ever since my attempt, my hair always looked like I just rolled out of bed. My dad hated it, but he was the only one who cared. If I wanted to walk around with messy hair and a ketchup stain on my white shirt, then I should be able to. It still was my life, last time I checked. I glanced at the clock, and finally time was exactly where I wanted it to be.

When I pulled into Beverly's lot, she was already be there waiting for me. I didn't see her at first, but when my headlights turned the corner, it displayed her all-black-clad self. I quickly unlocked the passenger door and she hopped in.

"Why are you dressed like a ninja?" I asked once we were back on the road.

She glanced down at her outfit. "In all the movies, they're dressed like this when they sneak out."

"Your mom wasn't even home—you didn't have to sneak at all."

"Don't kill the fun."

"No promises," I joked, straight-faced and focused on the road "Where do you want to go?"

She took a deep breath and stared at the car ceiling. "I want to go over Mikey's."

I almost braked the car in the middle of the road. "No way."

"C'mon, please."

"Beverly, do you know what the Basement is like? It's a bunch of losers who have nothing going for them."

"But you go," she argued.

"Are you trying to help my point?" I asked incredulously.

"How is it that you want me to be a reckless teenager but won't show me the holy grail of recklessness?"

She had a point.

"I don't want you to be a reckless teenager, Bev. You're perfect just the way you are."

I kept my eyes on the road. She had so many things going for her and one of the dumbest things I had ever said was that she needed to see the destruction. Why corrupt the innocent when they were the lucky ones? I'd feel like I was doing her an injustice.

"Thank you?" Beverly took a deep breath. "Please, Everest, I want to know what it's like just to be a teenager for a little while."

And with that, I caved.

* * *

I pulled into Burger Hut and ordered a bunch of burgers and a large cheese pizza. I knew these druggies were always eating so they'd appreciate this gift. After my car smelled like grease and diabetes, I drove to Mikey's, hoping that it wasn't going to be a crazy night. I held the food and told Beverly to knock on the garage. She looked at me confused, but she did it anyway. A guy I recognized as Sam opened the door; Beverly looked like she was holding in a cough as smoke came to greet us.

"It's Everest," he called back, and then his eyes glanced at the food. "And he brought food."

He grabbed the food from me, and I grabbed Beverly's hand. She quickly glanced at me and I could tell she was nervous. I still felt like she shouldn't be here, but I guessed everyone should have this experience. We walked in and it wasn't packed, but it still had a hefty amount of people. Twenty, maybe? I wasn't exactly sure. I spotted Mikey in the back, playing a game of cards. He was the best shark that I knew—beat me enough times to teach me that gambling wasn't a game for me.

"Well, if it isn't Golden Boy." Mikey smiled, showing all of his teeth. "And Beverly the Beautiful."

"Hey, Mikey," she said shyly.

He walked over to us with a beer in hand and a cig hanging out of his mouth. "What brings you guys to my humble abode?"

"Why else does anyone come here? To get away for a little bit," I answered him, and he nodded in approval.

Aurora came up from behind Mikey, and she had a small, black cat in her arms.

"I see you finally got a cat."

"Yeah, his name is Shadow. Mikey got me him for my birthday."

"Aw, he's so cute," Beverly cooed, gently petting the kitten.

"When's your birthday?" I asked.

"February the tenth." She smiled at Beverly and joined in on the petting.

"Your birthday isn't until months from now," I commented and watched as her face grew defensive.

"It's an early birthday present." She held the cat closer to her and walked away.

"Don't mind her, she's pretty sensitive." Mikey took a swig from his beer.

The room smelled like Doritos, sweat, drugs, beer, and fermented asshole. I kept telling Mikey to get some of those air fresheners that spritz by themselves, or to at least crack open a window, but I thought it went through one ear and out the other.

"Here, take a seat," Mikey told us, and as Beverly sat down, he slyly whispered in my ear, "Mary Jane is fifty percent off tonight." He was always up to business. It was quite admirable.

"Nah, man, I'm good."

It dawned on me that I hadn't smoked or drank in a while. It probably hadn't been doing me any good anyway. I sat on the ratty couch next to Beverly, and we talked and laughed at all the crazy stuff happening in the room. At first, I wasn't sure how she was going to take it, but she was fine. We were just a pair of flies on the wall—until we noticed a girl trying to take a swim in a fish tank.

"What is she doing?" I snorted.

"She's going to hurt herself." Beverly's voice was full of worry. I watched as she rushed over to the girl. I followed steadily behind.

"I want to be a mermaid." The girl smiled sloppily at us when we approached her.

Beverly grabbed the girl and supported her weight.

"Hey! You break it, you fucking buy it, Sydney!" Mikey shouted.

"Chill, Mike," Aurora yelled at him from the pool table.

"Mermaids are beautiful," Sydney said to Beverly, and I watched as Sydney took in her somber expression.

"Sure, mermaids are beautiful, but they could never be you. I can just look at you and tell you that you are absolutely stunning inside and out—always remember that. And if you still want to be a mermaid, think about how Ariel wanted to be a human so bad that she almost gave up everything to be one."

Beverly moved a stray hair away from Sydney's face and tucked it behind her ear.

Sydney looked at Beverly, and for a second it looked like she sobered up, before she grabbed Beverly's cheeks and pecked her straight on the mouth. I didn't have any time to react, it all happened so fast. Beverly's eyes widened and all I could do was just stare at her.

Beverly touched her lips then stared at her fingers like there was going to be something there. She looked at me and her eyes furrowed together before she burst out in laughter. I was extremely confused. She hugged me and laughed into my shirt, and I instinctively wrapped my arms around her. Then I grabbed each side of her head to look at her face to make sure she wasn't crying.

"Bev?" She was laughing so hard that her eyes were watering. "Why are you laughing?"

"She just kissed me, Ev."

Although this was weird, Beverly was looking pretty cute right now. I had never seen her laugh this hard, and I was still not exactly sure what she was laughing about.

"Yeah, I know, but why are you laughing?"

"My first kiss was with a girl."

She wiped her eyes and covered her huge smile with her hand. I immediately felt bad, like all of this was my fault. Beverly's first kiss was with a drunk girl in a basement that smelled like death, and it was all my fault. The girl was happily halfway across the room by now and we were still standing there frozen.

"Well, did you like it?" I joked apprehensively.

She slapped my chest and laughed. "Shut up."

"Are you really okay?"

"Yes, Ev. I think it's funny. I worked myself up thinking about my first kiss and now I realize it's not that deep." She had a few reeling chuckles, but overall, I saw that she was coming back to me.

We chilled at the bar, but we didn't have any drinks. For a couple of hours we joked and laughed and ate greasy food. No one did any drugs, and I was grateful for that. It was like everyone knew what kind of person Beverly was and didn't want to tamper with her. The most everyone did was smoke cigs and drink beers.

"Everest, I have to go right now," Beverly told me in a rush.

"What? Why?" I asked, halting my conversation with Sam.

"My mom is going to be home in, like, fifteen minutes. She just called me."

I immediately hopped up from the couch. "Well, what time is it?"

"Eleven forty-five, come on, we have to go." We hurried out of the basement and practically hopped in my car.

I drove quickly while Beverly was acting like a backseat driver and giving orders like "Not so fast, Ev," and "Please hurry."

Although she was worrying, she was laughing, and then her

laughter made me laugh. Then we became a couple of laughing teenagers speeding down the street. I pulled into her apartment complex in record time and she jumped out of my car quickly. She started to run to her door before I realized something was missing.

I rolled down my window and stuck my head out. "Since when do you leave without saying good-bye?"

She turned to look at me with that gorgeous smile of hers and ran back in my direction. She quickly jumped in and planted the sweetest kiss on my cheek and then ran back away.

"Bye, Ev."

"Bye, Bev."

I didn't stop smiling the whole way to my house.

27

BEVERLY

My mother didn't actually come home until six o'clock the next morning. The day before I'd had to nurse her back to health after she experienced a hangover more terrible than usual. I knew that she was just going to go back out again, but I couldn't watch her suffer.

"So, tell me about this guy you've been dating," she said as I handed her the coffee I always made before school. The mug almost fell from my grasp. I hadn't mentioned Everest to her, so how was it that she could have possibly known?

I decided to play it cool. "Just friends."

Her eyebrow quirked up and her lips pursed in disbelief. "You don't think I know what that means? I had 'just friends,' too, Beverly."

"No, Ma, we are literally just friends."

"Mmm-humm. Why don't you invite him for Thanksgiving?" my mother said. "Put your eyes back in your head."

"I don't think he wants to eat Japanese takeout for Thanksgiving."

My mother could cook, but for the past few years she'd just been ordering takeout. When I was younger, she used to do it really big, though, food far beyond the capacity of our table flooding in.

"I'll cook." She shrugged nonchalantly. "I have been known to cook. Remember when you were five? The turkey almost fell off the table, it was so full."

"Seriously?" I chuckled, happiness and disbelief shooting through me.

"Yes, girl, now go to school and invite your lover boy over for Thanksgiving."

She ruffled my hair before leaving the kitchen.

"Hey, Ma?"

She poked her head back inside. "What's up?"

"Has any mail come in for me?"

Yesterday there were two rejections from a couple of the many colleges that I'd applied to. I couldn't tell her, but I was disappointed, and worried that I wouldn't get in anywhere.

* * *

I approached Everest's locker with a certain excited pep in my step. Man, I missed him. I knew I that I had just seen him last night, but the fact that I couldn't just up and see him made me miss him even more.

"Guess who?" I asked, standing on my tiptoes and placing my fingers around his eyes.

"Is it Beyoncé?" his deep melodic voice answered with a slight tone of amusement.

I released my fingers and walked around to face him. "Really, Beyoncé?"

"A guy can dream." He smirked while putting a book back in his locker. "So, how was everything with your mom?"

"Consider me free." I grinned. "She didn't even come home last night. She came in this morning."

"Where was she?"

"Probably with my aunt Macy."

"Don't you think it's a weird that she's always gone?" he asked.

I felt my stomach drop. Little did he know I thought about that all the time. Everest took my books out of my hands.

"It is pretty strange."

Okay. Geez, Ev, I know it's weird.

"Hey, what's making you upset?" He stopped walking, and I didn't even realize he was talking until he softly grabbed my hand.

"Nothing. It's nothing, I'm fine." I fibbed. "I just remembered I have a test in bio today and I didn't study."

"Oh, you're going to do great," he scoffed like he knew for sure before grinning and quickly looking straight ahead. *Passing smiles are attractive*, I randomly thought.

"Thanks, Ev." I smiled a small smile, feeling sort of guilty for not telling the whole truth.

"This is it?" he asked once I stopped at my classroom door.

I nodded while he looked inside my classroom from the doorway. "Aw, you have Mrs. Anderson, she's—"

"Good morning, Mr. Finley." Mrs. Anderson came out of the room.

"—she's one of the best-looking, most respectable teachers in this entire school," he quickly said, and I pursed my lips to keep from laughing.

"Get to class, young man. The bell rings in the next forty seconds."

Everest quickly looked at the clock and swore. Realizing his mistake, he looked back at my teacher. "Oh fuck, sorry."

He closed his eyes briefly and scrunched up his nose. "I . . . didn't mean . . . to say f—"

"Just get to class," she said briskly.

"Right, okay."

He turned to me and kissed the side of my head before dashing down the hall at full speed, his flannel shirt floating behind him like a cape.

* * *

In the parking lot after school, I decided to ask Everest right then and there about Thanksgiving. My nerves were on high alert, and I wasn't sure why. It wasn't that I thought he'd say no; it was the possibility of him saying yes. I couldn't imagine what that would be like.

"Hey, Ev, quick question."

He turned to me as we walked over to his car. "I may have a quick answer."

The nerves kicked up their power, and I realized that I was just going to have to spit it out. "My mother wants to meet you, and was bugging me earlier about inviting you to our Thanksgiving dinner and—"

"Sounds good, of course I'll come."

"Wait. You're going to actually come?" My eyes widened.

"Why not?" He shrugged.

28

EVEREST

Confession: if I go to hell for killing myself, then I'll try to be like the most powerful thing down there. I'm not just going to be down there burning for all eternity. That sounds boring and like a major waste of time. I don't know, I'd probably try to overthrow the devil or some- thing and make my first law be that pure evil would only come to those who were downright disgusting up here.

—EF, November 11, 2018

"Where are you off to?" my mother asked, briefly grabbing my hand.

"I was just about to meet up with Beverly." Also, I really had no desire to sit and have breakfast with them.

"I made waffles-s-s-s," she sang.

"You *made* waffles?" My mother never cooked; I didn't think I'd ever seen her even pop popcorn.

"Okay, Miranda made waffles-s-s-s," she sang again.

I couldn't help my grin, but then she grinned back, and when I realized what we were doing, my smile fell as quickly as it came.

"No, thanks. I think I'm just going to go ahead and catch a bite later on."

The disappointment floated around my mother like a shadow. She immediately looked down at the diamond bracelet she received a few years ago for Christmas and fidgeted with it. Her eyes then met mine, a mild storm flooding within them.

"I'm trying, I really am." Her voice was soft and full of remorse, and an alarm suddenly went off inside of me. I was not ready to have this conversation. Looking at her for more than a few passing seconds, I didn't know what to do. Having my mother care was uncharted territory for me. She looked at me one last time before turning on her heel and heading to the kitchen. I stood there in the doorway as what seemed like a million years passed in a millisecond.

"Wait—" She turned to look at me and I took a deep breath. "I guess I can stay for breakfast."

Everything on her brightened and she clapped her hands together. "Great!"

She walked over to me and hooked her arm with mine to lead me into the dining room. Hadley, Susan, and my father were already seated. The already quiet room somehow got more silent.

I took the seat farthest away from my father. I hadn't seen Susan in a while. Never really liked her to be completely honest. I always thought that she was desperately trying to be Hadley's mother rather than her nanny. She was also a complete suck-up to my father.

Speaking of which, my father sat the end of the table, my

mother and Susan on each side of him. He was busy reading a newspaper, the large, thin papers shielding his face completely. I thought it was really corny how he was reading a newspaper. He could easily check the news on that phone he was constantly on. But my father, being my father, wanted to give off an obnoxious stance like usual.

"Hey." I playfully shoulder bumped Hadley.

"You're here."

"Yep," I answered, although it was an I'd-rather-be-anywhere-else kind of yep.

"Good. I'm glad. It was getting kind of lonely here."

And that was when it hit me—Hadley was always alone with these people, listening to the garbage that spilled out of their mouths daily, experiencing the harsh reality that in this house kids were ignored, their opinions and suggestions unheard; learning that her mother was tremendously materialistic, and viewed her children like accessories, and that her father was a judgmental corporate robot who only cared about money. My eyebrows furrowed together in thought. Guilt weighed down on me full force.

How could I have not noticed?

"I'm so glad we are all here as a family."

My mother spoke with blatant joy. My father brought the newspaper down and saw me.

"Son." He nodded his head toward me in acknowledgment.

"Frank." I repeated his movement.

"Since when do you call your father by his first name?" Susan asked with a motherly tone, and I wanted nothing more than for her to disappear.

"Isn't this a family breakfast? Why exactly are you here?"

My parents were both here and Hadley wasn't a small child incapable of taking care of herself, so I really didn't see Susan's purpose.

"Everest, don't be difficult. Please let's just eat and enjoy each other's company," my mother said.

As if on cue, Miranda came and set the waffles on the table. Now, besides Hadley, Miranda was my favorite. She never really talked, but I liked her a lot. She had done things for me that will forever stick. No one knew about how sometimes she silently prayed over me when she thought I was asleep, or about how when I was eleven and my father ripped my stuffed frog in pieces because he said I was too old for it, I found it sewn back together and in my bed the next morning. My frog, Green Bean, smelled like peppermint patties, and I knew it was Miranda who'd fixed it. We never spoke about it, but I would always remember that.

"I heard that you've been playing music, Everest." Susan's voice brought me out of my thoughts.

"You're still interested in that?" My mother sounded surprised. "You stopped going to your music lessons years ago."

Yeah, because Frank figured that football camp was more beneficial. There was a reason why I hadn't told my family, and I truly didn't appreciate Susan bringing it up. I didn't even care to question how she knew to begin with.

"Just messing around." I took a sip of my apple juice.

"You're really good," Hadley told me with a proud, sly smile.

"You've heard me?" I asked incredulously.

"It's kinda hard not to when you're putting on a full concert in the shower."

I chewed my waffle while looking at her with amusement, before my dad decided to make a comment to kill the mood.

"I thought you grew out of that. You know, there's not much money in that field."

I didn't want to repeat the stupid pattern this idiotic family has set. Play football, get into college with the help of my family's money, go to school for business, marry a girl I didn't love, run the family business, and have kids that I wouldn't have time for. I was completely fine with not doing any of those things.

"Yeah, I'm just having fun."

My father's phone lit up every three seconds with a notification. My mother noticed, too, and attempted sneakily to take a quick glance while grabbing her glass, but she was horribly obvious, and my father slid his phone closer to himself.

"That's nice, honey," my mother told me while glancing at my dad and looking unsettled.

The table grew silent after that, the only sounds the occasional pangs of metal hitting glass and the beeps from my father's phone, until my father got up from the table quickly, his phone flashing in his grip.

"I have to take this. Sonya has stumbled across a problem."

My mother stopped chewing and stared at my father. I anxiously anticipated that she would stand up to his crap for once. I wanted her to yell, scream, or basically do anything. Why was she doing this to herself? I begged her mentally to please just say something.

She swallowed her food, and for a moment I thought that this was when she would finally crack. All the toxins would be gone, and everything would be okay—that change was coming, and we could all be happy. In just that moment, I sensed hope. I was silently rooting her on, my grip on my glass so tight it was turning my knuckles white. Dabbing her mouth with a nearby napkin, she looked unsteady.

"I—"

This was it. The moment I'd been waiting for, where some of the infection that was this family would begin to be cleaned.

"I'll see you later for dinner."

My eyes instantly closed tight, disappointment hitting me hard. My father swiftly left, kissing Hadley on the head on his way out. It was disgusting, wasn't it? That that mouth of his, filled with sly lies and deceit wrapped in a box of sin, had had the audacity to touch something so pure and innocent. The same lips that he would touch those women with were placed on his daughter. And it seemed like I was the only one who was thinking this way.

I slammed my glass down with more force than usual, my fist clenched tight beside my plate as I took a deep breath.

"Everest, dear, these dishes are expensive. Please be more careful."

Was she just going to ignore what happened?

"Thanks for breakfast. I think I'm going to head out now. C'mon, Hadley."

I stood up from my chair. Hadley's head whipped quickly in my direction and her eyes widened along with her lips. She stood up from the table swiftly and stood next to me.

"Hadley? No. She has plans today," my mother said in a rush.

"Reschedule, cancel, tell them that her older brother wants to hang out with her today—I don't care." I turned to Hadley who could barely contain her smile. "You ready?"

"Wait, Everest. . . . Why are you . . ." My mother looked unsettled.

"You're trying, right? Let's not make a big deal of me taking my sister out."

* * *

"So, what's the plan?" Hadley asked excitedly from the back seat.

"Uh . . ."

There really wasn't a plan. I'd just winged that whole ordeal. I was supposed to meet up with Beverly.

"Where do you want to go?" I looked at her in the rearview mirror.

"You mean I get to pick?" she asked, surprised.

"Yep, anywhere you want. We can go right now."

"It's the fall festival in town?"

The fall festival was a huge event that took place in a different park each year. I'd gone a few times. It was one of the few events that Cara had dragged me to that I hadn't minded. The food was good, and the music was better.

Even though it was eleven o'clock, people were scattered all about the park. It wasn't too full, though, just a perfect amount of people, so we wouldn't have to wait in lines for a long time. There were different booths and rides set up. A pie-eating contest was scheduled for noon and pumpkin bouncy houses were scattered about. I bought both of us cheese fries and we sat at a bench.

"Okay, so tell me who you are?"

"I'm Hadley," she giggled, staring at me weirdly.

"Okay, Hadley, tell me about yourself." I pushed her playfully while chewing on a fry, using the same scenario that Beverly and I had months prior. It was quite sad how I didn't know who my own sister was. I had no idea what she liked or disliked, the things she dreamed about, her fears, or what kept her up at night.

She froze in thought, a smile on her face, before looking back at me. "That's a hard question."

"Let me start with something easier," I chuckled. "What's your favorite color?"

We traded questions back and forth, laughing every so often at our answers. I learned that her favorite color was pink. Favorite food was pizza. She said she hated when people didn't think she knew what was going on; it was an insult to her intelligence. Chocolate covered pretzels were the closest thing to heaven, and she adored dancing because it was like she was talking without the talking.

"I have a question for you," she said, mischief in her eyes.

"Shoot." I smiled.

"When are you going to quit being a punk and ask Beverly out?"

"Next question."

"Oh c'mon, Everest." She grabbed my arm and shook me a little. "She's so-o-o-o-o nice and pretty and smells good," she whined playfully.

"Oh yeah? Sounds like you should take her out on a date," I said, amused, getting out of her tight grip.

She giggled manically, and scrunched up her nose.

"Speaking of Bev, we were supposed to hang out today. I should call and cancel." I grabbed my phone from my pocket.

". . . or you can just invite her."

I looked at Hadley. "Nah, it's our day today."

I dialed the phone and it took Beverly longer than usual to answer. "Well if it isn't my favorite person . . ." I heard her voice through the receiver and practically felt her smile through the phone.

"You're blushing," Hadley mouthed, and I turned my head away from her.

"Hey, I just called to say—"

"Come to the fall festival with us!" Hadley leaned over my shoulder and yelled into the receiver.

I almost dropped my phone and had to adjust my grip. I moved Hadley from off my back and put the phone back to my ear to hear Beverly laughing.

"Sorry—" I said.

"Was that Hadley?" she asked.

I glanced at the smug-looking little girl next to me. "Yeah."

"Tell her I said hi," Beverly chuckled.

I turned to Hadley and spoke dryly. "Beverly said hi."

"I'd rather hear you say it in person," Hadley called out to Beverly.

I gripped my forehead and shook my head while Beverly chuckled. "Right now?"

"Yes, but if you're busy—"

"I'm on my way. I'll meet you by the pumpkin patch."

"So is she coming?" Hadley asked, throwing a fry into her mouth.

"She's on her way."

"Yay!" She smiled brightly.

Hadley and I finished off our fries. She was really excited to see Beverly, and although I wasn't showing it, I was too.

When Hadley saw Beverly, she broke out into a run then hugged her tightly. Beverly held her with equal enthusiasm, and I watched as she smiled fully and chatted a little with Hadley. Beverly looked so happy, with the colored trees around her, and her big, tan, fuzzy sweater. Her hair was in its usual spirals, and she wore a skirt with high socks and boots. I didn't think I'd ever seen her in a skirt.

"Earth to Everest?" Hadley called out to me, snapping me out of whatever daze I was in.

"Did I just get replaced?" I asked when I approached them.

"Oh, be quiet you." Beverly quickly wrapped her arms around my torso. Her hugs were so warm and comforting. It was like you never knew you needed a hug like that until you actually got one. I hugged her back, and I felt her nuzzle into my shirt.

"Well, if it isn't taco boy." I heard a voice come from behind me.

It was the kid who had been in the car that one day. "Hey, man," I said.

"Did you find the bathroom?" Beverly asked him, ending our hug.

"Obviously." He rolled his eyes.

"Hey, don't you go to my school? Manny, right?" I heard Hadley ask and I turned to look at him.

His eyes widened a fraction and he visibly gulped. "You know my name?"

"Sure, you're a genius."

"I think so too." Beverly smiled and reached out to ruffle his hair, and blatant embarrassment covered his face like a mask. Beverly came to stand next to me, and Manny scrunched up his face as he readjusted his hair.

We spent the next hour engaging in all the festival had to offer. From rides to face paint, we did whatever the kids wanted to do. By now the festival was in full swing, the stands filling by the second. Manny figured we'd get some food, and although Hadley and I had already eaten, we all got in line for more fair food. I was always in the mood for a corn dog.

"Everest?"

I turned to see Mikey and Aurora behind us in the line. Beverly went to hug Aurora, but Mikey intercepted the hug for himself.

Beverly smiled gently in his quick embrace. "Hey, Mikey."

"What are you guys doing here?" I asked.

"You know I love a party." Mikey winked, waving his hand like he was whacking a fly.

"Hello, children," Aurora said in monotone. Her hair was now a bright fury of red and I didn't miss how in awe Hadley was of her. While Manny gave them a normal greeting, it took Hadley a moment to get the words out.

"Yo, hey, guys." Lincoln and Lucky approached us with lighthouse-bright grins. I guessed everyone really was at the festival today.

"What's up, gentlemen?" Mikey did a handshake hug with Lincoln and fist-bumped Lucky.

"We were just about to play a set when we saw Everest and his big head," Lucky said, making Manny snort.

"Oh, you're playing?" Beverly asked.

"First timers," Lucky replied with a cheesy smile.

"How come you aren't playing?" Hadley asked me.

"I didn't know about it." I shrugged.

"You can play with us if you want," Lincoln said.

"No, I'll just watch. It's fine." I shook my head. "What are you playing?"

Lucky's eyes widened.

"'We Are the Champions,' the same Queen song we play every Friday. You sang it with us before, just do it again," Lincoln said.

"It's different." This crowd was three times as big. If I messed up, more people would know.

"You can do it," Hadley chimed in.

"Yeah, I second that," Manny said.

"Third," went Mikey.

"Fourth," came from Aurora.

I turned to Beverly and she grabbed my hand and walked us a couple of steps away. "Are you scared?"

"What if I'm not any good?"

"Hey, hey, you stop that right now. Remember when I said you're like a gloomy cloud?" she said. I scrunched up my face and glanced at the stage. She wrapped her arms around me and continued, "This is your rain, Everest." She looked up at me. "Are you ready for a storm?"

"I stay rain ready." I laughed into her hair.

"Ugh, just date already," Aurora groaned, causing us to separate.

I made my way through the crowd, pretending that I wasn't a bundle of nerves. I concentrated on the stage. It seemed so big, and so far away; it wasn't like the makeshift stage at 21 Daisies. This was an actual stage, with an actual crowd, and the stakes were a little higher. When I got on the stage, I had to remind myself to breathe. I looked out in the crowd for my friends, but it was too big. At the last moment, before we were to begin, I saw them muscle their way to the front, my sister and Manny close to the stage, their bright faces shining.

"You nervous?" Lucky asked from behind me.

I nodded, unable to speak.

Lincoln clasped my shoulder hard. "Well, it's too late to back down now."

The nerves clawed at me as I stood center stage. I was crazy. This was insane. But when the guys started playing their instruments, my blood rushed, and my face felt comfortably warm. I was engulfed in the aura of this magical place. It didn't even feel real, how the space was filled with nothing but happy people. When I began singing, I forgot why I was even nervous in the first place. I was having the time of my life. I gradually hit a soft, high note. The song was intense and beautiful. The chorus caught everyone's attention, and that moment right then couldn't have been anything less than rain. My dad loved this song. For a moment I wished he could see me. The girls were as caught up as I was. Mikey smiled and immersed himself in the music, thrashing his head like a maniac. I was so caught up in the performance that the crowd didn't scare me; they were just as mesmerized as I was, dancing and nodding their heads.

When I met everyone off stage once we were done, the good feelings continued.

"I still feel like that didn't happen." Lincoln shook his head.

"You were so good!" Beverly told us, and I grabbed her back in a hug again.

"No, but really, we should do this. You're the missing piece, Everest." Lucky shook his head, seriousness throughout his voice.

Still high off the crowd, I picked Beverly up and spun her around. "Can you believe that I did that?"

She laughed and held on to me around my torso while Hadley held on to the other side. "I'm so proud of you," Beverly said.

It was crazy how things could change but simultaneously stay the same. So much had happened in my life, but the mailman still delivered mail the next day, and my neighbor's dog still barked the same way. Spring still turned to summer and summer still turned to fall, and in a month's time, winter would still be here for us all. But there were these huge changes in my life, and it felt like my world had stopped and flipped upside down. One of the hugest changes in my life was no doubt the people. A year ago, I didn't know any of these people, and if you would have told me that we would be on a hangout, I'd have probably laughed.

A know-it-all class president, her band-geek best friend, the town's misunderstood local delinquent and his lost girl, an ex-star quarterback slash ex-suicide attemptee, the princess-loner in shining armor, and two bonehead musicians.

It was like life pressed the Randomize button and pushed us all together, and strangely, it felt right.

Afterward, we split ways and Manny and I went to win Beverly and Hadley these huge stuffed bears. I almost didn't want to get them because it would be a pain to carry them around, but I was glad I did when I saw Beverly's expression after I won. I knocked the bottles down with ease, and helped Manny with the secret trick to knocking down the bottles. After his fifth time, he finally got the other bear. I'd never heard a little girl squeal so loudly.

"Oh, look the photo booth just opened!" Hadley said.

My phone rang and when I answered, it was my mom. "Hadley has dance in an hour. Please bring her back home promptly."

"We'll be there." I hung up with sigh. Hadley was having fun. We were having a great time; better than we'd had in a while. When I ended the call, I could tell her mood had dropped.

"Was that mom?" Hadley asked.

"Yes. You've got dance in an hour. We've got to get home."

"Just let me take a picture with Manny first!"

Hadley threw her bear at me and grabbed Manny's hand to run to the photo booth while it had no line.

Beverly stared at me, asking me with her eyes if everything was all right. She worried about me too much. It shouldn't have to be on her to make *my* problems *her* problems. She was an angel for being there for me, but that shouldn't have to be on her. So to wipe the look of worry off her face, I wrapped my arm around her and hugged her close to me. The feel of this was comforting. The feel of the moment was too pure. My feelings were so strong. And, for the millionth time in the past two days, I was confused. I was confused because maybe, just maybe, I was having one of the best days of my life. I'd never felt more alive. And I was confused because maybe, just maybe, I thought I was falling for my best friend. I was confused because the future didn't scare me anymore—I saw it as a chance for opportunities now. I was confused because I was okay with not having a plan. I was confused because maybe I was free, and maybe, just maybe, things were going to be okay.

"We have to go," I whispered into Beverly's ear. "But I really don't want to."

I backed away, my thoughts managing to scare me senseless.

"Me either," she said softly.

"Why did only one come out?" I heard Hadley's voice.

"Not sure." Manny's voice spoke as they reached where Beverly and I were standing. He held the single strip of photos in his hand.

"I say you keep it." He stared at it for a while before holding the picture out to Hadley.

"No, you keep it." Hadley smiled.

"But—"

"I insist." She pushed the hand holding the picture to his chest.

He smiled shyly. "Okay. I shall keep it safe."

Beverly hugged Hadley. "I had fun with you today."

"You're leaving?" Manny asked, his face going slack.

"Yeah, Hadley has dance," I replied, and Hadley groaned.

"See you, Manny," I said, holding out my fist, and he fist-bumped it.

"I guess this is bye," he said to Hadley.

"No, it isn't. I'll see you at school, dork." Hadley smirked and playfully punched him in the shoulder.

He grabbed his shoulder in pain and forced a laugh. "That's a nice right hook you got there."

And with that, they left, waving as we went off in opposite directions.

"Before we leave, can we do one thing?" Hadley asked.

"Of course."

She grabbed my hand and led me to the pumpkin patch.

* * *

When we got home, Hadley convinced Mom to let her ditch dance for today. My parents never said no to her, so I wasn't surprised. Hadley was so excited to pull out her pumpkin. We sat on the kitchen floor and carved pumpkins together in comfortable silence.

"Today was a good day," she said finally.

I stared at her horribly carved pumpkin and smiled. "I think so too."

29

BEVERLY

My life went from being the same old things every day to every day being an adventure. It had been my favorite year yet, and I couldn't help but have high hopes for what was to come. Thanksgiving had always been my favorite holiday, and with the facts that my mom was cooking again and that Everest was joining us, I just knew it was going to be the best holiday.

I had been doing nothing but waiting and stalking time. I had already set the snacks out and prepared a chill playlist to play as the day went on. There were only so many times I could change my outfit, just to settle on the cranberry sweater and denim skirt I had already picked out two weeks ago. Everest wouldn't be able to come until his performance at the Thanksgiving benefit concert was over, so it wasn't like I could text or call him. As a matter of fact, the whole gang was busy. Mikey and Aurora had gone over to his father's house for the day, Nami and Tiffany were volunteering at a shelter, and Lincoln and Lucky were at the benefit concert with Everest.

I lay back on the couch, consumed with boredom. I painted the ceiling with my thoughts, drawing a story on the blank white canvas. Everest told me once that there was a story in anything if you thought hard enough. I projected my daydreams up high and dreamed about how this day would go. Everyone would get along, and the food would be better than ever. My mom would be trusting and not come off as unapproachable. I'd finally beat Manny at Scrabble and happily listen to all of Macy's crazy stories.

"That's Macy and Manny!" my mother screamed moments after the doorbell rang and I almost tripped over my feet rushing to the front door.

"Happy Thanksgiving!" I flung the door open and yelled with excitement.

"Geez, girl, you scream just like your mama. Here, I made some apple crumble cake." Macy shoved a bag in my arms before heading toward the kitchen without so much as a greeting.

I looked in the bag holding the crumble cake and didn't miss the price tag on the side of the box. "She didn't make it." I looked up to catch Manny in midsigh, before he stepped into my home.

"Yeah, I already kind of had a clue," I chuckled.

"I made some kimchi though." He stared at me with a mischievous smile before setting the jar on the table.

"Thank . . . you." I scrunched up my nose from the sour smell. My last encounter with the stuff wasn't something I wanted to revisit, and Manny knew this but refused to care.

"Don't try and put your fingers in my pans! Move, Macy," I heard my mother yell from the kitchen.

"I'm just trying to help you out! The turkey is looking a little dry." Aunt Macy matched my mother's tone. But as always, Manny and I remained unfazed. They were like that every time they were around each other.

"You know what's dry? Your lips. They're beyond the point of looking dry—how many times did I tell you that with this weather it's necessary to invest in some lip balm. At least lick 'em before you split them." My mother had amusement laced all through her tone.

"Oh, you wanna talk about dry? Remember your elbows yesterday? You could start fire with that a—"

"Happy Thanksgiving!" Manny yelled purposely to cut them off, making me laugh.

"Is that my Man-man? Come give me some love." My mom came out of the kitchen swiftly and pulled Manny into her arms.

"You smell like cholesterol." Manny winced.

My mother released Manny quickly after he said that and pursed her lips. "I'm going to go shower right now. Make sure *she* doesn't touch any of the food."

She untied her apron, pulled it off, and threw it on the couch before waving a stern finger in my direction to let me know she didn't want Macy anywhere near the kitchen.

"Make sure you brush your teeth," Aunt Macy called to my mother, at which my mother flipped her the bird before shutting the bathroom door.

"I have some snacks to hold us over in the living room." I waved at them to follow me as I sat back down on the couch.

I had set some cheese, crackers, grapes, and other snack foods on a tray on the coffee table. For a little while, we watched the recording I had of the Thanksgiving parade. Manny would shoot down every balloon I liked, calling each one stupid. He liked to make me feel like I was lame every chance he got, but I knew he didn't mean it. Anyone looking in would assume that he was serious because of his stern facial expression, but I knew he was just joking. I'd known the kid since his birth; I knew him better than anyone. Aunt Macy would have me watch Manny whenever she would go on dates—which had been countless times. She was a serial dater my mom would jokingly say, and had never been in a permanent relationship. But because of this, Manny and I were close.

"So, babygirl, where's lover boy?" Macy broke into my thoughts about her dating life and smirked. She picked up a grape and tossed it into her mouth with ease.

"Everest is coming?" Manny's eyes widened.

"Where have I heard that name?" Aunt Macy mumbled, staring at the ceiling.

"He's a Finley," Manny told her.

Coughing came next as Macy clutched her necklace.

"Are you okay, Mom?"

"Do you need some water?" I asked, trying to leave the living room as she grabbed my arm to force-sit me back on the couch.

"The successor . . . of Finley Corp . . . is having dinner with us?" Aunt Macy struggled with her words, looking quite shocked by whom my best friend was.

"Ye—*ouch*." She slapped my arm.

"Why didn't you tell me?" Her eyebrows furrowed and her lips pulled into a sneer. "Does your mama know?"

"Does it matter?" I moved an inch away from her on the couch and rubbed my arm where she had slapped it.

"Yes!" she huffed, exasperated.

"Why?" Manny took his turn to be confused.

She shook her head and sighed dramatically. "Wow."

"Anyway . . ." Manny trailed off, staring at his mother weirdly before looking at me with a nervous look. "Is um . . . is—"

"Hadley coming?" I smiled. "I'm not sure."

"Who's that?" Macy asked, almost like she already knew the answer but needed confirmation.

"His sister."

"The daughter?!" Macy yelped, exasperated all over again.

"Aunt Macy, calm down. I don't see what the big deal is."

"How did you two even cross paths? It doesn't make sense." She grabbed a cracker and bit into it with intensity.

"They go to the same school," Manny told her.

"It just kind of happened." I shrugged with a smile.

"Why are you getting so worked up?" Manny questioned his mother.

"Why are you guys acting so nonchalant? The son of the man who basically owns this town is having dinner with us. It shouldn't be something taken so lightly."

"Not that deep."

"Honestly." I agreed with Manny.

"I would've worn better shoes!" She smacked Manny's shoulder.

"Stop hitting my baby." My mother came around the corner looking stunning. She'd curled her shoulder-length hair to add a crisp wave to it. Her face was free of any makeup, and I could see the tiny freckles scattered on her nose. Her eyebrows were done, of course, but she hadn't filled them in, which I preferred. She wore a gray sweater with tightly fitted skinny jeans and her black heels.

"You look so pretty," I gushed, wondering if I would grow up to look like her.

"Oh, this old thing?" My mom smirked and turned in a circle, showing off her outfit.

"Why you got heels on?" Macy scrunched up her face. "Doing too much. I hope you fall."

My mother laughed unbothered and did another spin.

"I'm ready for wine," she said after she finished up her spin, and my aunt Macy practically jumped up from the couch when she heard that. They both went into the kitchen to get glasses, leaving Manny and me on the couch.

He turned on some football while I asked him a million and one questions about it. I did this every year, and just because we weren't having Japanese takeout didn't mean I would disregard the tradition.

"Please leave me alone," Manny grumbled, and I chuckled. He was just too adorable; I have loved him since forever. He was my first best friend, and I wasn't going to forget that. We may not have been blood, the same race, or gender, but he meant the world to me. I was his sister, and I always would be.

"That's impossible—"

My phone buzzed violently in my pocket.

> I'm gonna be there soon
>
> I'm outside
>
> Bev
>
> Beverly
>
> Beverly ffs I gotta get you a new phone

Text messages from Everest came in all at once, and I cringed when I noticed that the last text was sent fifteen minutes ago.

I leaned on the couch to look out the window and spotted his cherry-red Mustang. I smiled and waved at him. I waited for him to leave his car, but six minutes later he was still sitting there.

Um come in

Why he was just waiting out there? He could've easily just knocked on the door. The waiting in the parking lot was a bit strange. Finally, I spotted his figure getting out of his car and felt a surge of excitement radiate through my whole body. He was wearing a white button-down top with a black tie, and black bottoms. His tall shape ventured toward the stairs but then stopped. I raised my eyebrows and watched as he put a fist up to his lips and bit his thumb knuckle.

"*C'mon.*" I whispered to myself. Grabbing my phone, I sent him another text.

There's nothing to be scared of . . .

He pulled his phone out of his slacks and, wearing a mask of confusion, looked up at the window where I was.

I'm not scared

I received his text seconds later and sighed when he still didn't make any attempt to walk up the stairs. He ran a hand over his face, and I could just tell by his body language that he was nervous.

Despite his words, his body told me his true feelings. He had performed in front of thousands of people, had the weight of the school on his shoulders, and changed what was expected of him, but yet was afraid to meet my mom.

I tucked my phone in my pocket as I swiftly threw on my shoes. The autumn air swirled on my skin, and my breath came out in tiny puffs of white. I trudged down the steps until I reached Everest.

"There's no reason to be nervous," I told him, linking my arm in his and giving him no chance to say any words as I practically dragged him up the steps.

"I can't help it," he grumbled, finally giving in and admitting he was being skittish.

"Just relax," I assured him with a giggle. He was nervous for no reason.

"This is just the first time I'm going to have a real Thanksgiving."

I looked up at him and smiled. "It's going to be great."

I took his hand and opened the door.

"Everest!" Manny ran and hugged him, and I was surprised when Everest wrapped his arms around him.

"Hey." Everest smiled and ruffled Manny's hair, the tenseness he had shown earlier slowly fading.

Manny looked up at him with a scowl. "Why does everyone feel the need to touch my hair?"

"Because you're just so cute," I told him, giving him a hair ruffle of my own.

"I'm guessing Hadley isn't here." He pushed me off him and frowned.

"Yeah, she's in New Mexico with my mom and some family."

"So this is lover boy," my mom spoke, a smile on her face. She came out of the kitchen with a sharp knife in her hand.

I watched as he swallowed nervously.

"Yes, ma'am, but people usually call me Everest."

I wanted to laugh, but the tension in the room made me feel as though I shouldn't.

"Don't call me ma'am. It makes me feel old. Do I look old to you?" my mother teased him.

Everest looked at me for help, and I turned to my mom. "Really, the knife? Is that necessary?" I laughed, not able to hold it in anymore.

"I'm just introducing myself . . . and my knife," my mother added.

"Oh, leave the poor boy be," Macy chimed in, walking into the living room with a wine glass in hand.

"I get it. I wouldn't dare hurt Beverly . . . she's my . . . best friend," Everest explained, and I smiled. He'd never called me his best friend before.

My mother put the knife down. "Best friend? That's cute. Beverly has never brought anyone over before. I was beginning to think she wasn't ever going to."

"Yeah, don't scare him off. He's harmless," I said.

Everest glanced at me curiously before looking back at my mom.

My mother smiled. "Okay, well, good. Food is ready." She went back into the kitchen, and Everest turned toward me.

"Now your mom thinks I'm a priss," he told me, annoyed.

"Why would she think that?"

"*He's harmless,*" he mocked me.

I laughed. "You are."

He looked even more annoyed. "No, I'm tough."

"Okay, lean, mean, killing machine. Let's go eat."

* * *

We sat at the table, Everest beside me, my mother at the end of the table, and Manny and Macy in front of me.

"I've never seen a Thanksgiving table look like this," Everest said, eyes glued to the scene in front of him.

"Excuse me?" my mother asked raising an eyebrow.

"There's just a lot going on . . . is that kimchi?" Everest asked.

"Yes, yes, it is," I told him with a smile, sort of proud that I was able to show him something different.

"This all smells amazing." Everest's eyes glazed over from the array of food—mashed potatoes, creamed corn, baked macaroni, yams, ham, potato salad, green beans, corn bread, stuffing, rice and beans, three different pies, apple crumble cake, rolls, gravy, kimchi, and of course, a turkey.

"I know." My mom smiled at her hard work. "Just wait until you taste it. Now, let's go around the table and say what we are thankful for," my mother said, grabbing my hand. We formed a circle with our hands around the table. Everest's grip was warm and tight.

"I'm thankful for Bill Nye and Batman."

"I'm thankful for seeing another year and my beautiful boy, who is growing up to be something spectacular." Aunt Macy stared at her son lovingly, a proud look etched on her features.

"I'm thankful for being off today and seeing all of you around my table. I'm thankful for the love and support I get—oh, and wine," my mom said shortly after.

"I'm forever thankful for the clothes on my back, the food in my mouth, and the roof over my head. I'm thankful for this day. Just to sit in this chair and see all of you makes me complete," Macy said.

Everest looked uncomfortable.

"Just say something you're thankful for," Manny explained slowly. "I'm thankful for tacos, school, and my mom, of course."

"I'm trying to think." Everest looked as though he was going to fidget out of his chair. All of the eyes at the table landed on him and I felt bad. But all he had to say was one thing—surely there was one thing he appreciated.

"You don't know?" Macy raised an eyebrow.

Everest stared at the ceiling and visibly struggled with thought.

"Damn, that hard?" my mom chuckled.

Watching him, I wanted to get him out of that situation. He looked completely ill at ease and I couldn't stand that. Especially since we were in my home.

"He said music," I spoke up, and I caught the little sigh of relief he made.

"Oh." Macy laughed.

"I didn't hear him. Next time say it with your chest." My mom chuckled under her breath.

"Okay, okay, can we eat now?" Manny asked, aggravated, before I even had a chance to say what I was thankful for.

"I don't even know where to start." Everest scratched his head.

"You've been deprived. Here have some of this." My mother leaned over and added items to his plate. "And *this*, can't forget about *this*."

She added more and more food to his plate and waited for him to taste it. I grabbed his fork and gathered the macaroni on it.

"Try that first," I told him, gathering some macaroni on my fork as well.

"Oh, oh my God." He shoveled more and more into his mouth, his eyes practically rolling into the back of his head.

"Same," I laughed, watching his reaction to the rest of the things he tried.

"Not gonna lie, I'm a little afraid to try this."

"You've never had collard greens?" I asked with disbelief.

"No, not yet . . ." He shook his head, poking at the green dish with his fork.

"Just don't inhale the scent," Manny advised, scrunching up his nose. He never really was a fan of collard greens. It wasn't something that he was used to—he'd probably only had it a few times.

"Just eat the kimchi," Aunt Macy told Everest, shaking her head in disapproval at the collard greens.

"Everest, don't listen to them." My mom waved a dismissive hand and urged him to eat them.

"All right, I can do this," he chuckled before quickly shoving some into his mouth.

We all watched his face as he chewed, a certain determination laid out on it.

"Do you like them?" my mom asked, watching his features closely.

"Everest?"

His face was still in a state of something unreadable as he slowly chewed.

"You're chewing it for so long," Manny said, emotionless before grabbing a biscuit.

"Yeah, swallow it already," Aunt Macy urged him.

A slow closed-mouthed smile of pure amusement pulled at the corners of his mouth, and I watched his Adam's apple bob as he swallowed.

"Was it good?" I laughed.

There was about ten seconds of silence as we waited for his

answer before he swiftly shook his head with a chuckle. He grabbed the beer my mom gave him and washed down the taste.

"Yeah, I can't see how they can eat that stuff," Manny uttered under his breath.

"You should try it with some hot sauce." My mother moved the bottle closer to him.

Everest laughed, his face flushed red. "The taste was good, I just wasn't a fan of the consistency."

"It's like a gooey, smelly sock, right?" Manny whispered to Everest, but it was hardly a whisper at all.

"Don't get popped, Man-man," my mom threatened with amusement.

"At least you tried them and were honest," she said to Everest with a shrug, and added mashed potatoes to his plate. "You're just not used to them."

No one at the table was raised on collard greens except my mom and me. They were so rich in flavor, I wasn't offended at all by the others' view on them. That just meant that there was going to be more left for me.

"Yeah, he's not used to any of this. How's everything else though?" my mom asked after eating a forkful of mac 'n' cheese.

"Pretty good. My taste buds haven't had this much fun before."

"Oh baby, that's because your tongue has been programmed to Caucasian cuisine," Macy said, making my mom almost choke on her potato salad from laughing.

"You're stupid," my mom said to Macy with a snort, reeling from her laugh.

"My cook is actually Hispanic." Everest scratched his head.

"Cook? I forgot you Finleys got old money," my mom said with a smirk.

"Did she tell you?" I asked my mom but turned my head to look at Macy.

"Yeah, she did, but I already knew. I work at a hair salon, Beverly. Girls talk," my mother stated, lifting a brow. "But that's irrelevant."

"Excuse me . . . old money?" Everest said, confusion written across face.

"Money so endless your great-great-great-grandson would be set," Macy explained.

"None of that money is mine. I was just born into it."

"I wish I was born into some money," Macy snickered.

While my mother and Macy talked about the things they would buy if they won the lottery, I observed the scene. Manny barely talked as he ate, his facial expression blank. Everest looked relaxed as he chuckled every so often at my mom and Macy's banter.

"How did Beverly come to meet someone like *you*?" The way my mom said it forced a pang to hit my chest. Everest sensed it, too, because his nose wrinkled a bit.

"What do you mean?"

"Exactly what I said," my mother laughed.

"We met in the library," he told her before taking a sip of his beer.

"Now *that* makes sense." Macy laughed loudly.

"That sounds about right," my mom agreed, looking at Macy.

"So, are you guys using protection?" Macy questioned, and the air turned stiff.

"Protection for what?" I asked into the quietness.

Manny face-palmed and sighed. "Wow."

My mother turned to Everest. "Did your Indiana Jones go exploring?"

"Okay, that's enough." Manny covered his ears and I was more confused than ever.

"How you think you got here?" Macy told Manny, and suddenly it dawned on me.

"I'm leaving." Manny stood up from the table and began to walk toward my room, then came back to grab his plate before continuing on his journey.

"You still didn't answer my question," my mother said, making my skin turn hot.

"Ma, we—" I began but she cut me off.

"I want to hear it from lover boy."

Everest looked amused. "No, not at all."

"No what?" my mother urged.

"My Indiana Jones did not go exploring," he said slowly, before a chuckle slipped through his lips. To my surprise, my mom laughed along with him.

"What's funny?" my mom asked even though she was laughing.

"Why did you phrase it like that?" Everest covered his mouth, but his shaking body was an indication that he was still laughing.

"Be quiet, now, and eat your food," my mom told him with a chuckle, and in that moment, I felt like the awkward-meeting phase was over. I thought Everest might've just been approved by my mother at that point in time, which made it easier to play the board games.

Manny rejoined us as we played numerous games until Aunt Macy started to accuse everyone of cheating. After that, my mother whipped out her pageant album. I'd seen the pictures over a million times. She pulled them out every chance she got, and I willingly looked at them. Partly because I was in awe every time I saw them and partly because I liked how her eyes would brighten when she reminisced.

"You look like Beverly so much right here; your skin is just lighter." Everest pointed to a photo of my mother on a swing.

"Beverly looks like me, you mean." My mom inspected the picture.

"I've got to got to get some cigarettes," Aunt Macy said randomly, and my mother's ears perked. She hadn't smoked in a little bit because she'd "lost" her pack of cigarettes a few days ago.

"Stores are closed," Manny said, to halt their efforts.

"There's a ma and pa shop around the corner," my mother said as she put on her jacket.

"You're just going to going to leave us?" I asked.

"You guys are basically adults, don't be dramatic. Plus, I don't really know what I expected, but you know what? I like you, Everest Finley," my mother said, causing Everest to smile instantly.

"Does this mean I can call you Mom now?" His boyish grin caused everyone in the room to replicate his energy.

My mother and Macy laughed and laughed as they walked out of the door.

From there, the three of us sat on the couch. They boys watched TV, but I just couldn't get into it. So instead I went to look for some movies. It took longer than expected because the movies were scattered in random places in the apartment. No matter how many times I tried to make the movie selection neat, my mom would mess up the order without a second thought. During my search I heard Manny screaming and yelling at the television with Everest. After I gathered all the appropriate films, I went back into the living room to ask their opinions and saw Manny and Everest looking stressed.

"I got some movies," I said, waving them, but the boys didn't look at me.

"Shhh," Manny told me, his eyes glued on the TV.

Everest looked up at me and then glanced quickly back at the television before looking at me again.

"What kind of movies?" he asked.

"*The Fast and the Furious, Matilda,* all the Twilight movies . . ."

"Okay, let's watch *The Fast and the Furious.*" Everest shrugged.

"Shhhh!" Manny urged.

"I kind of wanted to watch *Matilda,*" I said sheepishly. I hadn't watched that movie in forever.

"Okay, *Matilda* it is." Everest grabbed the remote and Manny yelled when Everest changed the input on the TV.

"WHAT ARE YOU DOING! THE GAME IS STILL ON!"

"Beverly wants to watch *Matilda.*"

"You've got to be kidding me." Manny looked at me with disgust.

"I'm sorry, Manny," I told him, but he wanted no part of my apology.

"We can always watch the game later," Everest told him.

"You can, but I can't. There's no cable at my house." Manny looked like he was moments away from punching Everest.

"I'll tell you what—when your mom comes back ask her if you can watch it over at my house. I have a home theater." Everest lifted an eyebrow in suggestion.

"So? You think you can bribe me? I wanted to watch it now." Manny all but rolled his eyes. "You better provide snacks and refreshments," Manny said sternly before leaning back on the couch with a sigh.

I sat between Everest and Manny. I didn't know what it was,

but the essence of the room was very comfortable. Maybe it was our full bellies, or the warmth in the cold, or how close we were together, but everything seemed right. I was content in the state I was in.

"Beverly." My body was being shaken. I forced my eyes open. My mother hovered over me; her nicotine smell had returned to her scent.

"Everest." She then moved to the sleeping Everest, so we could be separated. My head was resting on his shoulder as Manny's head rested on my lap.

"If he's so tired, then it's time to go home."

I rubbed my eyes so I couldn't see who'd spoken, but I didn't have to see to know it was my aunt Macy.

Everest yawned and looked at his phone to check the time. "It's really that late?"

"Yeah, we've been gone for three hours. Stopped by a friend's house," Macy explained.

"*Geez*," I sighed. We'd wasted our time sleeping when we could've been doing something the three of us would actually remember.

"Beverly, go and help Everest find his way out," my mother told me while taking off her shoes.

Everest stood up and stretched, while Macy grabbed Manny and handed him his coat, assisting him in putting it on. Manny hugged Everest to say good-bye and Macy followed afterward. Shortly after that, it was just Everest and me. My mom stayed in the apartment to clean up a bit while I walked him to his car. The air was crackling from the cold, and the sky was dark.

The moon illuminated the slow smile that tugged on Everest's lips.

"What?" The words floated out of my mouth on a cloud.

"Thanks for this."

"You can't be serious," I laughed. My mother had been completely inappropriate, as I'd figured she would be. Macy had grilled him the whole time and Manny had held a consistent sassy attitude throughout the whole event. He complained about anything he could think of. I personally had no problem with it because it was what I was used to, but for Everest, I was sure it was a lot for him to chew on, to hear Manny's constant complaints.

"No, I am. I enjoyed myself," he told me without a second thought.

I hugged him after that. It just seemed like the appropriate thing to do. I would never get tired of hugging Everest. The feeling I got every time he pulled me in closer or when my hand landed directly over his heart was a feeling that I was addicted to.

"I'm thankful for you," he said so softly that I barely caught it. His arms squeezed me once before he released me, then turned on his heel and got into his car.

"I'm thankful for you too," I called as he drove away, not missing the smile on his face.

Upon returning to the apartment, I realized my mom hadn't done much. I wasn't all that surprised, though—cleaning wasn't her favorite hobby.

"Did he kiss you before he left?" my mom asked from the kitchen. I looked over to find her digging in the pans, and I shook my head.

"Why would he do that? We're just friends. I told you."

"I see the way that boy looks at you." My mother sucked on her teeth.

"Oh sure," I laughed as I began helping her clean. I started with the living room and grabbed the photo album we had gone through earlier. I knew she'd assumed Everest and I were romantic because of our closeness. I was convinced that no boy would ever love me. They hadn't before and I didn't see when they'd start. I'd kind of become accustomed to being alone.

"You have him wrapped around your finger and you don't even realize," she said from the kitchen. I shook my head as I placed the photo album on the bookshelf nearby, but when I tried to slide it in, it wouldn't fit. The photo album did have a large binding, so I pushed some books to the side to create space, but in doing so, I knocked over some books at the end of the shelf.

"What are you doing in there?" my mother called from the kitchen, but right as I was about to answer, I noticed a bunch of envelopes spill out of our household Bible.

My stomach flipped as I turned over the book, exposing the envelopes—they were all from colleges.

"Beverly?"

I didn't answer my mother and instead pulled out the first letter.

> *Congratulations, Beverly! We are pleased to announce you've been accepted . . .*

Next one.

> *"Dear Beverly . . . Congrat— . . . inform you of your admission"*

The next one I opened so fast that I ended up ripping the envelope.

Congratulations!
We are pleased to inform you of your admission . . .

My head hummed with a thick cloud of oblivion. I looked up at my mother, standing against the wall near the kitchen. Her hand was over her mouth, and concern was strung through her eyebrows. This couldn't be real. I knew it wasn't. It wasn't real. It was so ridiculous that all I could do was laugh. It was a joke. It had to be a joke.

"What is this?" I stared down at the letters clutched hard in my hand. I realized then that I was shaking. "Mom?" I could feel the tears building in my eyes, but I blinked them back. "Mom?" I asked again when she wouldn't answer me.

"I am so, so sorry, Beverly." She choked on her words, and it was then that I knew it wasn't a joke.

I felt like I was close to throwing up. I hugged my knees and hung my head low. In that darkness I tried to calm myself down. My heart hurt, like it was being slashed by a hundred thumbtacks. The sight of my mother crying suddenly made my blood turn hot.

"You know what? You don't get to cry. Explain." The tone of my voice shocked me. I wiped my face of the tears, even though a few still dribbled out of my eyes.

When she didn't make any move to explain, I nudged her shoulder. "You owe that to me."

She lifted her head slowly, her cheeks already puffing up from crying. "Bever—" She reached for me but I moved out of the way.

"I said you owe it to me. Why—" My voice filled with intense emotion and the tears began to build up again, so I let out a deep breath. "Why would you do that?" I asked after I swallowed down the pain and was able to get my words out.

"You wouldn't understand." I'd never heard my mother sound so broken before.

"So tell me! Make me understand." My ears rang from me raising my voice. The feeling of anger swirled in every inch of my body. The room pulsated at a rapid rate and all I wanted was for my head to stop spinning.

My mother dropped her head low again and cried, tears streaming down her face and making lakes on her sweater.

"I'm not ready for you to go." She tried to approach me. "I can't do it without you."

"God, I've got to get out of here. I can't stay here." I grabbed my coat from the rack and started for the door before my mother hopped in front of it.

"Where are you going?"

"Anywhere but here," I responded. "Did you really think I wasn't going to find out?"

"No," she stated simply, her eyes wild.

My emotions amplified tenfold. "I hate you."

The words slipped out before I could stop them. My mother flinched and then anger took root on her features. "If you walk out of that door, don't even think about coming back."

My mother stood back from the door, waiting for me to make the next call. She'd always been so in control. Even when she was drunk her air of confidence never wavered, but seeing her now was different. For the first time in my life, my mother looked lost and helpless—like a child who'd just got caught stealing from the cookie jar.

The moment was tense, and for a second, I saw nervousness swimming in her irritated eyes before a confident stance stood in them.

"Don't wait up," I said, shocking my mother and myself as I opened the door and walked out into the autumn cold.

I didn't know where to go, I just knew where I didn't want to go—no way did I want to bother Everest with this. He was so happy with the way the day had turned out, and I just couldn't ruin that for him. I actually didn't want to bother anyone with this. I walked, and cried, and walked some more, and cried some more, looking for somewhere to get away for a bit, until I landed at the garage that was designed just for that.

30

EVEREST

Confession: I could relive this day over and over again.

—*EF, November 22, 2018*

Everything about Beverly's family was the opposite of mine. Her family was raw and unorganized, not fitting into any specialized boxes. My family, on the contrary, did everything they could to fit into a perfect little box. Hell would freeze over before my family would behave the same way hers did. I loved it. Every second of it, even the awkward scrutiny I got from them. No fronts were made, and the people were real. No doubt, the realist family I'd ever been around in my eighteen years of living. I quite honestly didn't want to leave.

Sitting in this large, empty house made me appreciate a crowded home. I heated up a plate of leftover mac 'n' cheese while thinking of the day's events. It wasn't until I finished my last bite that I realized it was my favorite Thanksgiving in the history of all my Thanksgivings.

I could have written a book about every holiday disaster in my life, ranging from catching my aunt Loren snorting coke in the pantry to discovering my favorite uncle passing away. It was nice to finally have that holiday spirit that everyone seemed to talk about. I caught myself daydreaming about going over her apartment a lot more often—from what I gathered today, I left a decent enough impression to go over more.

After washing my plate, I began my nightly routine. I was down to just my boxers and socks when my phone rang. Sighing, I removed my socks and sank onto my bed. I was done for the night. It was a rare occasion that I slept well, and for once I was feeling legitimately ready for bed. So I decided to let my phone ring out . . . until it was clear as day that Mikey wasn't going to stop calling. I groaned when I declined the call and he instantly called back.

It was the perfect time to sleep—I was in an impeccable mood, my house was quiet due to the fact that I was the only one home, my belly was full, and the tranquility of the night had left me in a state of bliss. So leave it to Mikey to interrupt such a moment.

"Are you kidding me?" I finally answered the phone.

"Listen here, you little dipshit, I've been calling you because this is important—"

"This better be important," I interrupted.

"This *is* important. Come down to the Basement." His tone was harsh.

"It's two o'clock and I'm tire—"

"It's Beverly, she's real messed up righ—"

"What are you talking about?" I sat up in my bed.

"Look, I just got here after Thanksgiving with my dad, so don't try and blame shit on me. Sam told me she was hysterical, so he gave her something to take the edge off."

My blood boiled instantly. "What the fuck did he give her, Mikey?"

"Don't worry, don't hulk up, I already beat his ass. She's just loaded, apparently—she was drinking straight from the bottle. But that's beside the point, something real bad happened to her, Golden Boy. I don't know what, but something is seriously wrong."

"I'm on my way."

* * *

I pulled up in the driveway to see Sam standing near the entrance of the garage door, holding a bloody rag to his nose. That sight alone clarified that this wasn't a joke. I let out a deep breath before slowly getting out of my car. When Sam's eyes landed on me, he laughed a little to himself.

"Everest to the rescue."

My eyes only saw red, and for the second time in my life I punched someone in face.

Some girl immediately ran over to his side when he fell. He sat up and spit blood out of his mouth before looking at me with a bloody-toothed smile. "I'm actually impressed with that hit. Good work, *Golden Boy.*"

I shook my head with disgust before walking through the garage to find Beverly. It didn't take long—she was lying on the couch, her eyes red and puffy, looking as if she was seconds away from falling asleep. Mikey sat next to her, talking to her, but it was inaudible to me. It was like the pain in her demeanor was the only focus my body would register.

"Bev." Her name slipped out of my mouth automatically.

She looked up at me and a forced smile faintly etched the corners of her mouth. "Oh, hey, Ev."

Her words were slow and soft, and the smile was faker than a politician's.

"What are you doing here, Beverly?" I asked her hesitantly.

"What? I can't have a drink?" She shrugged uncoordinatedly; her speech was slurred.

Mikey looked at her with a wave of worry. It was almost eerie. The one person who we'd believed could never break was hanging by her hinges before our eyes. Our very own hope was facing her own darkness, and we had no idea why, or what we could do to help.

"What happened?" Mikey asked her, and I could tell by how she rolled her eyes it wasn't his first time asking.

"I'm okay!" she exclaimed with a laugh and a giggle, trying her hardest to convince us she was fine. "I'm okay, guys, stop worrying about me," she said again but softer, and almost like a sob was caught in her throat but she was trying to suppress it.

"I'm okay," she said again for the third time, quickly looking between Mikey and me.

"No, you aren't," Mikey told her.

Those three words caused her to burst into tears. She used her hand to cover her face and she bent over in sorrow. My heart immediately broke at the sight of it. I walked over to her and grabbed her free hand before squatting down to her level.

"Let's get you out of here, okay?" She nodded, and when I stood up, she followed me.

"Take care of her, bro," Mikey said, running a hand through his dark hair with a somber look.

I nodded before leading her out of the garage and to my car. She hadn't stopped crying, and I didn't know what to do. I thought that maybe her mom would know how to handle it.

"I'm taking you home," I said into the silence.

"No! I can't go back there, Ev. Please don't take me back. I'm never going back." She spoke with urgency through her tears.

"What happened?"

"Please, can you just drive around for a bit?" She hiccupped.

"You need sleep."

"I'm begging you to not take me back. Just trust me, okay?"

I ended up taking her to my house. She seemed to have calmed herself down but stayed as distant as she could. The occasional tear would dribble from her eyes and she would wipe it off with annoyance. I wondered what made her get like this. She'd been so excited for today and although I didn't know what had happened, I was very bothered by the fact that something had; she didn't deserve this.

Carefully guiding her through my dark and quiet house, I led her to the guest room. She sat on the bed and I sat next to her. I watched as she struggled to keep her emotions together and with each sniffle, my heartstrings shredded.

"Bev . . . are you gonna tell me what's wrong?"

She looked up at me, cheeks and nose tinged with peach. "I don't want to talk about it right now."

"Beverly," I sighed, stumped with how I should handle the situation.

Suddenly, she cried out into the silence, sounding like her insides were being torn apart with each passing second. I held her in my arms while she held me tight. Waterfalls of tears went down my sweater. She hung on to me like she was going to fall apart, and I wasn't sure if I could put her back together again.

"I got you, I got you," I kept repeating, stroking her hair as she cried into my chest. I could tell she was trying to pull herself together, but it was one of those heart-wrenching cries where you have no control. She tried to take deep breaths but they came out all shaky and distorted. I rubbed her back and tried to comfort her in the best way I could without talking. She needed to cry— she needed to release the powerful emotions running through her, but that didn't mean that it killed me any less.

"What did I do to deserve this?" she asked. Her eyes had a hurricane flooded within them. My heart was so heavy, sinking to the bottom of her pain, but I knew I had to be strong for her, because she needed me to be.

I held her away from me so she could fully see my face and told her what she needed to hear.

"I'll never understand why bad things always happen to good people. But I'll tell you right now that you did nothing wrong. This was completely beyond your control, okay?" I used my thumb to wipe away the single tears falling from both her eyes.

When I pulled back to look at her, she seemed to have calmed down substantially, which instantly took me back, but nothing could prepare me for what came next. I honestly had no clue what was happening as her face moved closer to mine. She then left an unanticipated soft kiss on my forehead, and I suddenly froze. I didn't stop her when she did the same to my right cheek and I didn't stop her when she did it to my left. I just stared at her, my thoughts—blank.

She scooted closer to me and left another kiss right under my jaw. Her eyes looked at mine each time she finished a kiss but would then stare at the next spot her lips would meet.

"B-Bev?" I found my voice when she kissed the base of my neck.

Shhh was all I got from her as she climbed onto me and straddled my lap, leaving a kiss at another part of my neck.

All of them were pillow-petal soft, and tantalizingly slow. Her lips brushed against my skin before she would leave the gentlest peck in place. I almost felt like I was dreaming, that none of this was happening. I should have stopped her, but I was too frozen to do anything.

She pulled back and stared into my eyes for the eleventh time in the past five minutes. I watched her eyes as they scouted their next location, and when they slowly drifted to my lips, I woke up. The girl I was falling for was on my lap, kissing me. And from silence, now I could only hear my heart thumping with anticipation. I felt my face getting warm, and my breath growing faster. I wanted it, wanted her. This feeling felt like the moment when I ran to the touchdown and knew I was going to make it. It was like those four seconds of reaching the goal and emerging victorious. As she moved closer to place her lips on mine, I selfishly didn't stop her. I'd dreamed of kissing her and I'd dreamed of being with her, and I woke up from all of them. But this time it was different, because I was awake and the dream was still happening. I was inches away from a dream coming true; four seconds away from the goal.

But this was just my dream, this wasn't Beverly. She was not herself right now. She was drunk and sad, and I refused to let my selfish mind go above what she needed right now. I used my one arm to direct her head onto my shoulder and put my other arm around her back and stood up. I pulled back the blankets and laid her down, making sure to arrange the pillows around her like I'd seen her do plenty times. Her eyelids were already drifting together, and I watched to make sure she fell asleep. It didn't take long. Once I was sure, I went to the kitchen to grab some water.

"What is she doing here?" I jumped slightly and turned to see my father with his usual disinterested attitude. The room was too hot, and I needed water more now than ever. But now, I wished I'd never gone into the kitchen. I sighed, preparing myself for the conversation. I really didn't have the energy to deal with him.

"She doesn't have anywhere to go right now." My heart rate increased and I watched as he shook his head.

"Everest—" he began, his voice stern.

"I know but . . . *please.* What do I have to do? I'll do anything. I swear, whatever you want me to, Dad, I'll do it. Just *please* let her stay."

"You'd start learning the family business?" He crossed his arms.

I gulped down my dreams while nodding.

"You'd give up music?"

I closed my eyes then, before nodding. I couldn't bear to see his face as I made this promise. "Yes."

"You'd do that for that girl?"

My emotions went from somber to focused from his words.

"Yes, I would."

He stared at me for a long moment before taking a sip from his mug.

"What a waste that would be." I watched as he turned off the kitchen light. "I'll call your mother and let her know she's here."

I stood there for moment, slightly in shock by the way my

father had handled the situation. It was out of character for him to act that way. I was positive that I was going to have to find a better alternative for her. Maybe my dad didn't hate me as much as I thought.

31

BEVERLY

My surroundings felt dull despite the autumn sun glowing behind a pair of gold curtains. I woke up to the sound of a couple arguing nearby. In no way shape or form did it soothe the raging headache I had. My mouth felt as if I'd had cotton balls for breakfast. Flashes of the night before rose into my memory, but only in broken pieces, like I was some type of artwork with scratches so you couldn't understand the picture. No, more like I was a record with spiderwebs traced all over it.

Tainted and dull.

I remembered walking to the Basement, how the moon was covered by gray clouds. The night had a chill and my toes were cold. The alcohol burned as it went down my now-scratchy throat. I remembered stepping on a soda cap, and thinking I was going to die. I knew I was crying because Aurora's cat, Shadow, wouldn't come to me. Mikey's eyes were angry, but that was it. That was all

I remembered beyond leaving the disaster that had exploded my life. Burping, I tasted all the foul contents of the things I'd ingested the night before, with a slight sprinkle of sweet potato pie. Sitting up in bed, I covered my face with my hands and groaned. Feeling my stomach rumble, my body moved before my mind did, and I lunged to the nearest bathroom. I didn't even know if there was even a bathroom, but I sure jumped up like I knew. Thankfully, there was a bathroom, but I didn't get a chance to get a good look at it because I basically stuck my head in the toilet.

With each upchuck, I felt weaker and weaker. Eventually, my body gave me a break and I held on to the toilet, attempting to gather myself together. Closing my eyes, I wondered how I'd ended up wherever here was.

Then I felt something nudge against the side of my head. "Here."

There sat Everest in the bathtub holding a purple towel close to my face. More sick than embarrassed, I accepted it, wondering if he knew the events of last night. He stared at me with tired eyes. The air was somewhat awkward but that might have just been on my part. His eyes were on me as I wiped my mouth.

"Where am I?" I asked after a long silence.

Ignoring my question, he laughed a little before asking me his. "What happened?"

It was strange how his face could be etched with amusement while at the same time looking so sullen. He looked just as tainted and dull as my surroundings, body, and thoughts. A force prickled the back of my eyes, but I held it in. I didn't want to cry anymore, but the pain continued to creep into my heart. Everest searched my face for recognition, but I couldn't pay attention to him when I was putting all my energy into pulling myself together.

"Bev, c'mon." His eyes were soft as they caressed my weakened spirit.

Taking a deep breath, I shook my head while staring at the expensive-looking floral wallpaper. "My mother has been hiding my acceptance letters."

The words tasted so vile and disgusting that I instantly felt sick again. Like somehow the combination of letters had manifested into some terrible illness. I couldn't help but throw up once again into the nearby toilet. The room was way too hot for comfort. I felt as if I were sweating bullets while I heaved time after time. My hair was lifted from my neck and I started to cool off almost immediately. When I was finished, Everest released the handful of curls he was holding.

He left the bathroom shortly after that and came back with a bottle of water.

"Why didn't you call me?" he asked shortly after that.

"I didn't want to bother you."

"Are you serious?" The way he said it made me feel like I'd made the wrong call to not contact him. From the look of it, inevitably, his holiday had still been ruined either way. He looked almost offended.

"Yes," I responded while getting up off the floor. I stood in front of the sink and splashed a little water on my face. I felt Everest's presence behind me and turned around, a little taken aback by how close he was.

"I worked all summer just so that I could afford to pay whatever costs my mom needed *and* pay for my college applications." Everest watched me intently as I recounted the night's events. "I was beginning to think that I wasn't going to get in anywhere. We ended up getting into this huge fight and I left. I'm pretty sure I'm not invited back." I sighed. "I didn't want to ruin your night just because mine was."

Everest stared at me for a few seconds before pulling me into a hug. He held on to me like he was afraid I'd float away. My arms were limp at my sides, which in turn put more passion behind his hug. He placed my head in the nook of his neck, and I could hear the steady beat of his heart. It reminded me of the hug we'd had last night, and I would be lying if I didn't say I wanted to stay in his embrace until it didn't hurt anymore.

"You can stay here." His chest rumbled.

"What?" I pulled back and looked at him.

"You're homeless. And I have a place where you can stay," he said like it was the most obvious thing in the world.

I looked around the bathroom, confused. "Where even am I?"

"My house."

I sidestepped to put space between us. "No, I'll just apologize to my mother today—"

"I think you should give it some time," he quickly told me. "This only just happened last night. The air needs to cool before you just waltz back over there."

I didn't have a chance to respond to that because shortly following his statement my mouth filled with vomit.

*   *   *

"Here, sit up, this should make you feel better." Everest came into view with a tray of food and set it on the nightstand. I sat up and yawned, and Everest sat on the edge of the bed.

"Hey, Bev?"

I stared at him.

"Do you remember anything else?" He ran a hand through his black hair.

"What do you mean?" I asked, wincing from how the words felt on my dry vocal cords.

"Like, do you remember last night in its entirety?"

I bit my lip and shook my head. "Everything after leaving my apartment is a blur. Why do you ask?"

He looked away and gulped. "Well, uh . . . nothing, it's just that . . . it's common for people to not remember things after they drink a lot."

"Oh, okay." I ran a hand over my eyes and groaned. "What time is it?"

"It's six o'clock in the evening. I really didn't want to wake you because you seemed to be really nauseous when you were awake but now you need to eat. Miranda made you your favorite."

He had changed from his outfit before into a red sweatshirt and gray sweatpants. I, on the other hand, was still wearing the same clothes I'd had on yesterday. I couldn't even begin to explain how icky I felt. I could honestly say I was as sick as my brain. My head had the worst dull, aching pain and my throat felt even drier than it had before.

I took the water from the tray and let it bring me back to life. It felt wonderful going down my throat. I didn't feel like myself again, but at least I wasn't going to die from dehydration. On the tray was a plate of chicken parmesan and a carton of cookies and cream ice cream. I wanted to smile from the sight of it but I couldn't—there was no energy to smile, and that thought alone made me want to cry again.

"I'm not hungry."

"You're still going to eat something."

I stared at him and he stared at me. Neither of us was going to let it go. I sighed before grabbing the fork and taking a bite. The food was warm but flavorless. I knew it should taste good due to the smell, but it tasted like nothing.

"Happy now?" I asked after finishing the one bite.

"No," he answered immediately. "But look on the bright side—you've been accepted somewhere you'd like to go?"

I slowly parted my lips. I couldn't tell him that it wasn't about that. What hurt the most was that she was willing to throw away my future so she wouldn't spend hers alone. I had sacrificed so much for my mom, and the fact that she could do that to me was just too much to stomach.

"I don't want to talk about it," I eventually was able to get out.

His eyes widened a little with realization. "Aw, I'm sorry, Bev."

I nodded and flipped the television on and combed through the channels with no intention of watching anything. Everest stared at me, and it was obvious that he didn't know what to do in this situation. Which was understandable, because I was new to this too. Nothing could have prepared me for that bomb. I'd been spending my time taking care of my mother and accepting her ways because I felt like they were justified, but now I couldn't seem to find my sympathy.

Who knew what kind of person I would've become if things hadn't gone the way they had? Would she have ever told me? What deadlines had I missed? Would anyone accept me now?

We spent our time together mostly in silence. A movie was playing but neither of us was really watching. Everest was either on his phone or looking at me like he wanted to say something but had decided against it, or I'd stare at the wall, the ceiling, or anything, really. The most productive thing I'd done all day was shut my eyes to fall asleep for the millionth time.

"Do you want me to stay with you?"

He'd been so attentive with me today. I knew he could have been doing much more exciting things than this. I felt horrible to say what I said next after all he'd done for me, but I needed it to be said.

"I'd rather be alone right now."

Something flashed in his eyes, and I turned away so I wouldn't have to look at him. Tears fell from my eyes when I faced the opposite direction.

"Oh . . . okay. I'll be back in the morning?" He stood there waiting for a response, but I didn't think I could open my mouth without it being extremely obvious in my voice that I was crying. Instead, I reached for the light and draped the room in darkness.

"Good night, Bev," he said with a certain tenseness before leaving. I cried so much that night. It rained in that room, but instead of the storm being in the sky, it lived in my eyes.

I spent the rest of the weekend there, and didn't even leave for school on Monday. I woke up that afternoon to Everest dropping off my schoolwork. He gave me an update on how the school day had gone and if I'd missed anything.

He didn't know it, but I'd decided that I wasn't going to apologize to my mom. I'd never felt pain like this before and I didn't want to be in that environment anymore. I'd just stay here until I left for college. I was going to pay his family rent, too, because it didn't feel right to just freeload.

For the rest of the day he stayed with me just as he had done the day before. The silence stayed but I was grateful for his company. He told me how the gang wanted to go bowling and asked if I would come too. Most of them hadn't seen me since Thanksgiving night, and he said they missed me. It warmed my heart to hear that.

"Good night, Bev," he said once again, but this time I said it back.

The next morning, I woke up earlier than I had anticipated. I showered and finally changed my clothes. I wasn't sure what got into me on this day, but I was tired of letting the misfortune take away who I was. Even though I wasn't quite ready for school, I no longer wanted to sleep all day and push away my life. I talked with Miranda, and she showed me how to make the nachos that Everest loved so much. As if on cue, when they were finished, I heard Everest's voice behind me.

"Hey, you."

I timidly waved and smiled just a fraction of a inch. "Hi."

"You're out of bed," he observed, a dimple appearing.

"I'm out of bed," I repeated with a slight chuckle. "Ready to go bowling?"

His eyes opened a bit and I didn't miss the flash of green go across the blue. "S-Sure."

When we arrived in front of Nesbits', my heart felt heavy, but it was bearable. It made me think of Manny and how he'd always wanted to come here but was too stubborn to. Manny was the type of kid who tried so hard to convince everyone that they were mature. At the end of the day, he was just an eleven-year-old kid who should enjoy being a kid. I turned to Everest, who was staring at me.

"Are you okay?" he asked with so much sincerity and vulnerability.

"I will be." I smiled and grabbed his hand. "Ready to get your butt kicked?"

"Yeah, right," Everest replied, laughing, as we walked through the doors to meet our friends.

32

EVEREST

Confession: although I've had eyes for eighteen years, only now do I really see.

—EF, December 10, 2018

The bar rang with drunken shouts of excitement. The lighting was dim, but the energy of the room was bright. The pumped-up patrons were canned together like sardines. Arms and bodies mimicked ocean waves as the music took over them. The air was smoky and the notes morphing together on the amp made my body hum. It would almost be a disservice to try and put the feelings I got when singing in front of a group of people into human symbols.

I was addicted to it.

Accomplishing something I'd worked so hard for in front of a group of people was surreal. Every time I performed, I had to take a moment to pull myself together. It was almost like a piece of me was given through song, and that moment I took was like restocking myself.

"Who should I return these to?" The red lace panties swung in Lucky's grip.

The crowd laughed and the insanely attractive girls at the front of the stage played innocent. I'd been playing gigs since Beverly put me on spot, and it was the best thing I could have done. I had only her to thank for this. Whenever my thoughts went rancid, she was the one there to distract me from myself.

"Thank you, everyone, for coming out tonight! We'll be performing at Point Square on the third. Catch us again if you enjoyed the show!" Lincoln's voice boomed through the mic, pulling me from my thoughts.

I waved good-bye and tried to focus. Falling in love with Beverly was like hearing your favorite song for the first time. She was like a tune that I couldn't stop playing. I couldn't help but think about her constantly.

She was eating when I spotted her, happily helping herself to a bowl of pretzels on the table backstage. She was wearing a peach sweatshirt and some blue jeans with, of course, her dirty sneakers. Her attire was so light and innocent compared to the outfits I'd seen in the crowd.

"So much for watching me," I said jokingly when I saw her. Her eyes widened and she turned around slowly with a mouth full of pretzels. Her hand held a fist of the intercrossed salted snack.

"I was . . . but then I got hungry, sorry."

She looked so cute with her eyes big and brown, sincerity plunged deep into them.

Suppressing a grin and failing, I took a pretzel from her and tossed it in my mouth with ease.

"I'm going to pack up real quick then we can head out and eat."

Just then, Lincoln clasped down hard on my shoulder. "O-o-o-o what we getting?"

"I'm in the mood for a sandwich." Lucky, too, entered the conversation. I turned to see him spinning his drumsticks between his fingertips.

"Oh, sorry, guys. My mom has been wanting me and Bev to be at Sunday dinner with her tonight. I doubt sandwiches are on the menu," I said with fake sadness.

"Wow, and she didn't want to invite us?" Lucky said with a soft, disapproving tone.

Lincoln snorted. "That's all right. We don't want to go to her crusty dinner anyway."

Beverly chuckled. "It's not crusty."

"You don't have to defend anything to him. He's having Subway for dinner," I said, taking another pretzel from her hand.

"Hey, there's some right here on the table, you know?" Beverly pushed the bowl closer to me, but I paid no mind to it because I wanted the pretzels she had.

"Don't even try and play Subway like that, Everest." Lincoln walked away with his guitar in one hand and his phone in the other. He was probably gearing up to talk to Tiffany—those two had been chatting it up a lot more recently. I could totally see them being a couple.

"You had a spicy Italian sandwich yesterday, you fraud." Lucky narrowed his eyes and threw a disgusted look my way.

"That was last week," I snorted.

"Whatever. Point is, you still had Subway." Lucky playfully hit me upside the head with his drumstick. After his miniassault, he left to go to the storage room.

I turned to Beverly, who was contentedly chewing on a pretzel. She had crumbs on her cheeks, and it made me remember the first time I'd hung out with her. She'd had crumbs on her cheeks then too. The sight alone, mixed with the memory, made me feel warm inside. I brushed the crumbs off her in a few swipes and she tilted her head upward so I could have better access.

"You're a mess," I said with an uncontrollable smile.

She stared at me and I could see the gears turning in her head. She had the kind of eyes that make you feel like she knew something you didn't. There was a depth in her brown eyes—a depth I hadn't discovered up until I'd met her. Beverly's mouth etched into a closed smile.

"Aren't we all?" she said after a moment.

I wondered the places her soul had been. Sometimes I wondered if she was secretly an angel. Or maybe she was an angel, but everyone suspected this except for her. She wasn't like anyone I had ever met before. I was so fascinated by everything she was. Beverly had me totally and completely hooked and she didn't even know it. My love for her went deeper than the depths of her eyes. I gently pulled her head toward me and kissed the top of it. "I'll be just a sec."

When I entered the storage room, I saw Lincoln and Lucky packing up their equipment.

"We're getting better and better every time we play together," Lucky said as I grabbed my jacket.

This was true. We were becoming a more cohesive group with each passing set.

"Jeff said he'll get us on tour across the country in no time."

I froze with that bit of information. My hobby was becoming more of a career than I ever thought it would now that we hired him as a manager.

"Seriously?" I asked as I put on my beanie.

Lucky nodded. "It could be as soon as this summer."

"Why didn't he tell me this?"

Lucky and Lincoln both looked at each other and laughed.

"What?" I asked.

"He did, but your mind is someplace else." Lincoln threw a rag at me with a laugh.

"Don't throw your sweat rag at me, Link. It smells like ass," I told him, throwing it back even harder.

"You're turning soft with all that hanging around Beverly," Lincoln said, sending a text, no doubt to Tiffany.

"Mhm . . . I'll see you guys later," I said with a smug smile before leaving the room.

It was true that I saw Beverly so much more than I had before. Wherever I went, she went. This was the fourth gig she had come to in the past week. My main goal was to try and make sure she was as busy as possible, so she didn't think about her home life.

It had been two weeks since the whole ordeal with her mom, and she seemed better each day, but I knew she was still fragile, especially since a couple of days ago when we dropped by to get her stuff and it was all scattered on the curb, ready to be collected by the garbage truck. She didn't cry but I think she wanted to.

"You ready?" she asked when I approached her.

I smiled; I couldn't even control it anymore. Being around her as much as I had only made my feelings for her grow stronger. "I should be asking you that. Hadley loves you there. She doesn't give you any space."

"I love her too. I've always wanted a sister." She shrugged. "I want to go."

"But why?"

"Do you not want me to go?" she asked with a teasing grin.

"No, no, I do. Believe me, I do. I'm just wondering, because your experience was so awful."

"The way I remember it, you were more affected by it than I was. Plus, your mom is actually sweet sometimes."

I looked at her strangely and changed the conversation. When we arrived at my house, I was pleased to discover my father's Porsche not outside my home.

We walked in to find my mom with a glass in hand and a joyous smile on her face.

"Oh, Beverly, dear." She grabbed Beverly's arm. "How are you, darling?"

"It's good to see you too," Beverly said shyly. It had been an experience watching how accepting my family had been toward Beverly. It made me feel good knowing that they cared for her as much as I did—or at least pretended well enough. I had a greater appreciation now for them.

"Hello, Mother."

"Good evening, my son." She kissed my cheek, no doubt leaving a mark. I looked at her glass again and wondered what number she was on.

"Come, come take a seat." When I reached the dining room, Hadley was already seated. But sat in place of my dad was our cook, Miranda, and beside her, sat her husband.

"Hey, Miranda." She nodded her head toward me in acknowl-edgment, a grandmotherly smile plastered on her face.

"Vic." Her husband waved at me slightly, acknowledging not only me but Beverly too.

It wasn't unusual for Miranda and her husband to have dinner with us. Whenever he was home from work and whenever my mother was in a good mood, she'd invite them to the table.

"I missed you." I heard Hadley beside me, practically squeal-ing as she hugged Beverly.

"You saw her yesterday," I deadpanned. Beverly had been in the car when I'd picked Hadley up from dance practice.

"It was only for a second," she threw back at me with ease.

"I missed you too," Beverly spoke with admiration. "I don't think I got to ask you about your trip."

The eyes of that child immediately glossed over as she excit-edly went into extensive detail about her trip.

My mom entered the dining room and set a blueberry pie on the table before taking a seat across from me.

Hadley looked at me before asking my mom, "Where's Dad?"

My mother stared at her with a who-cares look.

Miranda got up abruptly, the screech of the chair cutting through the awkward air. She returned with a pot, and when she lifted the lid, it was almost as if it lifted the mood of the room.

"That smells absolutely wonderful," my mother gushed.

Hadley leaned over the table to get a better look into the delicious-smelling pot.

"Oh my." Beverly practically drooled.

I leaned over slightly to see a perfectly cooked pot roast. Victor kissed his wife on the cheek, probably proud to have her.

"No hors d'oeuvres?" I asked, realizing that they hadn't been brought out. I couldn't even remember a time when I didn't have to spit out those shits on Sunday dinner; it was almost tradition in a way.

"Hadley told me you guys hate them. I had no idea. You guys never said a word. I would've had Miranda stop making those recipes I got from my book club years ago." My mother shook her head disapprovingly.

"You always got a kick out of finding recipes, so I didn't want to ruin it. But now that I know it's already ruined, I would just like to personally thank Hadley. Thanks, little sis."

"No prob." Hadley smiled.

"Beverly, how are you, honey?" my mother asked her politely. I didn't think my mother had ever been this polite to any of the people I'd brought home.

"Hungry," she said, staring at the pot, making those seated around the table chuckle.

Miranda served the plates after that. The roast was even better than the aroma it carried—it should be illegal for food to taste that good.

"How was your talent show?" My mother attempted to make conversation and show her interest in me. Even though it hadn't been a talent show, I gave her an A for effort.

"My set went fine, thank you for asking."

Beverly quirked an undercover smile before taking a bite of her food.

"Oh, I just remembered—Lucille told me to ask you if you can give her your autograph. Before you, like, blow up and become a star." Hadley spoke quickly.

"That's so cool, Everest. You even have fans in middle school," Beverly said happily and playfully nudged my arm.

"Honey, I didn't know you were on the road to stardom. I

would love to watch you perform," my mother said, giving me her full attention.

"Yeah, me too." Hadley turned to Beverly. "Did he do good tonight?"

Beverly nodded with a modest smile. "He always does good."

She was so cute.

"I want to go," Hadley urged, pulling my attention from Beverly.

Miranda and Victor told me with their body language that they wanted to come too.

I was not a hundred percent comfortable with the idea of them being a part of the audience. Singing was what provided me an escape from the life I knew. The attention the table gave me made my throat turn dry, my skin become itchy, and my hands get clammy.

"You know what I haven't had in a long time? A s'more." Beverly changed the subject.

"That does sound nice. We should make some after dinner," Hadley suggested, which meant it was going to happen. Being the youngest meant she was entitled to get anything she wanted.

For the rest of the dinner, the conversation ranged from college to the best kinds of coffee beans. The dinner was a pleasant one, and I couldn't place why it seemed so much better than all the Sunday dinners prior.

Miranda helped us find the s'more ingredients just before she and Victor headed home. I couldn't believe my mother allowed us to not only make s'mores in the den using the fireplace but to drink hot chocolate in there too.

She even took a cup for herself. At first, she briefly went upstairs to clear her face of all traces of makeup and changed into the cheapest set of pajamas I'd ever seen her in. They looked like she'd picked them up from a discount store. Such a dramatic change from her designer silk garments. Something was different about my mom—she was changing in a good way. She seemed like she was trying to become more approachable and instead of being judgy, she was attempting to be only accepting.

She sat on the couch, snuggled up in a blanket with Hadley up against her arm. I turned on *Home Alone* and the four of us watched it together. It was the first time in my life that I got a glimpse of a future—a future where Beverly and I would come to dinner every Sunday. A future where she was my plus one to every holiday, my mom and sister opening the gifts we got them for Christmas. I wouldn't mind this being my family. Just the four of us. Beverly was half asleep when I nudged her arm for her to get up. It was nice to see her at peace like that. My ray of sunshine was dealing with her own storm. Instead of her being the one to bring positivity to my life, I had taken her role. It made me realize in full all that she had been doing for me.

Before I left the den, my mother sleepily called me over to give her a kiss on the cheek. It wasn't weird like I thought it would be. Our family wasn't one for affection. It made me averse to acts of affection, but I realized now that I needed it. It made me feel loved. Which was something I never thought I would crave.

Beverly and I went outside to get some cool air. The sky was a midnight blue. It was dark but rich, with a velvety blue hue. The silver sparkles in the sky caused Beverly and me to take a moment to admire it.

The way the stars illuminated her skin was breathtaking. Looking at her as intently as I was, every atom in my genetic makeup tried to make sense of her beauty. Everything about her was so very beautiful. I'd never forget a thing about her—not even a single freckle on a face. Her curls swirled through the cool air. The wind carrying tiny frozen crystals and the snowflakes floating past her was a picture only artists could imagine.

She turned to me and watched the snowflakes as they fell from the once-clear sky. Her fascination was that of a toddler seeing a butterfly for the first time.

"It's snowing," she said, an immense amount of happiness dancing around her bright aura.

I love you, I said, but it came out as, "Yup."

33

BEVERLY

"So, did you mount Everest yet? You've been staying at his house for weeks."

The banana smoothie I was currently drinking got caught in the back of my throat. Leave it to Nami to speak so inappropriately in the food court with a bunch of people loitering around. They probably wouldn't catch the underlying message in her words, but still.

"What? Don't act like you weren't wondering too," Nami said to Tiffany after Tiffany hit her in the arm.

When Nami asked me earlier at school if I wanted to go Christmas shopping with her and Tiffany, of course I agreed. I'd never been to the mall with anyone other than my mother before. It was something I had always wanted to experience. Often, I would see a group of friends with lighthouse-bright smiles and bags stacked up on their arms, and I'd think to myself that I wasn't following some kind of protocol.

"Everest and I are *friends*. Friends, just like you and me."

"Oh please, you guys are basically dating. You do everything a couple does besides banging like bunnies. For all I know, you guys are. Which bring me back to my previous question."

This had to have been the hundredth time today she'd made a remark like this. Appalled, I turned to Tiffany. The look she gave me was as if she wanted no part of the conversation. Her teeth were clenched as she slowly shook her head and held her hands out in defense.

"You too?" I laughed in disbelief.

"Being around you guys is the equivalent to watching a Nicholas Sparks movie." Her nose wrinkled.

If only they knew how platonic our relationship actually was. We were just close, that was all. Everest and I cared about each other deeply, but it would be a stretch and outright silly to believe we were a couple. I leaned back in my chair and chuckled at their claims.

"You guys are ridiculous."

"Don't confuse me with you." Tiffany threw a used napkin at me playfully.

"So, you mean to tell me that you guys aren't a couple," Nami stated like she was running an interrogation.

"We are not," I said confidently to the interrogator.

"So, if someone asked you out, you'd go?" Nami's eyes narrowed.

I didn't understand why she was pushing all of this so hard. Being at a loss for words was a typical thing I experienced when being around Nami, but it still caught me off guard.

"Y-Yes . . . I mean, if someone nice came along, I—"

Nami abruptly got up. "I'll be right back," she said, leaving quickly before anyone had a chance to ask where she was going.

I watched as she headed toward the trash can to throw away her drink. Turning my attention back to my own drink, I heard Tiffany mumble, "What is she doing?"

Turning, I saw Nami talking to the smoothie cashier. From her body language, I could tell she wasn't ordering a drink.

What is she up to now? I couldn't help but think.

Tiffany and I watched the interaction between Nami and the boy. His eyes caught mine suddenly, as he abruptly turned his attention from Nami to me. His lips stretched into a smile and he sent a quick charismatic wave my way. Feeling like I'd done something wrong, I quickly turned to my drink. Nami talked to him for a few more long seconds before returning to us.

"What was that about?" Tiffany took the words from my mouth.

Nami began packing up her things. "C'mon, let's go."

"Ooooo-kay." Tiffany drew the word out, obviously just as confused as I was.

I stood up from my chair, feeling strange. I gathered the gifts I had purchased earlier, and the weight of the bags seemed heavier than I had remembered. I trailed behind Tiffany and Nami, who seemed to be busy in conversation. Walking past the smoothie parlor left me feeling tense. When my foot actually crossed over the line that set me past the store, I began to feel my body relax. Just as I was about to catch up, though, I heard a voice.

"Hey!"

Lots of people used that as a way of greeting or getting someone's attention, so I wasn't sure why I knew that call was for me. I didn't know anyone else in the mall, so there shouldn't have been a reason for me to turn around, but I did. I turned around to see smoothie boy coming from behind the counter. I seemed to be frozen, but I was able to turn my head a little to not miss the smug smiles of my friends. The first thing I noticed about smoothie boy was the unruly mess of dark-brown ringlets on his head.

"Hi," I said, my voice sounding foreign to my own ears.

"Hi."

"Hey, sorry . . . if I scared you." He grasped the back of his neck and rubbed it a few times out of nervousness. His smile was warm, like we weren't strangers.

"It's all right," I said, looking anywhere but his face.

"W-Would you like to catch a movie or something on Tuesday?" he blurted out suddenly.

Instantly, he had my full attention.

"That's a random day," I teased.

"Yeah . . . I guess it is, but I'm not working that night after school." He looked a perfect mixture of confused and amused.

"Did Nami put you up to this?" I asked.

His eyes shifted in confusion. "Who?"

"The girl who was just talking to you," I answered, wondering why Nami did this.

"Oh, that's her name." He chuckled in realization. "She noticed me staring at you and told me to make a move. I totally w-wasn't, like, staring at you in, like, a creepy-stalker-I'm-gonna-kill-you kind of way, but in, like, a you're-the-most-beautiful-girl-I've-ever-seen-in-my-life kind of way. I'm not a creepy stalker killer, I promise." His eyes clenched together for moment as if he was bracing himself to get hit in the face by a ball. "I'm sorry . . . I—made this so awkward. I'm just going to g—"

"Yes."

"Y-Yes what?" His eyes widened a fraction of an inch.

"To catching a movie or something."

He grinned. "Okay. Sweet cool. *Here,* give me your arm."

I stuck out my hand slowly while he dug around in his apron and pulled out a pen.

His fingers were cold but he was making my skin hot.

When I caught back up with Tiffany and Nami, their faces were focused on the boy I'd just walked away from. I stared at the numbers scrawled on my arm.

"What just happened?" I thought aloud.

"You just got asked out, Bevy-boo." Tiffany smiled coyly. "How do you feel?"

"I think I have gas," I said after a moment.

"Yikes, we need to get you a date outfit, then I'll drop you off at Everest's," Nami said nonchalantly.

My stomach gurgled.

Nami laughed. "Is this, *perhaps,* a symptom of betrayal?"

"Actually, I think it might be the food we just had. The noodles did look a little old."

On the way home, the date was all I could think about. It was kind of hard to forget when his number was printed on my skin and the constant ramble of my friends never ceased. The whole ordeal was giving me a case of serious gas. Holding it all in for the past ten minutes or so made me basically fly to my room.

"Bye, Beverly!" Tiffany screamed out the window of Nami's car.

"See ya later, Bevy-boo," Nami screamed after her.

I waved while running, my bags swinging violently on my arms. Strangely enough, when I got home, I had no traces of the bubbling gas I'd had in the car. I sighed while dumping the bags on my bed and dumping myself along with it. I was only lying down for what felt like a few seconds before my phone rang.

"How was shopping?" Through the ruckus of the background, I was able to pick out the words.

I melted into his baritone as it gave me instant comfort. "It was nice. You know Nami and Tiff."

"I sure do," he said with emphasis. "What you up to?"

"I'm about to start wrapping." I tore at the wrapping paper and began to cut the appropriate pieces needed to wrap.

"I wish I could help you."

"I can handle it, Ev. Plus, Hadley will be home from dance soon and there's no way she won't want to help." I chuckled, realizing he could hear what I was doing.

"*Everest, you're on in a minute*," I heard someone yell.

"*Okay, all right.*" His tone was annoyed.

"Sorry, Bev, but I have to g—"

"Are you ready for a storm?" I asked, embracing the feelings I got from the phrase.

". . . I stay rain ready," I heard him say after a few seconds. His tone was softer this time.

"Good night, Ev."

"Night, Bev."

Ending the call, I looked at the numbers on my arm, softly touching them and sighing. For a moment, I thought to wash them off without writing them down, but I realized that I had never been on a date before. I could've been possibly washing off an opportunity that could turn out amazing. I wrote the number down and took a shower before heading off to bed.

* * *

It wasn't strange for the gang to join Everest and me at lunch. Sometime after the fall festival, we began to eat together. It was never all at once. Some days it would be Nami and Tiffany. Other days, it would be Mikey and Aurora. There'd been a few occasions when it would be Tiffany and Mikey. The combination was something new every day. Of course, Lincoln and Lucky weren't included, being that one had already graduated and the other lived on the other side of town.

Lunch was my favorite part of school. It was the only time all of us were together. For some unspoken reason, we never spoke in school outside of those library walls. We seemed to dissolve back into the lives we had before we became friends. It seemed pretty silly to me. Today, though, was one of those rare days where we were all together.

"Now, why would you pack a tuna sandwich?" Nami's nose crinkled.

Mikey smiled childishly and opened his mouth to reveal the mush on his tongue.

"Real mature," Tiffany said, setting down the bag of chips she had.

"C'mon, man." Everest shook his head.

"People are eating here," Nami added with a disgusted look.

The typical scene made me smile a little to myself as I bit into my apple.

"Don't worry about what's happening on my plate, focus on your own food," he said to Nami.

"Oh, shut up, Mikey," Nami responded with a roll of her eyes.

"Well, that's rude." He smirked.

"Anyway, Everest, how was your set?" Nami shifted the conversation.

"It was fine," Everest responded, seemingly unbothered.

"So modest," Tiffany said with a sigh.

"I know, right?" I agreed.

"Everest puts on his cool act so he can lure the ladies in," Mikey said with a snort.

"I doubt he needs the act. Girls melt for a guy with a microphone," Nami responded.

"I bet girls throw themselves at him in masses. How many numbers did you collect last night?" Mikey asked.

Everest looked interested as he shrugged.

"*Dang*! That many?" Mikey snickered obnoxiously.

"Beverly got asked out," Nami told everyone abruptly, and I wanted to shrink into my seat. I subconsciously straightened my back.

Everest repeated my actions. "What?"

"Oh yeah, she got asked out on a date," Tiffany continued nonchalantly while she ate, while Everest turned to look at me.

Mikey turned to me. "What did you say?"

My mouth felt like cotton. "I-I didn't say anything."

"To the guy. What did you say to the guy?" Mikey asked while shaking his head.

Their eyes pulled me like magnets. I had their full, undivided attention, and I didn't remember asking for it.

". . . I said yes."

"Who is this guy?" Mikey questioned, like an older-brother figure in the movies.

I didn't know smoothie boy's name. How could I possibly let that slip my mind? I didn't know him from a can of paint, but I could have at least asked what his name was. I wondered if he faced this issue too—he hadn't asked for my name either.

"Nathan," Nami said, saving the day. "Remember?" she urged me and I nodded numbly.

"*Wow*, you don't know his name?" Mikey questioned in disbelief.

"I barely know him." I inwardly cringed.

Nami's hand clasped on my shoulder. "Yeah, but that's what dates are for, right?"

Shrugging her arm off me, I gathered my things, piling any trash I had and preparing to flee the scene.

"Where are you going?" Everest finally broke his silence. He grabbed my jacket to ensure that I wasn't going to leave without answering his question. The table focused on me once more.

"I have to go to Ms. Gregor's class early."

"Why?"

"I promised I'd help hang up art."

"Oh . . . yeah." He let go of my jacket.

"I'll walk you there," he said shortly.

"No, it's all right. Finish your food. I'll see you guys later."

* * *

After the awkward attention I'd got, I was in need of a breather. I left the library in a rush. Somehow, I felt like I'd done something wrong. I wasn't quite sure what that was, but I felt riddled with guilt. I was turning around to see if anyone had followed me when I suddenly bumped into a mass.

"*Ahg.*"

It was Nash. His eyes were puffy and red; he looked as if he'd been crying. Crimson cheeks and a sense of defeat was a look that was a foreign one on him. Sure, everybody cried—it was just too strange to see him like that.

"I'm so s—"

"Watch where you're going." He roughly pushed past me, cutting off my apology.

I watched as he walked in the opposite direction, not saying anything more or anything less.

* * *

"Hey, Betty," Lily greeted me. "Hello, Everest."

"Hey, Lil." Everest spoke for what seemed the first time in forever. After lunch, he'd barely spoken—not when he dropped me off at home after school or twenty minutes prior when he'd picked me up again. Something must have been weighing on his mind.

Everest had a shift that night, so I'd asked if he could drop me off at 21 Daisies. He'd agreed, but something was up with him.

"Hi," I greeted her. Lily had been glowing like a firefly in July these past few days. Her wedding was approaching quickly, and you could see the happiness that floated around her before her big day.

"I hear there's a special occasion," Lucky said from a foot away.

"Beverly is going on a date," Everest responded, walking ahead of me.

"With who?" Lincoln asked next.

"Wait, who told you there's a 'special occasion'?" I asked.

"Tiffany. Now, who is this guy?"

"Some guy named Nathan." Everest was talking more about me than directly to me at this point.

"When is he coming?" Lincoln looked at me with curiosity.

"Any minute."

"Wait, what's happening?" Lucky joined the conversation after coming out of the break room.

"Beverly is going on a date," Lincoln and Everest said at the same time.

I groaned. "Guys, please don't make this a big deal."

"Big deal? I'm calm, cool, and collected," Everest rambled distractedly.

"Beverly." I heard a voice come from behind me.

When I turned, Nathan was there.

"Hi, you look pretty," he said, and heat instantly rushed to my ears.

"What's your name, man?" Lincoln had an expression on his face that I'd never seen before. It was serious. Not only that, but also slightly intimidating.

"Nathan . . ." he answered, looking at me, slightly confused.

"C'mon, Nathan, let's go." I grabbed his arm in an attempt to flee the tense awkwardness of the room.

"Wait, not so fast," Lucky called out.

"Let them go. We have a set to play," I heard Everest say in a bored tone as he headed to the stage.

"Bye, Beverly," Tiffany said with a smile.

Nami chuckled. "Have fun."

* * *

When I climbed into the passenger seat of Nathan's silver Impala, it smelled of strong cologne with a slight funky undertone.

He tapped his fingers on the steering wheel. "Those were your friends?"

My eyes darted to him and then toward the road. "Yeah."

He didn't say anything after that, and for a few awkward min-utes, we sat through the silence. That was until Nathan flicked on the radio and piercing screams came through the speaker.

"Ah!" I screamed before quickly switching the radio off.

Nathan looked at me with an alarmed expression. "What was that for?"

My heart pumped through my ears. "There were screams."

His eyes were focused on the road, but I could see the confusion written all over his face. "Of course there were. It's music."

What.

"That was *not* music." I shook my head.

He glanced at me quickly before chuckling. "Sure, it was. It's screamo.

"Listen." He turned the screaming voices and harsh instru-ment sounds back on and thrashed his head backward then forward, and that was how my ride was all the way to the mall.

When we went into the movie theater, the overwhelming smell of popcorn engulfed me whole. The neon colors of vari-ous signs and arcade games caught my eye while Nathan bought the movie tickets. We didn't get any popcorn or snacks because Nathan figured we didn't want them, even though I did sort of crave the buttery kernels.

"What movie did you chose?" I asked as we walked toward the second ticket booth.

"It's a surprise. Don't worry, though, you're gonna love it."

I didn't love it.

Nathan picked the most gory, bloody, violent movie he could think of. Zombies were being slaughtered in gross detail scene by scene. But that was when I was able to watch the movie, which was kind of hard to do when he talked throughout the flick, about himself mostly.

"I always wanted to dye my hair. What color do you think?" he whispered in my ear. It was a good thing the theater was dark or else his feelings would have been hurt by my annoyed facial expression. I didn't answer his question in hopes he would give up and watch the movie that he paid for. But that only made matters worse.

"*Beverly.*

"*Psst.*"

He sat back and I thought he got over his prodding, but I was wrong. He reached into his pocket to pull out a balled-up gum wrapper to throw at me.

"What?" I turned to him with uncontrollable irritation but immediately felt bad and tried to not sound annoyed again.

"What colo—"

I forced a smile. "Blond."

"No, that's not going to work." He snorted and the person behind us gave him a shush.

Poke.

Poke.

My eyes fluttered opened and I remembered where I was.

"You're missing the climax."

Nathan's eyes were glued to the image projected on the huge screen and I immediately felt bad for falling asleep during a movie that he paid for me to watch. Soon after, the credits rolled and I felt relieved that I was going home soon. It was horrible for me to feel such a way while on a date with a nice person, but I did. I yawned into my hand when I stood from up out of my chair.

"Aw, you're a cutie," Nathan commented after he watched me finish my yawn. "You ready to head to the food court?"

I inwardly sighed when I realized that the date wasn't finished just yet. He looked so excited, and I felt compelled to nod my head to leave for the food court.

"This way, black beauty." A string of cringes swam down my spine.

When we got to the food court, Nathan bought himself a lemonade and some kind of panini. I ordered myself a banana smoothie as usual, but didn't have much of an appetite. He didn't pay for me, but he did give me a discount on the smoothie since he worked there, which was nice.

"My ex-girlfriend hated bananas. She always got the berry-blue smoothies," he said as we took a seat at a nearby table.

"Yeah?" I didn't really know how to respond.

"Yup . . . so, yeah, I think it's cool that you like bananas and stuff." He awkwardly took a bite of his panini, and the overwhelming smell of garlic hit my senses.

I nodded and wondered if something was wrong with me. Dates were supposed to be enjoyable, and all I wanted to do was go home. He was nice and cute, but none of this felt right. I kept waiting for it to get better, but it didn't.

"Did you like the movie?" he asked after a moment.

"It was great. How did you like it?" I asked politely. Zombie movies had never really been my thing, and I fell asleep a few times, but from what I had seen, it was all right—a tad too violent for me, but overall, an average film.

"Trash!" he exclaimed, and I got a huge whiff of the garlic onion panini scent on his breath. "There was no development. No growth. Quite frankly, their use of graphics was insulting—"

I felt like I was being tortured. The smell was so bad but there was nothing that I could do about it. I just sat there, taking hit after hit of his foul-smelling breath. Eventually, I tuned out of his review of the movie before realizing that the corner store in the mall sold mints.

"Beverly?" Nathan waved a hand in my face, pulling me from my thoughts.

I blinked a few times. "Sorry, I'm listening—it's just that my breath smells not that great. Do you mind if I go and get some mints?" I covered my hand with my mouth and began to stand up from my chair.

"Oh no, I need you to have fresh breath. Go get those mints, girl." He winked before folding his arms behind his head.

His response threw me off. It was as if he knew something I didn't. I forced a smile and went to the corner store. I purchased the mints swiftly, not wanting to waste any time. When I arrived at the table, I purposely opened the package in front of him. I tossed a mint in my mouth first before offering him one.

"No, thanks." He grinned and my soul sighed. *How long do dates usually last?* I asked myself in that moment.

As if someone heard my cry for help, an angel was sent to me.

I'm here

My phone buzzed with a message from Everest.

"Didn't you ever hear that it's rude to text while you're on a date?"

"Sorry—actually, that was my ride telling me that they're here. Thank you for taking me out tonight."

"Wait, that's it?" He looked surprised.

I felt bad for how quickly I was leaving.

"Okay, bye. Call me!" I heard him yell across the food court just as I was making my way out of it.

When I got in the car, Everest didn't say anything.

"So, how was it?" he asked when we were a quarter of the way home.

"I don't want to talk about it," I huffed, fighting to not let my words crash past my lips. I did not want to complain about my date, but at the same time, I did.

"Okay," Everest responded, like he didn't care much to begin with.

"He's nice. He's really nice and all, but I mean, he talked through the whole, entire movie. Do you know how hard it is to watch a movie while someone is talking to you? It's impossible. When we went to get food, he ordered this double onion, garlic, and ham panini, right? But refused the mints I offered him. And don't get me started on the fact that he called me black beauty. All I kept thinking about is the horse, Black Beauty, from a book I read years ago."

There was silence is the car before Everest busted out a compressed laugh. He laughed until he was red in the face. It all spilled out, like he was trying once to hold it back for a while.

"It's not funny." My ears turned hot from my sudden outburst.

He wiped his eyes with the hem of his shirt. "It kind of is."

His laughter filled the car once more, as if he'd thought about it again. It was if it had became uncontrollable.

"Stop," I said, while feeling the effects of his laugh. My stomach bubbled up with the fiercest amusement. Eventually, I joined him in the laughing fest. Being with him for just this moment was the most fun I'd had all night. It was easy being with Everest. We could be doing just about anything and I would never be bored.

So while the sky was dark and the only light was coming from the passing buildings, Everest and I laughed like it had been just him and me hanging out that entire night.

34

BEVERLY

There's this omen that has been passed on for years and years that whoever attends Winter Formal with a date will fall in love. It was as if Valentine's Day at Shady Hills Academy came early. I read somewhere once that love was the closest thing to magic, and I thought that was cool, because it meant we all had the potential to experience magic outside of movies and fairy tales. I wondered if Everest knew of this school legend when he asked me to go a couple of weeks ago. But Nami was able to secure the guys a performance at the dance, so that was most likely the reason he was going. It was a hopeless idea, but still I allowed my mind to wander.

I stared in the mirror and glided my finger along my face. My makeup was all right enough, I supposed. I was sure my mother would have something to say about it. I could practically hear her telling me to add more color. *Be bold.* I could feel her fingers sticking into my hair. She'd probably want it as an messy updo rather than a mess around my head. My pale-pink dress was fitted enough, but red would've made me stand out.

"Beverly, everyone is waiting for us." Everest knocked on the door.

I stuffed necessities in my purse in a rush and left. "Okay, let's go. I'm ready."

He was wearing a typical button down and tie, and somehow they outshone formal clothing. That morning I'd woken up early—spent hours getting ready—and it was unfair how he didn't have to do too much to look this good.

"Oh, you both look so nice!" his mother said on our way out the door. "Not so fast, let me get a photo."

We stood out in the yard to pose. Everest pretended that the whole thing annoyed him, but there was a smile hidden on his face. I noticed that Everest and his mom shared the same smile as she snapped the photos with delight. We were posing as if it was prom and not just a school dance. He held my hand, back to chest, and I told myself I was imagining his heart trying to escape. Meanwhile, I couldn't help but wonder where these photos would end up. Would I be a story she would tell her grandchildren as they flipped through albums? Or would they be deleted when I left? I couldn't stay at Everest's house forever.

"Okay, Mom, that's enough." He put his arm around me, and I was pulled instantly from my thoughts.

"Be safe!" she called from the porch as we drove away.

When we arrived at the school, the theme was automatically evident: winter romance. Golds, creams, greens, and some touches of red were everywhere. The decorations were doing their job of making it feel like a winter wonderland, and left me awestruck.

Everest had been to plenty of events, so he didn't understand my interest in everything going on around me. The gym was full of unfamiliar and familiar faces. Each person I saw was dressed to impress, and with a motive of witnessing magic. This time I wasn't all alone as everyone circled around Everest, looking for his attention. I had my own friends. Speaking of which . . .

"There you are!" Tiffany wrapped her arm around me. Nami stood behind her with her arms crossed.

"Oh, shut up, you arrive early to everything," Tiffany said.

We walked to the tables and I didn't miss the *ooohs* and *ahhs* that fell from the lips from just about everyone who was impressed by the decor. The ceilings were high, and Christmas lights hung in the most perfect places. Nami was on the dance committee, but she'd never mentioned how gorgeous the decorations were going to be. It was far better than homecoming. Red and white roses were everywhere in the space. An array of food was on each side of the room, with fruits and cheeses among other little snacks. Beautifully sculpted ice statues made me feel as if I was in a museum. Everest, being the goof that he was, had me take a few pictures of him messing with the statues when Mikey and Aurora approached us.

"Oh, look what we have here," Mikey exclaimed with his arms in the air.

Nami turned to me and sighed. "We really need to get a No Dogs sign."

Mikey laughed. "You know you love me."

"Down, cat. No need to have your claws out," Aurora said. I couldn't help but notice her purple hair was in glossy waves and she wore a red lip.

We found a table, sat down, and chatted. The conversation was always so light and easy with us. Everest had to split away from my arm when it was performance time. The band was playing the dance's first song. I thought their entire set was five numbers—a nice way for him and the guys to play but not have it take up the entire dance.

They'd set up at the far left of the room on a small platform. I watched from my elegantly decorated table how the boys joked and laughed while getting situated on stage. Everest's smooth voice floated through the room. His entire demeanor changed when he sang. He was usually so very calculated, but when he was on stage, he let himself become vulnerable. It was lovely and romantic.

Lucky counted them down and they launched into a version of "What a Wonderful World." I slow danced with the girls without taking my eyes off of him. His own eyes closed as he got really into the song. Everest could sing a song about pudding, and I would probably shed a tear. The chorus was upbeat—slow enough to show the meaning, yet still fast enough to dance to. His voice serenaded everyone in the room, and the music that came from Lucky and Lincoln was the perfect combination.

Everest used the passion of the room to fuel his words. He meant every word he sang and everyone knew it. Everest sang like he was telling the mic all of his secrets. Every time he sang, it was like that, but today was different—maybe the dance was making him into this love song. Lincoln and Lucky bobbed their heads to the beat, and Mikey twirled Aurora gracefully.

His set ended a few tunes later, and the amount of love that was in that room was enough to circle the world twice. Everest got several pats on the back as he made his way toward me.

"I loved it," I told him excitedly.

"Yeah?" he said with a shy smile.

"Yes, you were awesome."

"Do you hear that?" He pointed upward and his nose scrunched.

"Hear what?"

He grabbed my hand as the DJ started up. "Music. C'mon, dance with me."

And that sentence caused us to be on the dance floor for almost two hours. We danced to every single song. We danced, we danced, and we danced. We danced even if we didn't know the song. We danced even if the song was terrible. It was the most fun I'd had since the fall festival. Everest and I were completely and totally lost in each other. About an hour into downing the cider that was being served like water, Nami informed me that it was spiked and that I should slow down. I was feeling terribly hot from all the dancing. Everest looked overheated—his tie was nowhere to be found and his button-down shirt was unbuttoned a little. He strode toward the exit and nudged his head toward the door, summoning me to follow. The room felt so muddled and my mind spun as I followed. The Christmas lights sparkled gold. Everest pulled me outside, his face giddy and a glass of cider in hand.

"You need to slow down with the cider. It's spiked, surprise, surprise," I told him with a laugh, reaching for the glass.

He nudged my hand away and took off his suit jacket, placing it on my shoulders.

"Whatever, Mom." He smiled before taking another sip.

Snowflakes fell gently on his head while he smiled, and I wanted to take a picture. I wanted to doodle this moment in my notebook. I snuggled deep into his jacket; it smelled like a fight between cinnamon and alcohol.

"Having fun?" Everest asked. His lips were dangerously close to my ear, and the warm breath sent a tide of shivers down my spine.

He stood back up to his full height and stared down at me, awaiting my answer. His smile was righteous. Was the sky was black or blue? I couldn't really tell. The Christmas lights sparkled—the only things keeping me from looking right at him.

Not wanting to interrupt the scene or moment, I nodded my head softly, with the least amount of movement possible. Everest looked so pure; he looked as if he transcended the stars. And when his smile reached his eyes, I wondered what I'd done to deserve this. To deserve the pleasure of meeting him. Of knowing him.

"You look really nice," he said suddenly, and I froze. He'd never said I looked nice before, and him giving me a compliment affected me more than I thought it would.

"Shut up." I laughed in disbelief, realizing that he probably was joking. That maybe he didn't mean to say that. I never thought he would ever say such a thing.

"You don't think you look nice?" He moved closer, his breath coming out in puffs of white.

I looked away.

"Well, you don't," he said, laughing. I quickly looked at him, and instantly felt hurt. I knew he wouldn't ever look at me like that. He was drunk—he probably wouldn't remember what he'd said tomorrow. I began to pull off his suit coat to head back inside, before he grabbed my arm.

"You look beautiful," he said, searching my eyes with a breathtaking smile.

I stood shocked and unsure of how to react. His words knocked the air out of my lungs. Those three words did the weirdest thing to my heart. Heat rushed up the side of my neck and I just stood there.

"What would you do if I kissed you?" Suddenly his grip on me shot tingles up my arm. "Would that be okay?" he whispered and took a step closer. My external self stayed still but my heart tried to leave my chest.

I thought about this moment, and how I knew he would prob- ably forget it. But I wouldn't, I would never forget this. If I let this kiss happen, I would be the only one to remember it, and for the first time in my life I selfishly didn't care. There was always a secret part of me that was enamored with Everest. Every part of me wanted him. And although these were new emotions, it didn't feel like it. I should have realized it all along—what I felt for him, how much I cared about him.

Our breath mingled like clouds in the cold December air. The sky was dark and filled with stars. This was too perfect. How could I reject this moment? It was almost as if this was supposed to happen.

I grabbed his dress shirt and pulled his lips to mine. Piece to piece, we were a puzzle, fitting perfectly. I felt it. I felt *everything*. My fingers were no longer numb as my entire body ignited in a sparkling flame. He tasted of cider, and I was drunk. My mind couldn't form thoughts as he gripped my cheek, bringing us closer. His kiss was a paradox. It was urgent but slow; rushed but careful. His tongue gently traced my bottom lip, sending jolts of impulses through my body.

His eyes were still closed, and I couldn't seem to catch my breath.

"Do you know how long I've wanted to do that?" His eyes glittered.

I floated completely out of orbit. I wanted to feel his lips on mine again, again, and again. Because kissing Everest was the closest thing to magic.

So I kissed him again.

35

EVEREST

Confession: I'm so sick . . .

By the time the night after the dance came around, the coughing started. And that annoying little thing happened when one of my nostrils would be stuffed and the other would be clear. I was so sick, man. I didn't even know where it could have come from. For the following few days, I was a vegetable. I stayed in bed buried in sickness, and didn't think about anything. All I did was sleep. My throat was all kinds of sore. My eyelids felt too heavy to be on my face. My nose leaked out of both holes. My body ached and pulsed. My lips felt Sahara-desert dry, but I was too weak to do anything about it. I felt terrible.

Miranda, my mom, and Hadley all took turns tending to me. Usually, when I was sick, I dealt with it by myself. Most people wouldn't even guess that I was sick because I'd try my best to cover it up. So I wasn't exactly used to the treatment that I was getting. Miranda fixed my pillows, heated up tea, and brought this Antarctica-type water that was just the best thing on planet Earth. Hadley showed me pictures of the Christmas decorations around the house because I hadn't had the chance to see them. She was so happy to show me everything and just be around me. She was in my room the most, just watching movies or reading. I enjoyed her company more than I thought I would.

Sleep, sleep, and more sleep. I would wake up and it would be a new day. On the third day of me being sick, and probably the hundredth time where I woke up randomly, it was Christmas morning. My mom and Miranda helped me down the stairs so I could watch Hadley open up her gifts. It felt so good not to be in bed anymore. My bones felt like they were made out of popsicle sticks, and I felt grimy despite taking a shower the night before. But my overall mood was good. I so desperately wanted to pull Beverly aside during the opening of gifts so we could talk about Winter Formal, but she wasn't meeting my eye. The tree had so many presents underneath it that I figured the presents were being used as a stand to keep the tree up.

Hadley received dancing gear, clothes, a vintage pink bike and some other things that I couldn't remember. Luckily, I'd got my sister a care package stuffed with her favorite things before I got sick: chocolate-covered pretzels, a gift card to a local pizza place, Disney movies, and a gold necklace in the shape of a flower. My parents got me some expensive preppy clothing, like what I used to wear before, and a watch that probably cost more than my car. I kind of fell asleep at one point during the gift opening, and when I finally woke up, I was in my bed. I rolled over to switch positions and that was when I saw her. When did she come up?

Beverly was asleep with a box of tissues, vapor rub, and a blanket wrapped around her in the chair beside my bed. Her hair was frizzy underneath a knitted gray beanie, and her nose and cheeks were tinged a orangey pinkish color. She wore a red sweater and gray sweatpants with bright-yellow fuzzy socks.

"Oh, you're up. I was just bringing some tea for the both of you. Whatever you have, she has it too," my mother sighed sweetly. "Beverly, honey, I have some toast and tea for you." She spoke softly, and placed the tray on my nightstand with the rest of the supplies.

Beverly's dark-brown eyes fluttered opened slowly. "Thank you," she replied, her voice hoarse but sweet.

"Merry Christmas." I smiled, genuinely happy to see her, and despite the elephant in the room.

She looked at me and had that familiar softness in her eyes. "M—"—she broke into a coughing fit—"—erry." Then the series of sneezes began. "Christma—" She weakly held up a finger as she blew her nose.

I laughed before coughing myself.

"At least you two sick puppies have each other," my mother said with a shake of her head before leaving.

Beverly moved to sit up in the recliner, looking uncomfortable. At the sight of that, I lifted my covers and gestured to the space beside me. I didn't even have to say anything before she slowly worked her way out of the chair and into my bed. Even though I had just woken up, we both fell asleep after that. Her being close to me made me feel better.

I noticed when I woke back up that at some point we'd separated, probably because it got too hot. Her hat was no longer on her head, and she'd changed out of her sweater, which left her in a tank top. It was strange to have her so close again.

When my lips touched hers at the dance, it felt like anything was possible. For a moment, it gave me the courage to believe I deserved to be happy, and I knew for that moment, everything was going to be okay.

"I know you're awake," she said in a nasally voice. And even though her back was to me, I knew her eyes were closed.

I stayed silent until she turned around to check if I really was awake.

"Oh." She chuckled. "I knew I was right."

She looked terribly beautiful even when she was as sick as a dog.

"I'm sorry," she said, as if the words were in a hurry to come out of her mouth before she was ready for them to.

"For what?" I leaned on my elbow to sit up.

That moment felt like forever. Waiting for her to answer my question was the most anxiety ridden thing that I could have done. A new symptom rose in that moment—nausea. My stomach was wrecked at the thought that this could end terribly. Essentially, I was putting our friendship on the line, and I would hate myself if I ruined it. But at the same time, I would hate myself if I didn't push for something more. Life was too short.

Beverly made me feel things that I'd never felt before. No one talked to me the way she did, and no one looked at me the way she did. And that night at Winter Formal, I realized that no one had ever kissed me the way she did. After we kissed, I saw those pretty little blue birds spin around my head like they did in the cartoons. It was all so fast. The dancing, the kissing, the running away.

"I feel bad about it, honestly. You were drinking and weren't aware of what you were doing—"

"I knew what I was doing," I said.

"But you were drunk."

"I wasn't drinking that much, Bev. I actually wanted to kiss you, but you beat me to it."

I didn't know why all of this was coming out so easily, not when it had been so difficult before. She wasn't looking at me—probably too nervous to. But her lips twitched in a closed-mouth smile. It immediately soothed my concerns.

"*You* wanted to kiss *me*," she said slowly, as if she was trying to process it in her mind.

"That is correct," I said. "I really like you."

She let out a series of coughs. "I really like you too."

My heart did a backflip before I realized that she probably took that with face value. "No, Bev . . . I like *like* you."

She scoffed with a laugh. "I knew what you meant the first time."

"I wasn't sure," I laughed before sneezing.

"Wow." She chuckled while leaning over the side of my bed.

"What are you doing?" My mood was amplified by a thousand. I felt like a giddy little schoolkid. She leaned back up with a small little black box. "Marriage already?"

"Shush it." She smiled and pushed me playfully.

I observed that the little black cardboard box was tied with a red ribbon. I didn't even know what it was, but I knew that I loved it.

"Now, *you* shush it." I threw her words back at her before opening the box to see a guitar pick. It was dark blue and had my name painted in gold cursive on each side. The gift wasn't expensive by any means. It was cheap, but it was irreplaceable. I loved how personal it was, considering that I didn't have many things that had sentimental value.

Not thinking, I leaned over and kissed her on the lips. "Thank you."

Seemingly not expecting that, her eyes cast downward and her breathing picked up noticeably.

"That's going to take some getting used to," I said, staring at her while she stared at her lap.

"Yeah," she breathed out with a laugh.

I gathered enough energy to climb out of bed to get her gift out of my closet. I grabbed the red and gold gift-wrapped box and sat it on my bed before getting back under the covers.

"Oh, Everest, you didn't have to," she said, looking at the size of the box.

"I know," I scoffed.

She rolled her eyes before tearing the box open. Inside there was a new phone, a paintbrush necklace, and a camera. Her eyes practically glittered with stars. "Oh wow . . . oh my gosh. T-This is the nicest thing. How much did you spend on all this?"

"It doesn't matter."

She shook her head in awe of her gifts. "I'm going to get you something nicer, okay?"

"Anything else would be a downgrade." I waved her off, meaning it.

"Wow." She acted as if this was too much. I didn't even spend that much money.

"You needed a new phone, the necklace is so you can have something to remember me by when you're in college, and the camera . . . well, you're always talking about how you wish you could take pictures of things." Shortly after my explanation, I sneezed. "I forgot how awful I was feeling for a minute."

"To be honest, same," she said, with a mix of a laugh and a cough.

I picked up the TV remote sitting on my nightstand and turned on my Christmas movie playlist. "Let's just take it easy and get some more rest."

"Everest."

When I turned my head to look at her, she gave me a peck on the lips. "Thank you."

I couldn't help but smile. "Yep, definitely going to take some getting used to."

She laughed before snuggling up against me. We watched many movies that night, and, although I was the sickest I'd ever been, it was the best Christmas I ever had.

* * *

A few days after being sick beyond comprehension, we decided to go out on a little date. I was partial to just staying in and pretending I was unwell so my parents could let us stay in the same room, but Beverly really wanted to go out, and that managed to get us on track with our plans. If it was up to me, I'd have just stayed with her in at my house until I had to leave. But she was way too enthusiastic about ice skating. Hopefully, I wouldn't fall too much.

When we arrived at the rink, I tried to convince Beverly that it wasn't as complicated at it looked. She'd never gone skating before, and she did have a track record of being clumsy, but I did my best to assure her that it was all going to be fine. She hung on to the wall for a while before I coaxed her onto the ice and let her hang on to me.

"Just let go," I said, laughing. "It's fine."

Thud.

That's gotta hurt.

"Why did I agree to do this?" Beverly groaned, sprawled on the ice.

"Are you all right?" I asked before helping her up.

"I am, but my butt might have a different answer," she grumbled, rubbing at the poor thing. I instantly felt bad for not catching her in time before she crashed into the ice. It happened too fast. I wasn't the best ice skater myself, so we probably would have both went down.

"Dear Bev's booty, are you oka—" I began to say with a smirk.

"Stop it!" She laughed and tried to hit me, and almost lost her balance before I actually caught her this time.

"Okay, I think my girl has had enough," I chuckled. In the past forty minutes she'd done nothing but fall flat on the ice. It was like a fawn walking for the first time, all spread-legged and wobbly.

"You sure? We've got approximately an hour and a half before you have to leave me. What do you want to do?" she asked after glancing up from her watch.

I didn't want to leave her. I never did. I really wished she would come with me to my set, but she had to study for her finals with Nami and Tiffany. Although she'd already committed to a school, she didn't see that as a reason to stop studying. She'd always been focused on her grades. I couldn't remember how many times she had tried to get me to do my work. She always made sure to motivate me any way she could, so I tried to do the same. I made a point to help her any chance I got, which wasn't often. It wasn't like she needed my help, though.

"Hot chocolate?" I suggested, remembering she'd asked me a question.

"A man after my own heart." She grinned, and the ice beneath my feet melted a bit.

We found a nice little restaurant on the other side of the ice rink. The warm air hit my cheeks and wrapped me up whole. The walls were covered in the same boring red plaid I wore. Beverly chose a table by the window, the bright white snow matching the sweater she wore. We sat across from one another, catching each other's eyes and holding the gaze—an unintentional staring contest with no rules.

"Stop," she said with a smile.

"You don't like when I look at you?" I sat back and furrowed my brows.

"Not like that."

"Like what?"

"Like *that*."

"I can't help it."

She's so beautiful, repeated in my head as she stared at me and I stared at her. We were so preoccupied with just staring at each other and smiling that the waitress had to break my trance from my favorite brown-eyed girl. I ordered two cups of hot chocolate with whipped cream, along with grilled cheese sandwiches.

"What rhymes with pit?" I asked once the food arrived.

She thought for a moment. "Spit."

"Nasty, I like it," I marveled before I pulled my little notebook and pen out of my coat. "Let's keep going.

"Flame?" I asked, focused on the page.

"Game," she responded, after taking a sip from her hot chocolate.

"Heaven," I stated and she followed suit.

"Sin." She watched as I scribbled in the little notebook.

It knocks your insides out to a desolate pit
spits on your dreams
and put it in flames
A game rigged so you won't win
an illusion of rain
falls from your pain
while sadness overhangs
Pray to the heavens
to erase these sins

"Did you just come up with that?" she asked, shocked.

"Yeah," I said, biting into my sandwich. "What do you think?"

"Intense."

"But is it good?" I began to feel myself tense up from the thought that it wasn't perfect. Even though I hated that word, the ghost of perfection still haunted me.

Her eyes widened. "Yes, Ev, it's amazing. You know you are so talented."

She reached out and grabbed my hand, instantly soothing my nerves.

"I've just been on edge lately. The guys and I have been gaining more and more traction the more gigs we play, and I just don't want to screw this up. I don't want us to fail."

I was both the happiest and the most distraught I'd ever been in my entire life. I was so happy and proud of the things I'd accomplished and the people I'd met. I was happy for finding my passion and following my dreams. I was so happy for experiencing love—actual, obnoxious marry-me-right-now-soul-consuming love. I was happy because I was closer to my mom and I was closer to my sister. I was just so fucking happy.

But day by day, I was growing more torn by my happiness because I was realizing that it had a price—the increasing popularity of the band forced me to want to be the best. I couldn't fail. I wouldn't fail. My dream was right in front of me and I refused to ignore it. I was practicing any chance I got. I'd play any gig available. I wouldn't sleep until I wrote a lyric, melody, or song. I was hungry to succeed and I didn't want to starve.

I just didn't know how to break the news to Beverly that I was leaving on tour soon. The girl who started my story couldn't stay for all of my chapters. I tried not to think about that, but it was so hard not to. When I got the news a week ago confirming the deal, I put off telling her. I shouldn't have done that, because that only made things worse. The time for me to leave just kept getting closer and closer.

"Don't think like that, okay? There's no such thing as failure, only a lesson learned. You should be nothing but proud that you're making money doing something you love," she said while playing with my hands.

Saying nothing, I reached out and kissed her knuckles. Her words were the best at distracting me from my negativity.

"Excuse me?" A guy with blond hair and a green hat approached the side of the table. "Can I take a picture with you?"

Would you look at that, her eyes and grin said from the corner of my eye.

"Here, I'll take the picture." Beverly reached out and took the camera from the guy. Her smile could be seen from Jupiter.

"Sa-a-y che-e-esecake." She goofed around like she was the one in front the camera. Her smile instantly awakened my own.

When he left, Beverly could barely contain her chuckle as she took a sip of her hot chocolate. Her warm eyes and soft smile were a haunting reminder that we only had a few of these moments left. Guilt pinged my chest and I felt sick to my stomach.

"Bev . . ."

"Hm?" she hummed in response while taking another sip of her hot chocolate.

My heart clogged my ears and my eyes couldn't stare into hers. What if this ruined everything? We'd only shared a few weeks after confessing our feelings for each other. That wasn't enough. What if she wanted nothing to do with me after I told her? These were questions that ate me up every single time I tried to gain the courage to tell her.

"Are you excited for your birthday party?" I asked nonchalantly, sitting back in my chair while my heart boiled beneath my ribs.

You're a terrible person.

"I'm not having a birthday party?" Confusion was written on her face as she bit into her grilled cheese.

"On the contrary, I'm throwing you one."

Her eyes widened.

This doesn't make up for the fact that you're going to break her heart.

"You don't have to do that, Ev. I'm used to not doing much on my birthday. I'd be happy just to eat a cupcake and read a good book."

"Yeah, I don't doubt that, but this is your *eighteenth* birthday and that's a big one. We, as humans, only get a handful of big ones. And yours is coming up in a few days and it shall be celebrated."

"Okay," she laughed. "What are the details?"

"Seven o'clock at 21 Daisies on January 20—you know, your birthday. It's later because unfortunately I have a show. I'll be a little late, but I'll be there."

"Sounds good," she smiled.

"You excited?" I asked.

"Yes," she chuckled, and for the first time since I met her I wished I hadn't heard her happy response.

That feeling didn't come often. I loved hanging out with Beverly, and all of the group, and it made me sad to think that we'd part ways after this year. I wished we'd been friends sooner, that I'd known what real friends were before now. That I'd had Beverly, and Lincoln, and Mikey, and Nami, and all of them in my corner before. Before I was sad. Before I was depressed. Maybe things would have turned out differently, but without any of that, I never would have met any of them. Life was funny that way. This senior year was flying by faster than I thought that it would. I just wished I had more time.

36

BEVERLY

It was bittersweet to return to school after the holidays. It was sweeter than the ripening of strawberries in a garden, solely because I'd missed my friends. I hadn't seen much of them during the winter break, and I wanted to see if their time off was as magical and memorable as mine. I basically spent the whole time with Everest. I was completely in love for the first time and it was more beautiful than birds flying together in harmony, waking up to the first snow of winter, following your dreams and passions, the colors of the sunset, or even my favorite—a down-pouring rain. And that was why returning to school was so bitter. I didn't want the special time with Everest to end. He was out of town for the weekend for music gigs, but we video-chatted every night that he was gone, sometimes not going to bed until four in the morning, which was probably the reason why I overslept on the first day back. I anxiously got ready for school and called an Uber so I wouldn't be late.

"So, I know you didn't just walk past me without saying anything." Tiffany suddenly wrapped her arm around my shoulders on my way to lunch.

"Ah! I didn't see you!" I exclaimed in pleasant surprise, before squeezing her to bits. She looked cute today with her oversized brown leather jacket and silver rings stacked on her fingers.

"I'm so glad you're feeling better. I haven't seen my girl in too long," she said after we released one another from the hug.

"I know right? *Ugh*. Don't even remind me, I'll have flashbacks." I shuddered upon remembering the awful illness that Everest and I'd had. It was only bearable because the only person who was allowed to be near me was Everest and vice versa.

"Where's Nami?" I asked, trying to clear my thoughts of Everest.

"She's already in the library. Her fat ass couldn't wait," Tiffany said, lowering her voice so no one but me could hear.

"Mikey here today?" I asked, once we got into the line.

"Alive? That's if Nami didn't kill him in the library, but surprisingly, he showed up."

I laughed, and felt somewhat giddy that I was going to see almost all of my friends. Once we collected our food, Tiffany and I slyly left the cafeteria, but it wasn't easy. People were particularly chatty today. I got invited by three different people to have lunch with them, something that had never happened before. Even Tiffany got captured a few times by a few chatty people. It made me wonder if I should start packing my lunches or else I'd probably never make it out of the cafeteria.

When we were finally able to get to the library, my heart filled with helium and tried to float away at the sight of Everest sitting at our usual oak table. When he saw me, he instantly stood from his chair and rushed in my direction.

"Everest." I couldn't say his name without smiling. It was like an automatic trigger at this point. I couldn't fight it if I wanted to.

He came so close, with the intent to kiss me swirling around in his more green than blue eyes, before something flicked in them, and he stopped himself from getting too close, an almost embarrassed look etched on his features. And that was when I realized that everyone was staring at us.

Yikes.

Everest and I hadn't talked about exactly what our relationship was, or better yet, if we were going to go public with it. So, finally being in this situation made us both unsure of how to act.

"Hey," he said after clearing his throat, his stance totally awkward. He ended up giving me a cautious one-armed hug. He was rarely nervous, so seeing him act like that made me nervous.

"Hi," I squeaked and took my seat, my tray slamming unnecessarily loudly on the table.

"Hey, Nami," I said after I winced.

"Nuh-uh, what the hell was that?" She furrowed her thick brows, one hand holding an applesauce cup and the other a tiny spoon.

"What?" Everest asked with a bored tone, hugging Tiffany.

"Since when do you guys greet each other like that?" Nami snorted.

"Like what?" I asked, trying to ignore my heartbeat thumping in my chest.

Did she know?

"Like some weirdos," Tiffany added.

Just then the library doors swung open and Mikey walked through. "The gang's back together again."

His grin almost lightened up my tenseness. "Switch seats with me, Bev. I like the other side better."

He gestured to the empty chair next to Everest.

Everest suddenly became interested in his phone, most likely so that he wouldn't have to look at me or anyone else. I wasn't sure why, though, he was pretty good at hiding his emotions.

"Thanks, but I'm fine here." I forced a smile.

Mikey looked confused and then at Nami. "What's up with them?"

"Nothing," Everest and I said at the same time. Our eyes met and we both knew it made things look worse.

"What happened with you two?" Tiffany narrowed her eyes.

"We're fine-e-e." I laughed. "Stop being silly. How was break for you guys?"

My attempt to switch the conversation actually turned out to be successful. At some point while listening to how everyone spent their break, I zoned out completely. Everest became my only line of focus. It happened several times, not lasting more than probably five measly seconds. His energy was just so contagious and I was defenseless against getting pulled into his essence.

It was like he was unaware of the power he possessed—the power to draw me right in. His errant mess of faded black waves that turned an earthy brown when the light hit them just right. Unruly thick eyebrows that jutted in every which direction. That little scar he'd got when he was eight after falling off his bike, which was practically unnoticeable to the untrained eye, but that I'd traced enough times to find on his face from afar. His thick bed of lashes that I would probably only have in my dreams. Summer afternoon grass-green eyes that made me feel like I was burning up in the middle of January. My eyes scanned down to his pink lips, much smaller than mine, but softer than the kiss of a butterfly. Just thinking about his kiss made me uncomfortable in my skin. A wave of scorching-hot passion slithered beneath my skin and bones.

"Bev?" It was then I realized that Everest was talking to me.

The slither vanished in a rush, and I took a deep breath from the intensity. I cleared my throat. "Yes?"

Too high pitched.

I cleared my throat again. "Yes?"

Better.

"I have to leave early for my gig. Walk me to my car?" His eyes danced with amusement.

Too embarrassed to say anything, I nodded and gathered my things. Saying my see ya laters, I rushed to the door. Everest followed me, his aura swirling around me.

When we left the library doors and were in the desolate halls, he grabbed my hand, a slither of warmth wrapping up my arm like a sensual serpent. We didn't speak a word until we entered the parking lot.

"I thought you were out of town for another week?" It took me a second to get that out. The unforgiving winter aided in frosting down the heat brewing in me. I expected to be colder, but I wasn't.

"Had free time. I thought I'd come and surprise you." His hand played with my fingers.

"When do you go back on the road?" I shivered not from the cold, but from when his lips grazed my knuckles. It was insane how quickly the guys' popularity had been growing. From local festivals to weddings, they were booked and busy. They were constantly playing in the city, and had made a name for themselves. Life had such a funny way of working out.

"Tomorrow," he said. "But Felix and Lily are coming back from their honeymoon, so we're having a little party at 21 Daisies."

"We?" I raised a brow.

A passing grin flashed on his lips. "I'm picking you up at six. The whole gang is going to be there."

"Lucky and Lincoln too? I haven't seen them in a while."

"Unfortunately, I see way too much of them. Do you know how bad a tour van can smell? You never want to. You just don't."

I swiped at his chest, and he grabbed my other wrist. My heart manifested into a hummingbird when he gently pulled my arms to lace around his neck, bringing my face closer to his. His arms found their home around my waist. "I miss you."

Not past tense. Actively in the moment. I understood because I felt the same way. My missing him didn't flee or pass. I missed him when I was with him. That was how deep my roots were.

"I miss you," I responded, avoiding his gaze because I felt guilty for staring at him so much in the library. He was never at school anymore. Over the weekend he told me that he was going to sign up for online school for this last semester due to his now-busy schedule. It made me sad, but I didn't show it. I needed to be supportive of his dreams, even if it meant seeing him less.

From outside the building I heard the bell ring. "I have to go."

I made no attempts to leave, though, and neither did he. Instead, he pretty much did the opposite when he pulled me into a hug.

For the rest of the day, I endured the people in my remaining classes asking me a million and one questions. Someone had spotted Everest, and that fed the frenzy even more so than before. They asked if he was dropping out of school, if he was my prom date, if I had met any celebrities. It was honestly getting out of hand. Leaving school was harder because all of my friends were busy. Mikey had already left to do some business, Nami was doing some fundraiser work, and Tiffany had choir practice.

* * *

I was two steps in the door at 21 Daisies when Lincoln and Lucky wrapped me in a surprise constricting group hug.

"Awwww—I can't bre—" They released me so that I could get a gasping breath.

"Where have you guys been?" Poppy's hand was on her hip.

"Sorry, I lost track of time." I truly had. I had been studying for the longest while. Everest had told me six o'clock, but we ended up being an hour late.

"It's okay, I'm just glad you made it." Felix grinned.

I looked around the café. Blue and white banners hung from the ceiling. Treats that were once in the display cases were now on a table laid out for the guests. I saw my group of friends sitting on the red couch—a favorite of ours. Some recognizable and unrecognizable faces. Gold balloons spilled onto the floor. Everest had already stepped on two.

"You know there's balloons that come with helium, right?" he said amusedly,

"Lincoln was on balloon duty," Lucky explained, "so you know how that went."

"What's wrong with it?" Lincoln looked genuinely confused, which made the situation all that much more funny.

When we arrived at the red couch, it looked like all the fun and games had already began. They were playing some card game and from the look of Nami and Mikey, it looked to be very intense. Turns out the game was Spades, and I had no clue how to play. Everest taught me, sharing the same set of cards because I was in training. To be frank, I still didn't understand, but any chance to sit close to Everest and have the occasional touch of his hands made it worth it. Every contact we made surged that warmth that had occurred earlier today. It affected Everest too. His chest rose and fell a bit more than it had the minutes before. His eyes would flick to mine and would linger a bit too long. But he was always good at concealing his true feelings. I couldn't imagine how much concentration it took to experience this and play a card game.

"We need more drinks. Would you mind getting some more from the back?" Rose asked me, well into the third game.

I glanced at Everest before looking back at her. "Yeah, sure."

Inside the back room, my back was to the door. It was no bigger than a walk-in closet. Boxes sat on shelves of miscellaneous things. I ran a hand over my hair and took a deep breath. I had never experienced anything like this before. This *warmth*. It only came when I was physically around Everest. My face felt flushed before I began to look for the drinks. To my surprise, the door opened and Everest walked in.

"Need help?" He walked right up behind me. I could feel him without there even being touch. It was just that energy of his that clung to mine like a fly to a web, engulfing me whole, and the more I tried to fight or ignore it, the stronger it became.

"Sorry for taking so long. I was just—" His hand touched my waist, sending pulses down my side. When I turned around, my breath caught in my throat at our closeness.

"Oh, hi," I stupidly said—it was just the first thing that came to mind.

He grinned mischievously at my words, though. Taking my hands, he grazed my knuckles against his lips, and then laced my fingers around his neck, like he had done earlier.

"Hello." His voice was husky, practically a whisper. The grip on my waist tightened as he pulled me flush against him. My heart could be heard a mile away, warmth increasing and covering every square inch of my body. His head ducked low, and when his breath hit my neck, I shivered.

He paused before saying, "Remember when we were staring at each other in the library?"

His lips met my neck again, and I thought my body would catch on fire right then and there.

"Yeah."

"I wanted you too." I didn't even see it coming. It was as if I had no control over my body. I didn't know what was happening, but I also knew I didn't want it to stop. The intensity of his lips on my neck caused my thoughts and head to go all fuzzy. I wanted his lips on mine. For him to do what he was doing to my neck to my lips. I tangled my hands in his hair.

He pulled back and stars glittered and glimmered in his eyes. "*God*, you're so beautiful."

Electricity shot through me as my body reacted to his words. As if reading my mind, his lips hovered over mine. "I've been wanting to do this all damn day."

His lips lightly bumped against mine as he spoke. Not being able to stand it, I made the first move, our lips passionately crashing into each other. This intensity was nothing like the kisses we'd shared before. It wasn't laced with magic and softness. It was desperate and needy. He kissed me deeply. My lips told his how much I needed him. His lips told me the same. We kissed like it necessary for us to live.

"Oh goodness," I heard from behind, and I separated myself quickly.

My friends were all standing in the doorway with shocked looks on their faces.

"I knew it." Nami stared at me lovingly, and held a hand over her heart.

"What is wrong with you?" Everest snorted.

"It worked," she laughed. "I knew it would work."

My ears suddenly warmed up, and I felt myself sinking farther into the wall.

"You knew *what* would work?" Everest asked sounding confused.

"I set Beverly up on that awful date so you two would stop being stupid and get together," Nami said nonchalantly, seeming to calm down from her outburst.

"Wait, what? You set me up on an awful date on purpose?" I asked, shocked. I stepped from behind Everest.

"This is too much." Tiffany couldn't contain her smile.

"Well, yeah, Nathan owed me a favor. If it makes you feel better, he said he wished he could have been himself."

"I wish I could say I'm surprised, but I'm not," Mikey said to Nami, his grin not going anywhere.

"I don't know what to say." I was equally stunned.

"Oh, it's okay, you're welcome, Bevy." Nami beamed. "So when did it happen?"

"I don't know what you're talking about." Everest smirked.

"Oh c'mon," Tiffany groaned. "You're no fun."

I'd like to say that the conversation was dropped, but not exactly. The gang managed to wiggle more snide comments to get more out of Everest and me, but we didn't deny or confirm. I followed Everest's lead. Maybe he wasn't ready to take us public yet. I didn't mind, though. The rest of the night we drank and laughed. It was a day of awakening, A day of returning to my not-so-normal life. But whose day was normal anyway?

37

EVEREST

Confession: you showed me the beauty but I can't seem to hold up my end of the deal.

—*EF, January 14, 2019*

"I can't believe people actually say pop instead of soda," I said in response to Beverly ordering a Coke. She giggled in my lap, and I pulled her a bit closer, my head snuggling into the crook of her neck. I missed her. I'd been practicing with the boys nonstop. Coming to 21 Daisies and chilling with my friends was exactly what I needed to distract me from obsessing over music.

"Get with the culture or leave," Tiffany said from across the table. Lincoln was almost falling asleep at her side. No wonder it was so quiet in here.

"It just doesn't make sense though," I argued after sitting up, just as Lucky and I made eye contact. His expression told me that he supported my stance on the matter.

"You can't move to a small town and expect things to make sense." Nami, as always, had her two cents to add.

"Touché."

"Oh! Everest did you hear what Cara did?" Tiffany perked up like she'd just remembered.

"I. Almost. Forgot." Nami slapped her hand on the table to every syllable of her sentence.

"What now?" I sighed. It could be anything.

"She changed her party date to Beverly's."

They looked amused but I didn't find it funny. It was a deliberate move for sure. Cara's birthday was a whole two weeks after Beverly's. So why would she plan it so early? Surely because the attention wasn't on her. I shrugged in response.

"What's the big deal?" Beverly responded, her innocence gleaming.

"How do you not see that it's disrespectful? There was word of your party around school and she couldn't handle her party not being the topic of discussion. She made a power move, but good thing you have me on your team." Nami grinned, proud of herself.

"I'm scared to even know what that means." Lucky spoke for all of us.

"Nami what did you do?"

"I invited everyone to Beverly's party," she said with no remorse.

"You did what?" Beverly asked, looking nervous.

"Who's everyone?" Of course she invited everyone. I told her to invite some of the people whom Beverly approved, which wasn't a lot of people. Now the whole school thought they could drop by.

"When she meant everyone, she meant everyone. Don't be too shook when Mrs. Anderson drops by looking for a plate of cake," Tiffany confirmed.

Mikey laughed obnoxiously at that. "Man, screw her. She failed me last year."

I groaned. "I'm not trying to clean up after that many people."

"I'll help clean," Nami said quickly. "I have connections that will do the job. If that's the price to pay, it'll get done. Don't worry about it."

"Are you okay with this?" I asked Beverly directly. It was her party.

"Think about the gifts," Lincoln said.

"Yeah, we could charge people at the door and make a little bit of cash." Mikey grinned mischievously. Money was always on his mind.

"No, that's not necessary. I never had a party with more than four people, myself included. I kinda want to see what that's like," Beverly responded.

"You sure?" I asked. It didn't really seem like a good idea, but if that was what she wanted, then that was what she would get.

"I'm sure."

We left the café shortly after that. When we got back to my house, I let her go first, in the off chance that anyone was awake. My mom had already mentioned how much she disliked me being in Beverly's room for long periods of time, so I decided to try a new approach, but the house was quiet. I felt safe enough to follow closely behind to her bedroom. It was not in my interests to piss off my parents if I wanted to still have Beverly around here.

Sneaking into her room was the best way to play it safe.

"What do you want for your birthday?" I asked through my exhaustion, as I plopped on her bed. I'd already got her gifts; I was just curious about what she actually wanted.

She leaned up and softly kissed my jaw. "I don't want you to spend your money on me, Everest."

"It's entirely way too late for that." I ran my hand down her back, landing it on her waist and marveling in the comfort of her body next to mine. "Plus, who else am I going to spend it on?"

"Nami called you my sugar daddy last week . . . I don't like that."

I couldn't help but laugh.

"Stop it, it's not funny," she said sternly, but it was so sweet I couldn't take it seriously.

"Okay, sugar baby." I kissed the crook of her neck.

"Everest!" She tried to push me away from her, but our inter-twined legs stopped that from happening. I covered her mouth with my hand after her outburst. I couldn't have her blow our cover after we'd just snuck in.

"Don't listen to Nami, Bev. She just likes teasing." I rubbed my thumb softly into her lower back, and watched how she closed her eyes.

"Yeah," she responded in a sleepy sigh. I checked the clock and it read 11:46. "Happy birthday."

She opened her right eye to glance at the alarm clock on the nightstand beside us. "Not yet." Her grin was amused.

"I wanted to be the first." She chuckled at my words. "I also don't think I can make it to twelve. I'm exhausted."

Her hand reached out to softly trace my face, something she knew made me instantly tired. She traced every corner and every inch of my face. She traced my lips before pecking them. I would die happily if I died right now.

"You asleep? My lil' sunflower," I heard her ask but didn't respond. Was I asleep? I didn't want to wake up if I was.

She snuggled against me and rested her hand on the side of my face. "Good night, Ev."

When I woke up, Beverly was still cuddled up against me, her head snuggled into my neck and our legs in a tangled mess. It wasn't easy getting out of her grasp without waking her up, but I did it. After freshening up, I grabbed her bags of gifts from my car and hoped that by the time I got back to the room she'd still be asleep. Miranda raised her eyebrows when I left Beverly's room, but didn't say anything. Thankfully, Beverly was still asleep. Her position had changed, though—she took advantage of me not taking up so much space and spread out her arms and legs, selfishly hoarding all of the space on the bed.

"Bev." I found a small space to sit on the bed.

She made no move to wake up, so I had to take a different approach. I began to kiss her all over her face; when I reached her neck, her big brown eyes fluttered opened.

"Happy birthday." She looked confused before she smiled and laced her arms around my neck. She hugged me while she stretched. Her head nuzzled into mine. Sitting up, she rubbed her eyes. I already missed the brief hug she gave me.

"What's that?" she said, probably from hearing the bag crinkle in my hands when she hugged me.

"Nothing much," I said nonchalantly, as she eyed me knowingly.

The first gift she pulled out was a designer purse set my mom helped me pick out. I noticed how she never carried a purse, just an old, peeling book bag. The bigger bag came with smaller ones inside or something like that. I had put a couple of bills in the wallet for luck. I was worried she'd hate it, but the smile on her face told me otherwise. The next gift was a fresh new pair of sneakers. She told me straight after that she preferred hers looking worn.

"You can dirty up another pair now," I told her while she smiled in response.

"Thank you, Ev." She pulled back and stared at me with admiration.

"You're welcome, Bev." She was too happy. There was no way I was going to tell her the news and break this happiness. It would be cruel to do so. After she opened her other smaller gifts, she got ready for school. I threw on a sweat suit and beanie because I had to get ready later in the day anyway.

Straight after dropping Beverly off at school, I went to 21 Daisies. I only had a bit of time to get everything set up the way I wanted it to be. Nami even dropped in during her free hour to help out.

"Thanks for dropping by," I told her just as she was leaving.

"I did this for Beverly, not you."

"Well, could you do another thing for her? Take that bag on the table to her," I said.

"What is it?" Her eyes seemed to glow.

"Another one of her gifts I just picked up."

"I guess I could." She sighed but I knew she was just kidding.

"Oh, Nami?"

"What now?" she said with a roll of her eyes.

"You're going to keep her busy while I'm at the show, right?" There was no way I could let Beverly be alone on her day. I'd asked her if she wanted to come to the gig, but Nami had said she was going to take Beverly out. I was just double checking at this point.

"I got this," she said before she left.

The café wasn't open to customers because I'd rented it out for the day. Felix and Lily insisted on no payment, but that didn't feel right.

"So, did you tell her yet?" Lucky asked while we hung up streamers.

I almost answered but decided against it because I knew how bad it was. Hearing it out loud would make me feel even more ashamed.

"I'm going to take that as a fat no." Lucky laughed but there was no humor.

"Why? It's not a big deal. Just be long distance like me and Tiffykins," Lincoln added while struggling with the tape.

"For nine months? It's unfair of me to have her wait. 'Cause I know she will. We just got together." I suddenly found my voice; it sounded tougher than intended.

"So walk away? You're not going to fight?" Lucky set a pack of balloons down.

"She deserves more than that. I love her too much to have her wait," I said, realizing quickly that this was the first time I'd admitted loving her to someone other than myself.

"Shouldn't she get a chance to make that decision for herself?" Lucky said, not waiting for my answer. He walked past me and adjusted the centerpieces on the tables.

"He has a point." Lincoln spoke from behind me.

We finished up about an hour later. I went back home to get ready before Lincoln picked me up. This place was a bit bigger than the last. The energy off the rip was wild. It felt like they knew us. When we performed our first song, I could actually hear some of my lyrics shouted back at me. Our hard work was getting us somewhere. I couldn't tell you what that felt like.

The crowd screamed, and my blood rushed through my body. My mind was in an alternative universe. I sang better the more people I was around. If I was by myself, I didn't challenge my voice. I was hitting notes I wasn't able to hit during practice, my smiles appearing before I could stop them.

We only had time for half an hour, but it felt like five minutes. That stage. There was nothing like that stage. It was the only thing that could pry me from my best friend's side. I knew I couldn't give it up anytime soon. And the guilt I felt for even agreeing to the international tour was missing as we performed.

Lucky went wild on the drums. It was his best show yet, and I was proud that he evidently had been practicing as much as I had. Lincoln on guitar was insane; he could play with his eyes closed. The neon bracelet Tiffany made at band camp when she was twelve was around his wrist. I wondered how he felt about the tour; how he was going to handle being away that long. Just after our last song, I watched as the crowd screamed and cried out for us. Lights flashed through my skin and bones.

"We have one more song," I said into the mic before Lucky could say our sign off.

I turned my head to see Lincoln and Lucky staring at me in confusion before I made my following statement.

"Today is the day someone very special to me was born. Beverly, this is for you." The crowd yelled like they knew who she was or maybe it was because we weren't leaving the stage just yet.

The sound of Lucky starting the notes to "Happy Birthday" on the keyboard laced through the screams.

"I hope you all know the words to this one," Lincoln joked into the mic, throwing in his guitar sounds to the piano.

When we got backstage, Lincoln hit me upside the head. "Could you give us a heads-up next time?"

"I barely remembered the notes to that song," Lucky chuckled.

"You sounded great though." I wrapped my arm around Lucky's shoulder with a grin. My mood was happier than happy.

"Everest, we talked about this. They need to feel like you're attainable—no more talking about that girl," Jeff, our booking manager, scolded me when he met us, but I was barely listening.

"Anyway, great show! Excellent. This is it boys. The last show until tour." Jeff smiled once we got into the dressing room.

Please don't remind me.

My happy mood began to fade.

"February can't come soon enough," Lucky sighed.

Jeff's laugh was way too loud and way too throaty.

"I've never been anywhere," Lincoln said after he downed a bottle of water.

"The experience of a lifetime!" Jeff winked and smiled dramatically before leaving the dressing room.

"Let's get out of here." I spoke for the first time, annoyed by the conversation. I left the dressing room first and the boys followed. They knew what I was upset about but didn't say anything.

"What time is it?" Lincoln asked when we got into his van.

Pulling my phone out of my pocket, I read the time.

"All right, we have to hurry 'cause the party is about to start in thirty minutes. I told Tiffykins I wouldn't be late." Lincoln spoke his sentence as if it wasn't extremely cringy.

"Would you please stop calling her that?" Lucky grumbled.

"I second that. Also, could you just drop me off at my house? I have to shower. I'll just meet you guys there." I was all sweaty and wanted to look good for Beverly. Lincoln nodded and did what I asked. I asked if they wanted to freshen up at my house, but they declined.

"I'm good."

"Sweat is good for the body."

After I got ready, I decided to wear a navy-blue crewneck sweater that she had picked out for me a few weeks ago when we went shopping. I looked in the mirror and touched my sandy-brown hair. It was so weird looking like myself again— well, like myself but with the addition of tattoos. I was glad I had them, though. Without them, I looked like the preppy, snotty kid that I looked like before.

Picking up my keys, I hopped into my car. When I checked my pockets to shoot a text that I was on the way, my phone wasn't there. I looked everywhere. Underneath seats, in my house, in my old pair of pants, and around my room before I realized the last place I had it was in Lincoln's van when I checked the time. Now more than ever, I had to make it to the party. I felt naked without my phone.

"Let's go!" I yelled out the window, and honked my horn. Three cars ahead a sloth was driving in traffic that presumably came from out of nowhere. They weren't even going the speed limit. My luck was getting worse and worse by the second. My nerves were already jacked from leaving my phone in Lincoln's van, now I had to worry about being late.

That was when I remembered a shortcut. There was an abandoned park I used to hang out at all the time with Nash when we were younger. If I just cut through there, I should have a straight path to Brisklin Street. At the idea, my body automatically went into gear and headed in that direction. I had so many memories of High Point Park. It was one of my first hiding places when I first moved here.

The sun was beginning to set and turn dim. I glanced at my clock and realized the party had started about forty minutes ago, but I had told Beverly that I'd be a little late, so I should still make good time.

When I approached High Point Bridge, I saw a guy staring down at the water before taking off his shirt. And then I noticed something strange—a scar running down the side of his torso. The only person I know with that scar was—

Nash?

Bruises laced the right side of his face, his right eye blooming purple by the second. I stopped the car by the side of the road and raced out to meet him in the middle of the bridge.

"Everest?" he whispered, his stance swaying slightly. He'd been drinking, I could tell immediately.

"What you doing, Nash, man?"

He looked out at the lake, a vacant look on his features. "I'm about to go for a swim."

That was when I knew something was seriously wrong.

"You're afraid of water, Nash," I said as I walked closer to him.

"Stay back!" he shouted.

I stopped in place.

"Okay, okay." I held my arms up and took a step back, fearful that he might jump.

"What happened?" So many questions swam around my head, but that was the only one that came out. Who caused those bruises? Why was he out here? How could it be that we'd run into each other like this?

"You wouldn't understand. No one understands what I'm going through!" he cried in anguish.

"Okay, well, make me understand," I said in attempt to make him talk about what had happened.

"You won't get it." He shook his head before facing the water.

At that my emotions coursed through me.

"Are you kidding me? If anyone understands, it's me. Okay? It's me. I've been there, Nash. I lay awake antagonizing myself. I've cried until I could barely breathe. I actually did it. I went through with my attempted suicide just to live. I've dealt with being on the edge and coming back from the dead. I've faced the disappointment and disgust that followed my recovery. I understand all too well." The last sentence of my rant got caught in my throat. Tears of my own were desperate to escape.

"You won't talk me out of it," he said quickly before climbing over the railing and standing on the other side. I almost panicked but I quickly realized that would make the situation worse. The ledge was very small. His grip on the railing in front of him was the only thing keeping him steady.

"If you jump, I'll wear plaid to your funeral," I said, knowing he hated plaid more than he hated himself, and taking the opportunity to take a few steps closer.

"Now is not the time to make jokes." He looked disgusted.

"You're right. I'm just scared. I don't want you to jump. Please get down."

There was a pause. He stared down at me, and his eyes pleaded with me. Pleaded with me to help.

"For what? There's no point." His voice was soft.

"The point is that life isn't pointless. You think me showing up at this *exact* time at this *exact* place was a coincidence? You think it was a coincidence that if the ambulance was called ten minutes later on the night of my attempt that I'd be gone? We are here for a reason. You are here for a reason. I know it sounds strange, and unlikely. But I swear, I swear to you, Nash, that it's true. I didn't believe it at first, either, but I believe it now. You have to know that you'll never find happiness if you die with sadness.

"I can't tell you that you'll be immediately fine," I continued. "Or that you're okay. Because, clearly you aren't. But I will say that it gets better." I took slow steps toward the railing where he stood.

"What suicide prevention flyer did you steal that from?" An empty laugh followed. "I said stay back! Not everyone can have a success story like you. Give up football and become a rock star the next day." His grip faltered for a moment but he caught it.

"Success? I still struggle. I still get sad and scared. I don't have everything figured out. Every day there's this lingering emptiness where the depression used to be. I'm still recovering. But I'm glad I'm still here. I'm so glad that I'm not dead. Because I'm giving myself a fighting chance to be happy. Because I'm healing day by day. Because I wouldn't be here on High Point Bridge stopping you from jumping."

My heart beat wildly in my chest, thumping all the way up to my eyes, triggering my breathing to pick up. He couldn't jump; he would drown.

"It's over for me. They know. The guys know. It's only a matter of time before word spreads. They'll never accept me for who I am. I'm disgusting. Jacob even refuses to talk to me. I have nothing."

I took in the scene and froze for a moment. Because for once in my life, I knew exactly how someone felt. That was me once upon a time. He wasn't just the guy who'd deserted me. He was the fourteen-year-old kid who'd convinced all of the football team that I wasn't some prissy rich kid, and that I could actually play a hell of a game. He was the kid whose house was like my second home when things were bad at my house. He was the kid who'd stuck up for me before I had the chance to stick up for myself. Yes, he was a jerk for turning his back on me, but that didn't mean he didn't have his moments.

"This isn't over. Fuck them. Fuck everyone who has made you feel like you aren't enough. You are not disgusting. Anyone who doesn't accept you isn't worth any more of your time. Consider it a blessing they leave."

Another pause.

"Don't act like you care," he spat at me with so much hurt I didn't understand.

"Of course I care, Nash. You were my best friend, man. It wasn't always bad. We had some good times. Despite it all, I never wanted this for you. I know we haven't talked in a while but that doesn't mean I don't care about y—"

"Oh yeah?" he said aggressively, cutting me off. "Is that why you tried to leave?" His eyes were reddening, tears piling on top of each other to escape his eyes.

His words tore open my heart.

"Is that why you tried to leave me behind, Everest?" He repeated his question, his grip on the railing loosening.

"I didn't try to leave you, Nash. I wasn't thinking about anyone that night. Just how you aren't thinking about what this will do to your dad—"

"I could care less—"

"What would your mom think about this?" For a moment I felt like I'd said the wrong thing because something harsh flickered in his eyes.

"Don't you dare talk about my mom! Don't you dare act like you fucking know me!"

"But I *do* know you, Nash. I know you better than you know yourself." I took a step closer, my voice rising a bit. "You're afraid of water because you almost drowned at Gold Oaks Country Club when you were ten. To this *day* you won't go near water. You listen to George Strait every day like it's a part of your religion. You're allergic to gerbils. Only gerbils. You cut the crust off all your sandwiches like a weirdo. That little tattoo of a bird on your thumb is a matching tattoo you got with your mom when you came out to her. It means freedom, but after she passed, you never granted yourself that . . ."

He flinched from my words.

"I'll be free after this," he said calmly, but his eyes were wild.

"No—" I quickly took a step forward, my heart beating wildly in my chest.

"Why are you doing all this? We aren't friends."

I stared deep into his eyes even though it pained me. "We were. And honestly, what does that matter? I still care about you. I'll always care about you."

I walked close to where he stood on the bridge and held my hand out.

There was a moment before he grabbed my hand. But somehow, he lost his footing and dragged me over the railing. The only thing keeping us from flying into the river was my shoes digging into the concrete.

"I got you. I got you." I breathed roughly out of my nose.

The look of wild fear in his eyes was proof enough that he didn't want to die. He scrambled in my hold. My lower back strained trying to gather all my strength to pull him over, but his constant moving and weight was pulling me apart.

"Stay still," I ordered, and pulled with all my might so he could get his hands on the railing so that he could pull himself up.

I thought everything would work that way, but I failed to remember his drunken state. His reflexes weren't up to speed, and he missed the railing completely. I tried to grab his hand but I missed it by half an inch. There was nothing I could do. I'd never felt so helpless in my entire life.

His face of sheer fear, battered and bruised, had me glued to my spot. I wanted to help. I wanted to do something but I was frozen. All I could do was watch as his body dove into the winter river.

The impact melted me away from my mind. I was so scared. Slamming down on the railing, I let out a string of curse words. I took a deep breath before I kicked off my shoes and jumped sixty feet after him.

Falling, I screamed louder than I ever had before. My legs kicked and scrambled, desperately looking to find stable ground. As I fell, I thought about Beverly. I thought about my family. I thought about my friends. The rushing air made it difficult for me to catch my breath. My bones crackled from the harsh temperatures of the water. Thankfully, this part of the river hadn't frozen over, but the water was still ice cold. I opened my eyes and saw only darkness despite the sun still barely out. I swam to the surface and took a huge breath. My adrenaline kicking into over-drive, I looked around me for signs of movement, but the river was as still as could be.

"Nash!" I yelled, frantically looking at all angles. I went back under the water, afraid that I'd never find him.

I came back up and yelled his name again. "Nash!"

My calls became desperate.

Taking another breath, I let the water cover me once more. I wasn't even searching that long before one of the last of the sun's rays shone directly on his limp body. Using every bit of strength I had, I swam after him. By some miracle, as soon as we reached the surface, I heard him sputter. It was music to my ears to hear him cough because that meant he was breathing.

Swimming to shore was harder that it sounded. The distance looked so far away, and although I knew I was tired, my mind ignored all that. Nash's cough was all the energy I needed to get us to shore. My arms burned and felt like mush, but I had to push through because if I didn't, we would both be gone and we had too much to lose. When we reached the bank, I used my last bit of energy to push Nash ahead of me before I plopped on the mud, trying to catch my breath.

It never felt so good to lay face first in dirt, and to feel my fingers grasp blades of grass.

I thought I might have been hallucinating for a moment because I heard laughter instead of coughing, but when I saw Nash, he was actually laughing.

I groaned into the mud. "You idiot."

This only made him laugh harder.

I reached out and weakly hit his shoulder before he hissed in pain. Instantly I sat up. "You okay? You all right?"

He held his shoulder with a frown but his mouth was amused. "It could've been worse."

I stared at him blankly, entirely confused before shaking my head. "Fucking idiot."

After we caught our breath, I trekked back up to the bridge, following a short trail to bring my car down to the bank. Nash was injured so I didn't want him moving more than he had to, but he was alive.

We were alive.

He wanted me to drop him off at his house but I wasn't trying to hear it.

"No," I stated simply. "You need medical attention and supervision."

"I can't. No one can know about this, Everest. My dad would kill me if he found out what happened this evening."

"Screw him. You may be seriously hurt," I said, getting upset.

"If I go to the hospital, this would be blown up tenfold. I already have to worry about the team outing me to the whole school. I don't want to have to deal with my dad finding out I tried to kill myself tonight."

I understood that he wasn't ready for all that was coming his way. Pushing him to go to the hospital would open up questions. Questions that I knew he wasn't ready for.

"I'm still not leaving you."

"You really helped me tonight. I'm not going to do anything, okay? Almost dying made me realize I don't want that. I just want this day to be over."

He wrapped himself tight in the spare blanket I left in the car for Beverly so she didn't get cold. The heat was on full blast.

"Promise me." He never broke a promise. I never broke a promise. That was one mutual thing that stuck deeply with us. Our fathers always broke their promises, and we'd vowed to never be like them.

"I promise," he said with such sincerity I had no choice but to believe him.

I couldn't let this question go unanswered. "Who did that to your face?"

He looked as if he was going to fight his secret, but gave up. "Jacob."

I didn't want it to be true, but I knew it was.

"Cara's party?"

He stared at me before nodding.

When I pulled in front of his house, he sat in my passenger seat for a long moment, making no move to leave.

"I-I'm sorry." He clearly struggled to say so, his arrogant demeanor nowhere to be found. "Thank you. For everything."

He then left the car in a rush, and I didn't stay to watch as he entered his house. I had a party to make it to.

The sky was no longer orange, but now blue. The streets seemed quiet, too quiet. I pulled into Cara's driveway, anger lacing through my veins. Red cups littered the lawn. People could be seen from every opening. The music wasn't loud but loud enough. The front door was open, and as expected, people filled every corner of her home.

"Oh my gosh, is that Everest?"

"Is it raining outside?"

"Yo, Everest is in the building."

"I knew they were still messing around."

I pushed past the people with only one person in mind. It didn't take long for me to find him; I knew where all of the athletes hung—the office. My old team was in there, smoking Cara's dad cigars and taking swigs from his liquor stash. They were all laughing among themselves.

Jacob sat on one of the leather chairs, a vacant, empty look on his face.

"Hey, Everest." Some of my old teammates greeted me, but I ignored them all. Jacob was who I'd come here to see. He didn't dare meet my eye.

"My man, you just missed it. Nash was wilding out. Got too

many drinks in his system and he got fruity," Gabe snorted. "Tried to feel up on Jacob."

"Oh yeah? That's crazy," I said staring right at Gabe. My clothes could've been dried by how much my blood was boiling. I looked a mess, but everyone was too intoxicated to notice.

"I actually came here to talk to Jacob real quick, if you guys don't mind."

Jacob looked at me in that instance, and his jaw ticked. I thought respect for me had long since diminished, but the guys piled out with no question.

I started to roll up my sleeves. "Stand up."

He snorted. "For what? To fight? I'm not going to fight you."

"Either you stand up and defend yourself or stay there. Either way, we're fighting." I didn't even sound like myself. I was just so angry. So fucking angry that he was the reason that Nash was pushed to that point. That if I hadn't been there, he would've drowned while people partied.

"Is this about Nash?" He stood up confused. "I—"

"He almost drowned tonight because you humiliated him. The only person he's ever loved after his mom. You piece of shit. How dare you?" My breathing began to pick up.

"Drowned?" He looked even more confused, but he had guilty written all over his face.

"He tried to jump off of High Point Bridge tonight because you weren't man enough to be true to yourself."

The image of Nash's hand slipping and me not being able to catch him flashed in my mind, and tears pricked my eyes.

Jacob took a step near me, his eyes sad. "Is he okay?"

"What do you think? He almost died tonight." The tears began to fall.

He covered his face and leaned against a bookshelf. When he moved his hand, tears rimmed his eyelids.

"What are you getting upset for? He's disgusting right?" I shot back.

"That's not fair. Don't, Everest. Just don't. You don't under-stand—he was going to blow our cover. He almost did a few weeks ago, standing up for this gay kid and getting into a fight with Richardson. Then tonight, trying to kiss me in front of our team? He's becoming reckless, I got scared."

"You think because you beat on him and called him names in front of your friends, it's going to make you a man? You're tough for beating on someone who would never think of hurting you? Nash has more balls than you will ever have."

The door to the study opened to a very drunk and happy Cara. "You showed up."

I sighed at the sight of her. This was just too much. Too much in one day. Her friends stood behind her in shock, whispering to each other like I wouldn't notice.

"Are you gonna sing happy birthday to me?" she slurred.

Birthday. Beverly. Fuck.

I got out of there in a rush. How could I forget about my baby? Today was her birthday. She was going to hate me. Literally hate me, and there was nothing I could say or do to fix it. I slid past Jacob and Cara and her gang. My mission with Jacob was accom-plished; my words hurt him more than any punch would, but I'd failed the love of my life.

I thought maybe if I sped, I'd make it there in time for at least cutting the cake. I was only four hours late—it couldn't be too late. It shouldn't be. I couldn't get there fast enough. My good luck of the night was nowhere to be found. I got a ticket for speeding, the slowest of cars seemed to want to lead the way, traffic lights lasted eternities, and a turtle even got in the cross hairs of my driving. I literally had to get out of my car to take it across the street.

"I'll be there," I kept repeating. As if that mantra would help the universe help me.

When I pulled into the parking lot of 21 Daisies, I knew I was too late. The lights of the building were turned off. From the windows I saw Nami and Tiffany wiping off tables. Lincoln, surprisingly, was sweeping the floor, and Mikey and Beverly were headed out the door to take out the trash. She looked so distant as she walked, Mikey bumping into her side playfully, but all she could give was a distracted smile.

Dreading the disappointment, I parked and hopped out of my car, then walked slowly toward her because I'd already caught her eyes. One look at her and I knew I'd messed up.

"I'm so sorr—"

She dropped the trash bag at the sight of me and crossed her arms. Tears instantly began to flood her big brown eyes. "When were you going to tell me you were leaving?"

38

BEVERLY

Eight hours earlier.

It was barely a kiss. His soft pink lips lightly brushed against mine. As if he wanted me to cave from the intensity. He knew I wasn't going to kiss him in front of people, so it was up to him to make that move, and he knew exactly just how to abuse it.

"Everyone's always staring," I sighed as I came down from cloud nine, ignoring his burning gaze from my peripheral. Everest without fail studied my face every time he kissed me. It drove me crazy and he knew that too.

"Let's give them a show," he suggested with a smug smirk while his lips lightly touched mine as he spoke. Embarrassment clung to me like a perfume and I quickly took a step back. I couldn't even look him in the eye as I headed straight toward the entrance.

"Have fun at school!" he called from behind me, a dangerous grin no doubt etched on his face.

When I went inside Shady Hills Academy, it seemed like everyone knew it was my birthday. They most likely did, thanks to Nami. I was getting wishes in every class, after every bell, at every bathroom break. It made me nervous about my party later on. If I could barely handle the attention at school, how could I endure the attention in a intimate environment? I was way to awkward to be this well known.

Mikey offered me a birthday blunt that I politely declined. Nami and Tiffany showered me in gift cards. As the day progressed, my outlook on the attention changed. I was having a pretty good day. After a bit, that aspect was actually kind of nice. My existence was noted. People would notice if I was gone, and I found that quite warming.

"Another gift?" I exclaimed, unable to hide my grin. Setting my apple slices down, I tried to contain my joy as I stared at the plain brown, slightly dented box.

"Sorry if it's smashed. I tried to seat belt it because it kept falling," Nami sighed, taking a seat next to me.

"He didn't!" I screamed internally. Excitement and giddiness filling my heart. When I unwrapped the box, it was a bouquet of sunflowers. How could he have known that? I'd specifically made a note to keep my pet name for him to myself. I was far too shy to call him that aloud.

"Aw, he got you flowers." Tiffany grinned.

"I'm telling you, Beverly, that kid Everest probably doodles your name in arrow hearts." Mikey sat back in the old library chair, his hands laced behind his head.

"Oh stop it." I was still not completely over the fact that someone had romantic feelings for me, let alone Everest.

"Seriously, though, you should have seen him at 21 Daisies

today, being a little diva about the decorations being perfect."

"That's so precious," Tiffany gushed, while I was right along with her. This party couldn't come soon enough.

Shortly after school, the girls treated me to a movie date. It was a romantic comedy that did nothing to help to cure my Everest thoughts. It only made me just miss him even more. I wondered if he was thinking of me too. I would've rather have gone to the boys' show, but there were errands we needed to take care of before the party.

"Chips?"

"Definitely chips," I responded while we stacked the bags of our choice on top of all the other snacks we needed for the party. Although there were already finger food options available, you could never have too many snacks.

"Now we just need the cake." Nami and Tiffany had been so helpful throughout this party process. I was blessed to have such great friends at this time in my life when I needed someone the most. Last year for my birthday, I'd watched reruns of *The Nanny* and finished a whole tub of Nutella.

Almost immediately after Nami set the cake neatly in the cart, she looked back at me with a hopeful look on her face.

"Well, what do you think?"

My upgraded cake this year was gold and blue with elegant swirls. I smiled instantly from the sight of it. It really felt like my birthday just then. I was used to this day not really meaning much, but seeing all the people involved already made it more memorable than my last ten birthdays.

"I think I truly couldn't have better friends."

Tiffany wrapped her arm around me swiftly. "Well, duh, that's a given."

"I love facts." Nami smiled. "Now, c'mon, we have to somehow, by some miracle, get cuter than we already are for this party."

"Oh wait, we forgot candles," Tiffany pointed out when we made it to the checkout aisle.

"I'll get them," I exclaimed in a rush before they could object. Those girls hadn't let me help with anything. I knew they wanted me to be some kind of queen today since it was my birthday, but it only made me feel useless. I was used to helping, not fading into the shadows.

My rush was ultimately reckless when I turned into the baking aisle, because I bumped directly into someone who was leaving just as I was entering. The baking supplies in his arms fell to the ground. I immediately bent down to pick up what had fallen. "I'm so sorry."

The man was kind about it, though, offering me a string of "It's all rights"s and "It's okay"s. I handed him the last of his dropped items and started mentally cringing at myself.

"Slow down," I told myself as I searched for the candles.

"You still talk to yourself? I guess people never really do change."

"Manny?"

When I slowly turned around, I was met with two faces I'd seen more times than I could count. Macy and Manny looked the same, but different; their faces weren't new but the feelings were.

"Beverly, oh wow, is that you?" Macy said, almost shyly. For an instant, it hurt that we felt like strangers bumping into each other, and it hurt because Macy was never shy. Especially around me.

"How are you guys?" I tried to keep it cool.

"Great. Everything is great. I got a raise at that new job, and Manny is still a mini-Einstein." She ruffled his hair and he frowned as if on cue. She paused. "What about you?"

"Congrats. You know, just making it by as usual." Now it was my turn to pause. "How's my mom?"

Macy first looked like she was unsure before settling on, "She'll come around."

I nodded, knowing that was as good a answer I was going to get. "I graduate June fourth."

I threw it out in hopes she would catch it, but she only nodded and grabbed Manny's hand. There was no good-bye in the exchange, but Macy wasn't really known for her social skills. Manny stared at me as they were leaving the aisle before he ran to me and wrapped his arms tightly around my waist.

"Manny!" Macy called for him, but that only made him squeeze tighter.

I immediately embraced the hug. It felt like a piece of home.

He pushed back away from me. "Happy birthday. I didn't forget."

Then he was gone, running back to his mom, who looked guilty and relieved at the same time.

"Thanks, bud," I whispered as I watched them leave the store.

"Did you grab the candles?" Nami asked just as I got back to the line. I nodded and tossed them to her, choosing not to say what happened moments earlier.

* * *

The girls dropped me off at the house to get ready while they set up the snacks for the party. I put a little extra effort into my look due to the sheer fact that eyes for sure would be on me. The dress and black knee-high boots were what Everest chose for me to wear in the morning. At first I didn't think it would look good, but I needed to start listening to his fashion advice more because it looked great.

"Beverly, did you check the band page?!" Tiffany practically yelled at me when I got into Nami's car.

"What?" I chuckled at her blatant anguished happiness.

"Lover boy sang happy birthday to you at his concert," Nami explained, and I instantly whipped my phone out. I watched it on repeat, thankful that I hadn't been there or else I would've most likely fainted. I wanted to give him a hug as soon as I spotted him.

When I entered 21 Daisies, my stomach fell to my knees. The place was already more full than any karaoke night ever. Lights were strung all through the place like captured stars on string. Gold balloons spelled out my name, and pictures of me were at every booth and table as a centerpiece. The snacks were neatly laid out on the largest table. A DJ had even set up on stage. Music was flowing and cups were pouring. My very first birthday party was even better looking than it had been in my dreams.

"Happy Birthday!" The boys left their growing circle of fans to pull me into a hug.

"Where's Everest?" I realized shortly after the embrace that he wasn't in sight.

"Don't worry, he'll be here soon," Lucky assured me.

"He's getting all dolled up for you." Lincoln grinned before asking me where Tiffany was. From the looks of the video, Everest already looked great. He didn't need to get all dressed up. I just wanted him here.

"Beverly! Take a picture with us." Nami called me over. After that, we danced. I was pretty much dragged onto the makeshift dance floor, but it was fun—so much fun that I almost stopped looking for Everest through the crowd.

When an hour had passed and Everest still hadn't arrived, I went outside and called him. He always answered my calls, but for some reason today he didn't. I got called back into the party after my third dial. Dancing didn't seem all that fun anymore. Everyone seemed to be in their element, and I'd never felt more like a fish out of water. The party was just beginning and I wanted it to end. I sat at a nearby booth checking my phone every so often in hopes he'd send me a quick text.

"Hey, birthday girl." Mikey sat in front of me. "Why the sad face?"

As if on cue, I felt my features immediately soften.

"Everest?" he guessed, an eyebrow arching upward. "I called him a bunch of times for you, but I think his phone died or something."

I nodded, while he waved it off.

"Ah, don't worry about it. You got that boy so whipped, you could stick him in the oven and bake a cake. He's coming. In the meantime, I got you a little gift since you rejected my first one."

He reached into his jacket and pulled out a metal container. "Here's some fun juice. You look like you could use some fun."

"What is it?" Taking it from him, I unscrewed the cap. It smelled extremely chemically fruity.

"Are you deaf? I already told you. Don't drink it too fast." He winked before sliding out of the booth.

I took a tiny sip and it tasted of regular fruit punch until it hit my chest slightly. There was a minuscule tolerable burn. I took a few more sips until eventually that burn made me want to dance.

"Happy birthday, Beverly." Megan, my chemistry partner from sophomore year, began to dance with me. We were hardly friends, but that was like most of the guests here. The power of

Nami to pull it all together. That girl knew everyone, no joke.

"Thanks." I smiled back, and she turned to dance back with her friends.

Nami suggested cutting the cake to get my mind off of Everest not being around. It did make me feel better to see all the effort my friends were going to for me. People started drinking, and urged the birthday girl to take two shots of "fun juice."

Normally, I wouldn't have entertained it, but all I could think about was how Everest wasn't around for my birthday. It was keeping me distracted. Eventually the fun juice wasn't that fun anymore. I found myself at the booth again, watching other people enjoy themselves. I felt so alone. Here I was again in a room full of people still feeling like it was just me. Perhaps even more alone. Everyone was going on with the party and I was just at the booth. So many times, someone would ask where Everest was and I had no answer. The party was winding down, and every minute that ticked by, I grew more confused and concerned that I hadn't seen or heard from Everest.

"I just thought you should know that Everest is at Cara's party." A guy who had asked me earlier about Everest's location told me on his way out the door.

Huh?

"Lie again." Nami smacked the guy in the shoulder, making him turn around and return to our booth.

"Golden Boy wouldn't be there." Mikey narrowed his eyes.

"Look for yourself," the guy said, turning his phone to face us.

I shouldn't have looked.

In the picture was a sloppy-tired looking Everest and a happy-looking Cara, staring at each other. The worst part was the caption that read: These two are meant to be. I instantly felt sick and rushed from the booth to the break room. I sat on the couch and stuffed my face into a pillow, gripping the edges while I was on the edge of tears. My stomach pulled inward while I fought my sobs. So this was why didn't come? The door to the break room slammed closed as quickly as it flew open.

"Lift your head up now," Nami's voice ordered.

"Leave me," I cried into the pillow.

She lifted my head up, and staring into her eyes made me feel even more ashamed. I just cried even harder.

"I'm not like her. I'll never be like her. She's everything I'm not with her blond hair and blue eyes. Why did I think that I had a chance with him? That's why he didn't show up to my party. She's beautiful. They're perfect for each other. Is that what you wanted to hear?"

Nami looked at me and pulled my arm harshly. "You listen, and you listen good because I'm not going to say this to you again. I know you only mustered up that bullshit because of that fun juice. So this is only addressing tipsy Beverly.

"I know you feel like you are unworthy. But that's not true, because there is no real image of beauty." She wiped my tears, and I started to feel myself calm. "We are all just caterpillars trying to be butterflies. It all starts from the inside, and that process is your cocoon. Once your insides are beautiful, it shines through your skin. You will be beautiful, and not by anyone's standards but your own. You won't get insecure when you see someone else who's gorgeous. Because you're just as lovely. Beverly, you dumb bitch, you have the most breathtaking heart, and you're fine as wine. I don't want to ever hear you talk down on yourself like that again."

I wanted to hug her, but I knew she'd probably punch me if I did. "Thank you."

"Don't mention it. But that bitch isn't even a butterfly, she's a moth in makeup. There's got to be an explanation. Don't you trust him?"

I didn't get a chance to answer because the door to the break room opened once again and a intoxicated Tiffany flew in. "Oh my gosh, Beverly, it's okay. The boys going on tour is a good thing, you don't have to be sa—"

Nami's eyes widened dangerously, and she took the pillow from my hands to hit Tiffany in the head.

"The boys are going on tour?" I said.

Why hadn't anyone told me? That was great news. Maybe this night would have a happy ending after all.

"Isn't that what you're crying over?" Tiffany scratched the back of her head.

Nami sighed deeply. "She's upset that Everest hasn't showed yet."

Now Tiffany's eyes widened, as if she'd ruined a surprise. "Oh, I think Lincoln is calling me so I'm just gon—"

"Not just yet! I didn't know about the tour. That's amazing. Where are they going? When is it?" I wiped my tears and sat up ready to hear the details that Everest was probably too busy to tell me.

Tiffany looked at Nami somberly. "You already spilled the beans. It's too late now."

"It's international, they leave in five days. For nine months." She rushed to leave the room but Nami held her in place.

I shook my head. "No, that can't be right. Everest would have told me—I mean, nine months?"

When Tiffany's eyes turned sorry for me, I knew it was true. I so wanted it to be a lie or a drunken story, but the way Tiffany and

Nami were looking at me proved it to be otherwise. Nine months? International? I felt like he had just broken up with me. Told me every hurtful thing he could say. Stomped my heart into dust. I had yet another breakdown. I snatched the pillow from Nami and started to cry even though I had just finished my first breakdown. This time Nami let me cry it out, Tiffany taking a place at my side.

"I just want this night to be over," I groaned, my mind and body feeling groggy from my breakdowns. Tiffany and Nami calmed me down in the break room, letting me cry it out until I couldn't cry anymore. Once I finished crying, a part of me desperately hoped that Everest would be waiting in the lobby for me. Despite how angry I was at him, I still wanted to see him. He probably wouldn't be waiting, and for the first time that night I began to come to terms with it.

"You're sleeping at mine. We'll eat ice cream and talk shit. It'll be great," Nami told me with assurance.

"First this party has to die," Lucky added.

There were about six people left chatting about and I couldn't leave until they left.

Mikey stood on the table. "All right, y'all don't have to go home but you gotta get the hell up out of here."

We started to hurry and close the restaurant. All of us had had enough of this failed party. Lincoln even escorted people out. As I took down the decorations, I wondered and thought about what this year would have been like for me if I'd continued to be the ghost girl. Would I still endure such heartache? I opened the front door with a heavy heart. Did I not deserve to know? Maybe we weren't as close as I thought.

"I'm sure Golden Boy has an explanation." Mikey tried his best to reassure me, but even his charming smile was unsure.

* * *

Lights flashed, bringing my attention to the car I'd been search-ing for all night. Everest pulled into the parking lot. The sight of his car caused the compressed emotions within me to bubble up my throat. His sandy-brown hair looked chocolate brown in the moonlight. His clothes were wet and there was a tear in his sweater that hadn't been there this morning. That mouth of his started to move but I couldn't hear what he had to say. There were other things on my mind. *How could you not tell me? You're really leaving? Were you ever going to tell me?*

My voice found the words I wanted to say so desperately and I couldn't stop them even if I wanted to. My poor heart beating in pain.

"I—who told you?" He staggered back.

"The real question is why didn't you tell me?" It was then I felt my tears start to make an appearance.

"I didn't know how." He took a step closer to me.

Nami came outside just then. "Where have you been?"

"Long story." He answered her but stared at me.

"Can we go somewhere private to talk?" His soul silently pleaded with mine. He made me breathless. He stared at me with such intense longing and sorrow, it made my stomach twist and turn.

"She has time," Mikey said and lightly pushed me toward Everest.

"Do you want to talk to him?" Nami grabbed my arm, her protective stance thick and stern.

I nodded. "It's okay."

I followed him to his car. It smelled of earth and salt. The front seats looked like they had been wet but had been wiped down. He opened the rear doors and I followed suit, wondering where this conversation would take us.

"I know you're angry. Someone needed my help."

"Cara?" I hated the way her name sounded in my mouth.

"What? No." He looked confused, and grabbed my arm to look directly at me.

"Nash. He tried to jump from High Point Bridge."

My stomach leaped and suddenly I felt sick.

"What?" I turned toward him, hoping for it to be a cruel joke.

"Yeah, I had to jump in to save him. Then once I found out why, I had to see the person responsible. That's why I was at Cara's party. Trust me, I'd rather have been with you all night."

"Wow. I'm s—" I felt guilty for being angry. He was going through so much tonight and I didn't even realize. The apology got stuck in my throat from the shock of his words.

"No, don't you dare apologize. I'm sorry. I'm so sorry, Bev. I'm sorry I missed your party. I'm sorry I didn't tell you about the tour. I'm sorry I let you down. I'm sorry. You don't deserve any of that. I didn't tell you because I didn't want to make this strained or tense. It's one thing to be gone a couple days of the week. But nine months?"

"So we won't. We won't make it strained. Let's just enjoy the time we have left." My heart tried to leave my chest. "You should have told me. If we're this team you speak of, communication can't be taken for granted."

"You're right." His eyes swam with hurt.

"We still have five days, three hours, and twenty four minutes." Being with him now made me forget why I was so upset in the first place.

"Well, let's make every second count."

That night I convinced myself that wasn't the beginning of the end.

39

FEBRUARY

Don't cry.

I hate that phrase.

I tell myself that a lot but I'm living out my dream so there's no reason for me to feel sad anymore, but I'm really missing my life. I wish there was a way to combine the two. A lot of people in the industry are convinced that my father bought my way in, and that is too frustrating to deal with sometimes. Crying is necessary. It's a fucking human necessity and I am no exception. Crying does not make you weak. I pray that all of this gets easier and becomes worth it because for now I'm struggling. I'm struggling adapting to this new life that I have and I miss you. I miss you dearly but I respect that you stopped responding to my messages. Call at 2 a.m. may be standard for me but that doesn't work.

—a journal entry from Everest

40

MARCH

Dear Ev,

It's been almost a month since we last spoke. It didn't end well and I am completely to blame. I have too much pride to just be your friend. I honestly don't think I could be strong enough to not be able to love you freely. My mindset was everything or not at all, and I wish I could go back in time and change that, because it's better to have just a little bit of you than to not have you at all. I've been listening to the songs that you showed me all those months back. I didn't really like them at the time, but now they're all I ever listen to. I miss your voice, laugh, smile, terrible jokes, and just you. I miss you, Everest. I stopped staying at your house. I just didn't think it was right anymore. I'm trying to act like this is normal, I promise I am, but I don't think it gets any better than you, Everest Finley. I didn't realize what I had until it was gone, and the mere thought of you with some other girl makes me sick.

It rattles my bones and sends tornados through my insides, and I feel sicker than sick.

I think about you at 3 a.m. when it's just me and my thoughts. I don't just think about you when it's that weird time between morning and night. I think about you when I'm making cereal or doing my English homework. I miss you when I'm watching movies or when I'm talking to people other than you. I miss you when I'm tying my shoes or doing laundry. I miss you all the time. I miss you when I can't seem to find me. My biggest fear is being forgotten and it's here and true. Did you forget about me? Because I'd never forget about you.

—found in iPhone notes, but never sent

41

APRIL

We're in London now. Every two days is a different city. They have funny accents here but the food is all right enough. I think about you a lot. Of all the places I know you'd love. I'm sorry I couldn't visit like I said I would. Another show got added to the list and we didn't end up flying back for this leg. I hope everything is all well and good with you.

—a text sent at 11:41 p.m.

42

MAY

I see you're doing really well for yourself. I'm so proud of you and the guys. You're calling yourselves Brisklin Street now. That's really cool. I miss you. Just calling to tell you that I graduate a week from today. I know you said you couldn't make it but hopefully the universe brings us back together again.

 —missed call; voice mail.

43

BEVERLY

When the sun came through the window and randomly lightened the whole room, I always adored it. I could be anywhere—classroom, bedroom, library—and the sun would just brighten the room, and I would feel peace. That was until Nami threw a pillow at me. "Wake up! We're graduating today."

I rolled over into the couch. "Not until five." It was no later than eight in the morning.

"There are preparations to be made, Beverly." She exuded flamboyancy. "You know this."

"I'm up, I'm up." We had to decorate for Nami's graduation party. She was adamant that it be finished before we got ready. I didn't mind. It was the least I could do since her family took me in. When we got to the school, it felt like an alternate universe. The halls were filled with exuberant students. The principal led us single file out onto the football field.

I'd dreamed of this, and yet I didn't feel prepared. I stood in line full of jitters. The stands were full of families. I looked up but didn't see anyone that would be here for me. As I took my designated seat on one of the many chairs on the football field, I saw Mikey, sitting closer to the front, waving violently to get my attention. I couldn't help but laugh. I was in that chair for what seemed like forever, the June afternoon sinking my legs into my seat. When my row got called up to the stage, I felt important. Taking deep breaths so I wouldn't pass out from all the attention calmed my nerves. I passed the stands and Aunt Macy jumped out to take a quick photo.

Beverly Davis

My ears crackled and my skin was prickled in goose bumps as I accepted my diploma. The principal shook my hand and for the first time I felt like all eyes truly were on me. I wasn't invisible anymore, and perhaps I never had been. After the final speech, suddenly all the caps were in the air. The sky was so blue. I looked at my peers, faces I'd probably never see again. There were tears that I never accounted for. Suddenly, there were arms are around me, and I was surrounded by the people I'd grown close to these past months, and it was sad to think that it was over.

Tiffany grabbed my cheeks. "Stop crying."

I tried but somehow the words fueled more of them.

"Aw, Beverly," I heard Nami say. "I'm so glad that I met you, and I'm angry we weren't friends sooner. I guess we just have forever to make up for it." I laughed and wiped my tears.

Hugging the two of them harder, I said, "I love you guys."

"We love you, too, Bevy-boo," they said as if on cue.

"Care if I interrupt?" I managed to hear above all the commotion. Of all the people in the world, she was who I wanted to see here. My mother opened her mouth to speak, but I just wrapped my arms around her instead. I'd dreamed of this happening. I'd waited for this day. In her arms, in that moment, I couldn't remember why I was mad. Her body grew limp for a moment before she held me tight. She held me like she was afraid it was the last time; I'd missed her smell. I could have cried again, but I didn't.

"I'm sorry, Beverly." She stroked my hair. "I'm so sorry."

I pulled back and wiped her tears. "I know."

"Beverly!" Manny and Hadley pulled my attention away from my mom.

"We'll talk later." She nodded in understanding and winked. "At *home.*"

"Okay," I said instantly, smiling from her words. It was time. It had been time. I had a summer to spend with my mom before I left for college.

I walked over to my two favorite eleven-year-olds and met them in a hug. Hadley handed me flowers that her family got for me. They were extravagant but beautiful. The note read "You are the sun." I cried again and I hugged so many people from then on. Just like that, high school didn't matter now. That chapter of life was over and everyone knew it, but we had memories that would *always* be with us. I was so incredibly thankful for the people I'd met and the memories we'd made. For the friendships that would never die and that I would cherish for the rest of my life. I would continue to be fearless and continue making life experiences because I'd gained so much just from doing it for one year.

My eyes moved past the football field and the setting sun until they stumbled on Lucky and Lincoln standing a few feet away from me. My chest clenched as we made eye contact, and I just knew. I knew with everything in me that he was here. I looked around, making a full circle. Blood rushed to my cheeks and my heart skipped. I felt like I was dreaming but I knew that I wasn't. "Hey, Bev."

My earth shattered. I felt like I might float away. I had so many things that I could have said: I'm sorry I pushed you away. How's the tour? Did you miss me? You look good. Why are you here? I'm sorry for being stupid. I missed you every day. I'm so proud of you.

Instead I smiled. "Hey, Ev."

THE END

ACKNOWLEDGMENTS

The manifestation of this book you possess would not have been possible without the belief, determination, and support of all the fans who have been on this journey with me since the beginning, as well as the many people involved in its evolution. I wish I could list them all, but I suppose this will suffice for now. This couldn't have been possible without Deanna McFadden, the best editor I could have asked for. Thank you for the endless revisions and requests that sucked the life out of us both but ultimately shaped something quite beautiful. Thank you for not only your patience but your passion. Whenever I felt like I couldn't, you told me I could. Special thanks to Alysha D'Souza—I will never forget the kindness and everlasting support. And to the many others at Wattpad HQ who worked hard on the preparation of this book.

Dejah, Italy McClurkin, C. M., Summer Jones, Mignon, Lynn Mcmeans, Royal McClurkin, Kyceen Ragland, my high school French teacher, whose class I used as a writing workshop rather than studying my adjectives. My fifth grade teacher, who was rude as heck but pushed me to prove myself through literature, and lastly, Ty and Keith, for creating me. We truly have them to thank, I guess.

Tap by Wattpad

Take a universe of interactive stories with you.

Tap by Wattpad is creating the future of interactive stories. Download Tap today and discover the latest.

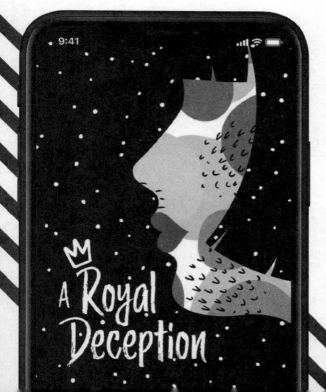

wattpad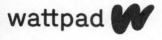

Where stories live.

Discover millions of stories
created by diverse writers from
around the globe.

Download the app or visit
www.wattpad.com today.